CONTENTS

Notes For a Magazine 9
Notes for a Special Issue 11

MERRIL MUSHROOM
   Merril Mushroom Meets *Common Lives/Lesbian Lives*
   (and falls in love) 13
TRACY MOORE
   A Decade of Common Dyke Publishing 15
JO FUTRELL
   When *Common Lives* Came to an End 27
JEAN TAYLOR
   Common Lives/Lesbian Lives Lives On 29
Jean WEISINGER
   Melanie DeMoore 33
THE COLLECTIVE
   Celebrating Joan Nestle 34
KIM PAINTER
   Remembering Anne Lee 35
ANNE LEE
   Rest Cure 37
CANYON SAM
   Cross 42
DIANA MILLER
   Untitled 48
JOANNA BROWN
   The Dishwasher 49
TAMARA HOLLINS
   Airport 50
JAN HARDY
   For Pat Parker 51

AISCHA DAUGHTERY
    Girls Like Me 53
ALISON LUBAR
    Hyper-Pop Apocalypse, OR, nonbinary lesbian blues 55
MEL CONNELLY
    Do You Consider This Blue? 57
MISTINGUETTE SMITH
    Rain. 59
CHRIS CINQUE
    Self-Portrait 64
RANDA DOWNS
    Queen Cluck 65
ANANYA GARG
    The Year 2068, Age 71 71
AMY SPADE
    Canzone 72
EVE JASPER
    Other Half 74
DIAMOND MARIE PEDROZA
    I Met an Imagined Woman 75
C. ELLIOT MULLINS
    Straight school for dykes 77
ROWAN HARVEY
    Dykes Like Me 79
MERRIL MUSHROOM
    Butch Cologne 85
TANYA OLSON
    Forget Me Not 89
TAMARA HOLLINS
    A pandemic death 94
PAPUSA MOLINA
    Loveless Love 95

CINDY CLEARY
  Entwined 101
PAPUSA MOLINA
  Poema del Amor, amor 102
CHERRY MUHANJI
  What It Takes!!! (aka Billy in the First Person) 108
ABBY LYNN BOGOMOLNY
  July Joy: 1775 121
LEONORE WILSON
  Naciye 123
MARGARITA MEKLINA
  Cadet Cap 126
MARY AVIYAH FARKAS
  Margaret's Death and Plunder 133
WINDFLOWER
  She said 137
  A Beginning with No End 138
REBECCA HENDERSON
  Chama Notes – August 1989 139
MI OK SONG
  Traps in Water 146
  Me & Puffins 147
STEPHANIE SAUER
  Maybe It's The Only Way 148
EVERLYN HUNTER
  Almost Everything I Know About Healthy Relationships
      I Learned From My Cat 154
SANDRA RENEW
  Dykes of the seventies send a message to the 2020's
      via villanelle 157
LISA SCHOENFIELDER
  Common Lives/Lesbian Lives Cover #1 158

ALISON BECHDEL
   Literary Dykes to Watch Out For 159
LINDA SHEAR
   Long Time Love ... Song, 2021 161
PALOMA RAFFLE
   Santa Cruz Sunset 163
TESS CATALANO
   Woman in Arms ... Song 164
LORI CURRY
   Sunflowers 165
MARIE CARTIER
   My One Wild Life: Class 166
SUE KATZ
   The Slogan Fetish 171
SABRINA MCINTYRE
   Untitled 173
SARAH WALSH
   The Wing of Fire 174
DAGMAR JILL SPISAK
   Gap 176
   Moth Light 177
TAMARA HOLLINS
   elders 178
MARIA MINGUEZ ARIAS
   Laundry 179
JACQUELINE WOODSON
   Limbo 180
BETH BRANT
   Seeking My Own Vision 181
ZÖE BRACKEN
   Bath 186

Anne Lee
    Somebody's Childhood 187
Quinn
    New York Politics & Friendship with Blue Lunden 192
Everlyn Hunter
    Recovery 198
Olivia Loscavio
    Goodbye To(morrow) 206
Aaron Silander
    A Dyke to Watch Out For: Iowa Dyke March, June 2018 207
Rabbi Lisa Edwards
    Rainbow Flags: A Speech 211
Katie Leah Hewett
    Love Poem with Old Thermometer 215
Melinda Goodman
    After 911 217
Jan Phillips
    Perpetual Emotion, Novitiate Training, 1968 221
Rainbow
    Terradyketil Kitchen 229
Shari Katz
    Backing Forward 230
Kimberly Esslinger
    My Weather is Female 237
Jules Taylor
    When Obama Repealed Don't Ask Don't Tell 238
Mary Vermillion
    Jam-Packed 239
Dodici Azpadu
    Paper Trail 246
    Sleep Map 247

KIM ESSLINGER
   The Last Lesbian Bar In The Wold Is Closing 248
SUE KATZ
   My Gratitude for *Common Lives/Lesbian Lives* 250
JESSE JOAD & ANN BONHAM
   Remembering Dirt Bag 252
TRACY MOORE
   Photos of Linda Knox (Dirtbag) 254

   Contributor Biographies 255

NOTES FOR A MAGAZINE

I am so pleased to present *Sinister Wisdom* 134: *Lives of Common Lesbians*. The editorial collective for this issue has done a great job bringing together new writing that reflects the spirit *Common Lives / Lesbian Lives* as well as reprints from its published issues.

The journal *Common Lives / Lesbian Lives* has interested me since I first started reading lesbian periodicals in college. In the political cauldron of the 1980s during a presidential administration hostile to lesbians and feminists and amid perilous economic conditions in the US, *Common Lives / Lesbian Lives* articulated class consciousness as a vital part of feminism, particularly elaborating the meaning of working class in feminist and lesbian politics. Within the pages of *Common Lives / Lesbian Lives*, whiteness and consciousness about the privileges and obligations of whiteness emerge, another vital contribution of this journal to broader conversations in lesbian-feminism. Through the publishing work of *Common Lives / Lesbian Lives*, writers interrogated the construction of whiteness and explored its relationship to woman of color feminism in the 1980s, how whiteness is inflected with class consciousness, complex relationships to whiteness and ethnicity and religion, including awareness about Jewish women, and explications of the intersections between class, race, ethnicity, and religion in the United States. Finally, *Common Lives / Lesbian Lives* demonstrates the ways that cultural work built lesbian communities in the 1980s and highlights the significance of those communities outside coastal cities.

This is *Sinister Wisdom*'s second tribute issue to a lesbian-feminist periodical from the past. The first was *Sinister Wisdom* 123: *A Tribute to Conditions*. As a part of that work, we ensured that there was a robust archive of *Conditions* available to contemporary readers. Conditions is digitized and freely available at www.LesbianPoetryArchive.org/Conditions. Currently, *Sinister Wisdom* volunteers and interns are exploring another periodical, *Feminist Bookstore News* (FBN). *Sinister Wisdom* volunteers have digitized all the issues of *FBN* and made them publicly available at www.LesbianPoetryArchive.org/FBN. Volunteers compiled an extensive database of articles in *FBN*. Now we are working on a bibliography of all of the books mentioned in *FBN*. This archival and digitization work is I believe crucial to preserving our past and prompting greater understandings of it. Deep engagements with lesbian print culture are a valuable part of collective life at *Sinister Wisdom*.

This work has not been done on *Common Lives / Lesbian Lives*. There is a partial archive of the issues as a part of the Independent Voices collection at JSTOR, but it is incomplete and there is no way to easily and efficiently search the archive. I hope that people reading this issue might take up the challenge of archival and digitization work on *Common Lives / Lesbian Lives*, preserving it for future generations.

I also hope that this issue of *Sinister Wisdom* will not be our last tribute to the lesbian past. I invite proposals from other editorial groups to consider other lesbian-feminist periodicals, books, collectives, and other constellations of the lesbian post. I am interested particularly in work that engages with vibrant readings and re-readings of the journal in a multi-generational conversation.

Sinister Wisdom has planned another wonderful season of events to celebrate the issues of the journal and explore and understand more about lesbian culture in the world today. I hope you will join us for as many of these events as you can. It is a pleasure to see beloved *Sinister Wisdom* subscribers, friends, and supporters on the screen.

As always, the fall and the end of the year brings our annual fundraising campaign. I hope that if you value the work we are doing in the world for lesbian and queer women's literature and lesbian and queer women's culture you will give as generously as you can. I am always humbled by the support for *Sinister Wisdom*. Thank you.

In sister- and sibling-hood,

Julie R. Enszer, PhD
Fall 2024

NOTES FOR A SPECIAL ISSUE

The book you are holding is a tribute to *Common Lives/Lesbian Lives (CL/LL)*, a magazine whose 15-year publishing life wove a design into our lesbian cultural fabric that is still relevant.

The women who conceived and created the magazine were new to Publishing. Our thirst for more lesbian identity motivated our passion for the richness of lesbian culture and dedication to our community.

The idea was sparked in October 1980 by a group in Southern California, three of whom moved to Iowa City to produce the magazine with other inspired lesbians.

The large lesbian community there had a history of activism around women's and lesbians' social and political issues, as well as lesbian-owned publishing businesses.

CL/LL documented the rich and diverse experiences and thoughts of lesbians, presenting the lives of ordinary women who had struggled to survive and create a culture. That work continues in this volume, a testament to the ways we imagine our lives and bring them forth...in defiance of a dominant culture that advocates against our very existence.

Forty years later, the following pages reflect the lives and thoughts of contemporary lesbians. Woven throughout are pieces from the original magazine, juxtaposing threads of ideas, concerns, and feelings then and now.

Editorial Collective: Cindy Cleary, Jo Futrell, Rowan Harvey, Papusa Molina, Tracy Moore, Aaron Silander

Editorial Contributors: mj corey, Rabbi Beth Lieberman, Merril Mushroom, Juno Stillee.

We are delighted to feature original artwork for this issue by:

Chris Cinque
Lori Curry
Britta Kathmeyer
Diana Miller
Jean Weisinger

Cindy Cleary
Rachel Feury
Sabrina McIntyre
Paloma Raffle

We also reprinted artwork first published in *Common Lives/ Lesbian Lives*. The following artists represent the many generous contributions made to each issue by lesbian artists and photographers:

Alison Bechdel
Sudie Rakusin
Jean Weisinger

Morgan Gwenwald
Mi Ok Song
Sue Parker "Rainbow" Williams

Their combined work, along with others, graced the covers and pages of many issues over 15 years, bringing to the journal its depth, beauty, and signature look.

We especially want to recognize Lisa Schoenfielder, whose art brought joy to the magazine over the years and, who generously brought her creativity to this book.

For its first five years, *CL/LL* was solely created by Iowa City lesbians: typesetting and layout by *Annie Graham*—owned and operated by Judith Pendleton, who was responsible for designing the unique look, feel, and heart of the magazine. *CL/LL* was printed by the *Iowa City Women's Press* and bound by *A Fine Bind*. Members of the first Iowa City collective were Nancy Clark, Cindy Cleary, Anne Lee, Linda Knox, Cindy Lont, and Tracy Moore.

MERRIL MUSHROOM MEETS *COMMON LIVES/ LESBIAN LIVES* (AND FALLS IN LOVE)

Merril Mushroom

During the decade of the 1980's, I was in a primary relationship with a lesbian literary journal. There were other lesbian literary journals in my life then, too, like *Feminary* and *Sinister Wisdom*, but my predominant relationship was with *Common Lives/ Lesbian Lives*. For a good while toward the end of the 1970's, I'd been hearing some buzz on the lesbian news and information circuit about the possibility of a new publication. Catherine and Harriet, editors of *Sinister Wisdom*, had been urging lesbians to create more places for our stories to be shared. This was before the internet, cell phones, or other accoutrements of mass communication. Our dyke communication system depended on U.S. Postal, telephones, lesbian bookstores and festivals, and other in-person meetings. Since I was by then living in the middle-of-nowhere, Tennessee, I was dependent on communication from the dykes I was connected with elsewhere to get any lesbian news or scuttlebutt.

Then, on one of my visits back to NYC, I went to visit my old friend Joan in her apartment, and she told me that indeed there was a new journal publishing lesbian stories. It was called *Common Lives/Lesbian Lives* and that was exactly what it was all about—our common lesbian lives. The first issue just had come out, and she had a story in it. So I got it, and I read it—every word—and I loved it a lot: the stories and poetry, the bios, the lesbian ads, the notes about the *Common Lives/Lesbian Lives* collective, who they were, what they hoped to be, how they functioned.

They welcomed manuscript submissions, either typed or handwritten on real sheets of paper and mailed flat in a manila envelope with SASE included. (That would be a Self-Addressed Stamped Envelope—oh, I sure do miss those).

Best of all was the information that every contributor would get two free copies of the issue she appeared in. My budget was tight to the penny and did not allow for magazine subscriptions. I had written for other publications in exchange for copies, and sometimes even for money. Now I was captivated by the thought of writing about people, places, and events I'd experienced in the lesbian culture of the 1950s and 1960s. I knew so many stories, and here was a place to send them!

I found that writing personal stories of my own lesbian experiences was fun and satisfying, the mind-tripping and reminiscing delightful. My first piece, "How To Engage in Courting Rituals 1950s Butch Style in the Bar," appeared in issue #4, and after that, I was hooked. From 1982-1990, thirteen of my stories found their first homes on the pages of *Common Lives/Lesbian Lives*.

So I feel as though we have had a long-term relationship; and I also feel as though I had long-term relationships with—unbeknownst to them—many of the lesbians who had pieces that appeared in different issues of that journal—lesbians whose work I have seen since then in many other places—even if we never met or had any sort of personal communication. But I knew who they were! Even now, I know who they are.

Other lesbians whose work appeared in "*Common Lives/Lesbian Lives*" I *did* know, and some of us remain friends to this day. I am a fan of all of them. Thanks, *Common Lives/Lesbian Lives*. I was sad when you stopped publishing.

A DECADE OF COMMON DYKE PUBLISHING
Tracy Moore

From *Common Lives/Lesbian Lives*, Issue 40, Fall 1991

The Beginning

The inspiration to start a lesbian magazine came from the co-founders of *Sinister Wisdom*, Catherine Nicholson and Harriet Desmoines. In February 1980, as part of a tour focusing on lesbian publishing, they spoke in Los Angeles at a reading by local lesbians they had published.2 Insisting that publishing was something anyone could do, they called for the establishment of more lesbian periodicals. Their stories of the writing and artwork going unpublished for lack of our own lesbian media convinced us that the need was pressing, and that ordinary women could make it happen.

Cindy Cleary, Anne Lee, and I formed the core of the group of eight lesbians that started *CL/LL* in the LA area in the fall of 1980.3 The three of us were planning to move to Iowa City in June 1981, so in the intervening ten months the group did everything we could to launch a magazine. We spent hours describing what we wanted: an inclusive, non-academic, beautiful journal documenting the widest possible range of lesbian experience; a magazine that ordinary lesbians would acclaim as their own. Our office was a couple of milk crates in Cindy's living room, and meetings alternated between Long Beach and Pasadena. Although Anne Lee was a writer, no one but Tracy had any publishing experience.4 Our primary guides were our goddessmothers, Catherine and Harriet, who sent us an audio tape about everything they had learned in their five years of publishing *Sinister Wisdom*, plus the SW office manual. Carol Seajay, cofounder of Old Wives' Tales bookstore in San Francisco, gave us a complete education in dealing with bookstores. Her most emphatic advice—that we earn credibility by sticking to a definite publishing schedule—became a solid value and served to motivate us through the years and not a few tough times.

Of all the details we had to figure out, the major question of printer and typesetter was always answered: the Iowa City Women's Press and Annie Graham Publishing Services,[5] both lesbian (and in the case of the press, union) shops, would produce the magazine. The possibility of an all-lesbian publication, both content and product, was inspiring. Having our own press and typesetter available had everything to do with our empowerment to start the magazine, since there was never a worry about censorship or the probable oppression of dealing with straight people or men. In the middle of winter, we visited Iowa City to establish the relationship. Their help then and though the years was invaluable. Press women advised about paper, costs, time schedules, etc., and the typesetter (who is also a book designer) did everything from choose the perfect font to coach us (sometimes lecture us) in how to prepare manuscripts and plan and mock up an issue. And all of this at dyke rates.

Back in California, we began making flyers calling for submissions and offering subscriptions, and the amazing part was that lesbians subscribed. It wasn't amazing that lesbians submitted their writing and artwork—the assumption that the work was out there was why we got started—but gathering those pieces for #1 awed us just the same. On the business side, we made lists of all the feminist and lesbian publications we could and wrote to them to exchange ads. Talented lesbians held fundraisers. We sold t-shirts, and talked about it to everyone we could. The preparation definitely needed ten months!

An early stumbling block was the magazine's name. We had no idea what to call her! Long lists of powerful, female, mythical, evocative adjectives and nouns were compiled. In desperation we consulted the Ouija Board, and asked the spirit to go look around in the future and tell us what the name of our magazine was. After only nonsense ensued, someone asked if the spirit could read. The needle slid directly to NO, so we went back to the lists. The situation was urgent because *Sinister Wisdom* was announcing the birth of the magazine in her Spring issue, deadline December 1.

We were sure the word *Lesbian* had to be in the title (this was going to be an Out Magazine!) and we wanted to use the word *Common*.6 So we simply combined two suggestions, *Common Lives* and *Lesbian Lives*, emphasizing our vision of bringing to print and to light the existence of lesbian experience in all its forms.

When the magazine moved to Iowa City, we had a little bank account, subscribers, enough material for a 112-page issue, and a waiting collective.7 Lesbians there volunteered to help network, collate, mail out, and keep books. The momentum and support proved important, as they helped carry the magazine through the deaths of Anne Lee, in July 1981, and Linda Knox, in February 1982.8

Roots of Grass

CL/LL started as, and remained, a grass-roots magazine. She was run by a collective of lesbians,9 and no one ever "owned" her, in any sense, and certainly not through monetary investment. There are only a few true collectives anymore, and "collective" has taken on different meanings in different contexts. For *CL/LL*, collectivity meant that consensus must be reached on any decision, and consensus means that everyone is willing to own the decision, even if it isn't her first choice. It's a slow process, but one that served the collective well. Consensus shaped cohesion of direction and forced us to deal with our differences, and not just "register" them with differing votes. Consensus also prevented one lesbian, or even a faction, from being responsible for a decision. Critics are frustrated when there is no isolatable target to blame, and it is true that collectives can find collectivity a useful shield at times, and this one has. But to the survival of the group and thus the publication, the degree of protection provided by collectivity has been crucial. Horizontal hostility10 threatens political activism and projects while collectives support one another and deal internally and externally with criticism, better than individuals and hierarchies.

Using collective structure allowed us to learn skills, empower each other, and resist the trap of specialization that chains of command are built on. Although for the past five years new *CL/LL* members have had to learn the skills and methods of collective decision-making on the job, the *CL/LL* collective sees the process as important to lesbian future, and not an anachronism.

Over the years, *CL/LL* collective members have not usually been academics, or even wide readers. They tend to be activists who relate to the cultural politics of the publication and have never imagined they could act as editors (though they typically know what they like!). As a result, there is a process of consciousness raising that happens just in joining the collective, and that continues as the skills of collective process and publishing the magazine are acquired. The diversity of interests, jobs, and education among collective members contributes to the common character of the quarterly.

Staying Alive

Before an assessment of *CL/LL*'s successes and failures is made, it's important to account for her survival—not for ten years, but for five, or even two. The forces working against such a project are legion: outright opposition and suppression by the dominant culture, meager funding, the relative poverty of women/lesbians and scarcity of "leisure" time in which to do our political work, the competing claims of other, seemingly more urgent causes; internalized sexism and homophobia, self-doubt; the critical scrutiny of the lesbian community. It's a wonder we ever do anything! But our hardy needs and passions lead us to resist and to create.

The reasons for the continued existence of *CL/LL* begin with something the '80s taught us to call "infrastructure." Iowa City is an excellent context for the project because of the counter-cultural and lesbian support systems that have been growing there for decades. The Women's Liberation Front (WLF) in Iowa City, first self-identified in 1968, grew out of the New Left/anti-war/civil rights activism of that era.

Immediately lesbians began extending their culture, through the "gay cell" of WLF,11 the "publication cell"—lesbians and straight women who produced *Ain't I a Woman?* For 45 years, women's dances held at the Unitarian Church, the Free University,12 the Women's Center,13 leadership roles in the daycare movement and the free medical clinic, producing lesbian talent shows and concerts, setting up a free car repair garage. And as mentioned, there were lesbian printers and a typesetter, who were joined in 1981 by a lesbian bindery.14 The Iowa City lesbian community's do-it-yourself tradition meant that lesbians looked for ways to be involved in their culture. They worked—always for free—on any number of projects. This ethic helped assure *CL/LL*'s survival.

The other important factors in *CL/LL*'s birth and survival were the race and class privileges her white, middle-class members operated from. Access to credit, friends with some money to share, college educations, and the cultural assumption that doors will be opened combine to bridge the leap from "if only" to "I can."

Business Stuff

The work that goes into producing each issue of the magazine is considerable. Working from 3-6 hours a week, a collective of 5 lesbians coordinates the organization, does the selection and editing of the contents, and makes business decisions. Poetry editing is usually done by a separate group, cover design by an artistic dyke. For the first seventeen issues, the magazine was hand collated by a crew of dykes who ended up giddy and hysterical from walking in circles around tables piled with 16-page "signatures" of the mag's contents.15 Not until the third year was anyone paid to help with office work; since then, there has usually been a half-time office lesbian working for $5/hour to process the mail, do business correspondence, banking, etc. *Most* of the business gets done by volunteers, however. Distribution to bookstores, bulk mail to subscribers, bookstore accounts, "handling" manuscripts (logging in, acknowledging, tracking), all require the regular assembly of dedicated dykes.

Financing the magazine comes mainly from subscriptions and bookstore sales.16 Our friendly printers and typesetter allowed us to spread the costs over the three months between issues. For two years VISA checks floated us over the rocks. Donations have been important, but never enormous; the largest were two $500 gifts, while most were an extra couple of bucks added to a sub. Revenue from sales lags far behind the arrival of the bill, so it was hard going for a long time. By the fifth year, cash flows had caught up to expenditures. However, because subscriptions promise future magazines, there is always a liability on paper, *CL/LL* never received a grant because we've never applied for one—not out of some political analysis, but because there never was the time to incorporate, a requirement for a grant. Once incorporated, you have to keep books and be a lot more accountable to the government than seemed important to bother with. And since *CL/LL* always operates in the red, the collective basically knows where the money is and goes.

Expenses are low. The Women's Center provides an office (in the mouldy basement until 1987, now on the first floor in exchange for occasional use of the magazine's PC). Collective members financed the computer initially and then were paid back. The biggest windfall—though perhaps not worth the price—came as a result of settling *CL/LL*'s censorship lawsuit against the University of Iowa,17 which agreed to print three issues of the magazine for free.

Although you'll see ads for *CL/LL* in various women's and lesbian magazines, marketing (indeed all "business functions") is not really attended to except as someone has the energy. Planning focuses on getting out the issue at hand and perhaps the one following. As a result, circulation has stayed constant at around 2500. With concentrated effort—mass mailings, trips to festivals and bookstores—who knows? The point is that whoever is on the collective brings her interests and abilities and available time, and these determine how business is directed.

And then we published…

The concept of *CL/LL* 18 is the basis for most of her editing and design characteristics. Once something is in print in a beautiful journal, it's easy to imagine that the author or artist or photographer is someone really different, someone you'd never know yourself. We knew the lesbians we were publishing were just dykes from any town, and not famous "stars" to be othered as in the capitalist system. We printed authors' bios right after their pieces, so readers could associate what they'd read with an individual. We also asked that bios be personal and not patterned after academic bios that are written in the third person and list publishing credits. After all, most of the lesbians in *CL/LL* have never been published before. First person bios that include the contributor's ethnic/racial heritage are required, and after that, any personal info she would like to share.

Editing is not done to a given style. Authors are asked whether or not they want their spelling corrected, and any changes made for clarity are first OK'd by the writer. The hope is to retain and honor the integrity of every woman's language. Selection is specifically made for reasons of inclusion. A lesbian whose experiences or culture or point of view has been underrepresented in *CL/LL* or the world in general gets priority. Those who have never been published rank higher than those who have. Submissions are handled with respect: when received they are acknowledged with a letter that explains the selection and editing process, and decisions are made so that no one waits longer than six months.

Forty issues provide a litany of milestones. With #5 the subtitle was changed from "a lesbian feminist quarterly" to "a lesbian quarterly," gaining praise and criticism in equal measure. #8 documented (on special glossy paper) artwork by 21 Iowa City lesbians. Hundred-word book reviews of self-published and small press books began in #11, #12 featured a "Lesbian Family Photo Album" (the closest *CL/LL* ever came to having a theme issue), and #14 printed (in purple!) a Lesbian Songbook, lyrics and tunes by 6 Iowa City dyke musicians. #17 was the final issue to be printed by the Iowa City Women's Press, killed by Reaganomics. After printing #18 and #19, our new (straight) press at the University of Iowa refused to print #20 because of Noel Furie's beautiful photographs of lesbians making love; another press was found, and *CL/LL*'s complaint and suit led to total vindication and a gratifying settlement.19

The collective consciously decided not to have special issues by theme. In addition to avoiding the extra time and work special issues demand, we felt our role was to be selectors of what came at will from lesbians, not as guides to what we wanted to see in print.

Disappointments

The major shortcoming of *CL/LL* has been in our attempts to broaden the diversity of the collective.20 White, middle-class lesbians have always comprised the majority. While there has always been a minority of poor or working-class lesbians, only two lesbians of color have ever served, and since the founding group, one Jew. No one over fifty or under eighteen has joined. Fat lesbians have been well represented; disabled lesbians have not. The collective has dealt with this reality in a number of ways. We've made sincere attempts to reach out to lesbians from underrepresented groups, though never enough. Editorial selection policies that give priority to lesbians based on their historical exclusion from media are on strategy, and local lesbians of color and Jewish lesbians have acted as guest editors of work from their cultures. None of this addresses the issue of credibility. In addition, those who run a publication are able to solicit work from their communities; more to the point, they are seldom able to do so outside of them. *CL/LL* has relied on networking among its readers and contributors and its own publishing track record to attract diverse contributors. The collective is proud of its vigorously good intentions and continually humbled by their inadequacy.

Some of our goals were unrealizable. When the journal began, our passion led us to dream of a national network of cultural workers who would take it upon themselves to tell everyone they knew who wrote or drew or took photos or kept a diary to send their work to *CL/LL*, and after that they would go out and tape oral histories with their favorite local heros, and then they would transcribe them and photodocument it all. We urged women to edit their correspondence and journals, and published a few. The Iowa City art and music collections were done both to honor our own community and to model that possibility for others, but it must have looked too overwhelming. Without in-person contact, it's really hard to persuade women who have never thought of publishing the stuff of their lives to do so.

At least our underrealized dreams aren't due to failures of imagination.

Achievements

Forty issues: 4,784 pages of lesbian experience reflected in memoir, history, fiction, journal, poetry, drama, music, photography, painting, drawing, cartoon, interview, letter, erotica, science fiction, biography, fantasy, essay, review, treatment, joke, anecdote. If we knew the numbers of lesbians published, volunteer hours, dollars taken in and spent, we'd tell you. I do know that roughly 100,000 individual copies of the magazine have been printed and, presumably, read. Now ain't that a kick?

Anne Lee always said that a people must have a literature, and that it must be vast, so that people may find entertainment and nourishment, and so that the truly great works have a medium in which to be sustained. She pointed out the role periodicals play is to develop the authors of that literature, by providing rich and varied collections of creations in many forms. Many lesbians who first appeared in *CL/LL* now have published books, and surely many more will. When you pick up a lesbian book or anthology, just notice how many credit CL/LL as first publisher.

Still, this quarterly is for the common lesbian. That is why every manuscript and every copyable artwork submitted to CL/LL is copied and sent to the Lesbian Herstory Archives in New York City, where it is preserved in the *Common Lives/Lesbian Lives* Special Collection.

Fights and the Future

That last paragraph was supposed to be the end, but I haven't talked about a bunch of things—which is bound to be the case. Fights and the future seem to be the most glaring omissions. We didn't have a lot of fights, especially after we made a rule that lovers couldn't serve on the collective at the same time. Also, we learned that it's really important for a group to measure the energy it put into dealing with detractors (as opposed to principled critics), because no matter what you do somebody isn't going to like it, which doesn't mean you shouldn't do it. Most of the times we were criticized we dealt with it in the magazine, apologizing as responsibly as we could for the errors we were bound to make.

As for the future, I think it's *always* a miracle that our literature and art get published. Lesbian publishing is a fragile enterprise that a very small disaster could derail—especially because lesbians no longer own our own printing presses.[21] The good part is that the CL/LL collective is like an institution, in that it has some life and structure of its own and doesn't entirely depend on any one individual.

This is a personalized history of this quarterly and probably full of factual errors as well. I'm grateful to have had the experiences and to have been asked to write about them.

Endnotes

1. With much appreciation to Cindy Cleary for her morale support, important suggestions, and memory.
2. Held at The Church in Ocean Park, Santa Monica, 2/2/80, featuring Terry Wolverton, Anne Lee, and Alice Bloch.
3. Members of the LA-area founding collective were Jan Monical, Moire Martin, Joan Leech, Chris Selgren, Cindy Freedman, Cindy Cleary, Anne Lee and Tracy Moore.
4. From 1971 to 1974, Tracy worked on the collective of *Ain't Ia Woman?*, a Women's Liberation Front newspaper published in Iowa City.
5. Founded in 1971 and 1980, respectively.
6. Carol Sejay was the direct inspiration for this word, with Judy Grahn's "Common Woman" poem providing the cultural referent.
7. Members of the first Iowa City collective were Linda Knox, Cindy Lont, Nancy Clark, Cindy Cleary, Tracy Moore, and Anne Lee.
8. See issues #2 and #4 for more about these women and events.
9. The *CL/LL* collective usually numbers five or six lesbians, although there have been more (luxury!), and in hard times, only three. Collective members are named on the copyright page of each issue.
10. *Horizontal hostility* is a phrase used to describe the effects of internalized oppression that lead oppressed peoples to "do the work of the oppressor" by cutting down leaders and infighting so much that nothing gets done to further the revolution. Naturally, then the white heteropatriarchs look blameless and uninvolved, while achieving their goals undisturbed.
11. The first public lesbian group in Iowa City. Its purposes were consciousness-raising and social.
12. Called Action Studies, it was headed by various lesbians who conscientiously used it to funnel University resources to lesbians and other grass-roots groups in town.

13. The Women's Center (later Women's Resource and Action Center) was founded in 1971 on the University of Iowa campus. Most of the leadership was lesbian.

14. Founded as *A Fine Bind*, it later became part of the Iowa City Women's Press.

15. *CL/LL* was printed on large sheets of paper, 8 pages to a side, folded into "signatures," collated, bound, and trimmed.

16. Originally $10 (1981), subs went to $12 after two years, and in 1991 were raised to $15. Cover prices were $3.50, then $4 and $5. Bookstores get a well-deserved 40% of the cover price, and distributors 15%. *CL/LL* began using distributors in 1987.

17. More about *CL/LL's* censorship lawsuit against the University of Iowa in issues #21-28.

18. For the full statement of the *CL/LL* concept, see issue *#40*.

19. The University Press agreed to print three free issues and was compelled to write clear guidelines of acceptability of material. However, the process was draining and obnoxious. The collective was prepared to drop the suit if it threatened *CL/LL*'s survival.

21. Poetry selection groups have reflected far greater racial and ethnic diversity than this collective.

22. Though lesbian publishers may use the word Press in their names, they do not actually print books themselves, but hire printing companies to do so.

WHEN *COMMON LIVES* CAME TO AN END
Jo Futrell

I joined the *Common Lives/Lesbian Lives* collective in 1992. To boost my coming out in Iowa City, Sandy Pickup had invited me to join the collective—as well as a lesbian softball team, named for the lesbian restaurant Grace and Ruby's.

I worked on *Common Lives* until I moved to Wisconsin, returning to help when the journal folded in 1996. Our distribution company, Inland Books, had gone bankrupt and took us down with them, along with many other small publications.

The end of a magazine is messy: there are subscription fees to return, back issue orders to fill, gently telling those who'd kept it afloat that we were done. We had to undo 15 years of publishing lesbian voices while honoring the subscribers, contributors, collective members and readers. Because we didn't want our legacy to disappear, we donated full sets to the Lesbian Herstory Archives in NYC and the University of Iowa Library Women's Archives. Anyone who requested issues, got them—and then it was over.

Piles of dusty boxed issues had been stored in the Women's Center basement. One weekend we hauled them to Sandy's garage and walked away. When Sandy needed her garage back, I hauled the boxes to my Wisconsin farm, where the barn housed them for years.

Life with boxes of *Common Lives* convinced me that this was "the magazine that wouldn't die." Recycling wasn't an option at the time, so we got creative. We tried to mulch the garden, but the glossy covers wouldn't decompose. We started a burn pile, but the covers took too long to burn. Finally, when a groundhog burrowed under the pallet of boxes in the barn, *Common Lives* had to go.

In the end, we *still* had boxes and boxes of journals. So, I took the boxes to the Michigan Women's Music Festival. After multiple trips from my truck camper to the festival downtown, hefting boxes onto flatbed shuttles, I set up near the community center with a sign, "Free Issues of *Common Lives*!" They were gone within hours. Just like that—a fitting ending for the final inventory.

It was a bold act to announce yourself in this journal, to put your name on a piece of prose or poetry, art or photography. It was a bold act for the collective members representing lesbian lives and sharing the voices of women loving women. It was a healthy time to publish lesbian material, but it could still be dangerous. *Common Lives* carved a space for itself, for common voices and the courage of expression, for representation, for the hunger to see who lesbians were. Without an internet, we created a community for those who didn't have the resources or support to connect otherwise.

Created by and for lesbians, sustained for sixteen years, folding at a time when none of us could bankroll the journal ourselves. And if we could do it again? What would we receive now, what would women be writing about, and creating art about, now? Our best answers appear in this new space, thanks to *Sinister Wisdom*.

Common Lives/Lesbian Lives, Issue 25, Winter 1988

Photo Credit: Tracy Moore

COMMON LIVES/LESBIAN LIVES LIVES ON

Jean Taylor

Before writing this tribute, I checked with my book *Stroppy Dykes: Radical Lesbian Feminist Activism in Victoria During the 1980s*, to see if I had known this US lesbian magazine existed. It was sometimes difficult in Australia to get news about overseas publications so I was delighted with the following:

"The first issue of new lesbian quarterly *Common Lives/Lesbian Lives* was produced in August 1981 by a lesbian editorial collective in Iowa City IA USA. The magazine aimed to document lesbian experiences and included fiction, photos, herstories, biographies, graphics, correspondence, journal writing and essays and gave lesbians the opportunity to publish their creative and political work."

I'd have written more if I'd had access to the internet, to trawl through this on-line herstorical lesbian archive that informs me that the full set of these magazines is being held and have been made accessible by scanning each page and stored at the Charles Deering McCormick Library of Special Collections, Northwestern University in the US.

There have been many lesbian magazines, journals, and newsletters over these past fifty years in the US, UK and Australia. While most have come and gone, a few, like *Sinister Wisdom*, have managed to continue into the present day. To explain, the collective wrote in the first issue of *CL/LL*: "Our inspiration came from Catherine Nicholson and Harriet Des Moines, the founders and editors for five years of *Sinister Wisdom*." The no-holds-barred, well-written and in-your-face stories in *CL/LL* attracted attention, a great start to a magazine designed to attract a broad lesbian audience as writers and readers. A few examples:

In 1981, the wrap-around cover of the first issue of *CL/LL*, created by Lisa Schoenfielder, shows five dykes in a top-down sports car, the first of many such eye-catching cover graphics.

In that same issue, Joan Nestle, one of 21 contributors of stories, poems, photographs, drawings and essays in this first 116-page issue and co-founder of the Lesbian Herstory Archives in Brooklyn, published *Esther's Story, 1960*. She wrote, "I had heard of Esther. She was tough, a passing woman whose lover was a prostitute. Sea Colony talk. We all knew stories about each other like huge ice floes we would occupy the same ocean without touching. This night we touched."

Among the 56 issues of *CL/LL*, the cover of Issue #17's three old womyn wearing Sage straw hats caught my eye. And *CL/LL* had already become so popular and newsworthy, issue #15/16 had sold out, much to their surprise, and added: "Consider this: PO Box 1553 is a very small room in a medium-sized town at the heart of the Midwest. Just a front and back door, the front with a small window overlooking knees and linoleum and the occasional crown of a small child's head. Big deal. Now consider this. Without it you wouldn't be reading this page, because that's how we talk to people, through the mail."

All the work for this community-run lesbian periodical back in the day was hands-on. Every single job, from opening the mail and negotiating with contributors to typesetting all the contributions according to the magazine's format to organizing with printers to get the magazine printed for the lowest possible price and then posting them out to subscribers and fundraising on top of everything else, was done by willing lesbian hands.

In the double issue, Elana Dykewomon included her short story "Staking Claims":

"Sophie and I were sitting at a table with a view of the bay. It was just late afternoon, but we were ready for dinner. We'd never been to the restaurant before, it was new, clearly fashionable, and had a huge menu of attractive foods.

"Ordering food is a tricky business."

We're immediately drawn in by the writer who wants us to appreciate an aspect of the everyday lives of lesbians so that we can identify with the characters, learn something of benefit to know in our own lesbian love lives that most of us, let's face it, have had to make up as we go along, as we hope for the best and learn by our mistakes.

And lest anyone imagine that the indubitable excitement of producing a successful lesbian periodical would be more than enough to carry the editorial collective through all the obstacles that inevitably occur in even the best of endeavors, I noted the collective boosted their morale in issue #33: "A long overdue weekend retreat happened for our busy, tired and shrinking collective. We spent two days away in the woods relaxing, laughing, walking, dreaming and talking about *CL/LL*. A very needed time of reflection and self-praise for the journal occurred as we looked through the last fifteen issues of *CL/LL*. The overwhelming consensus was that a very small group of dykes from Iowa City put together a terrific journal."

"*Notes to our readers*... Welcome to issue #45," presented the radical lesbian activist and writer Judy Freespirit's amusing poem, *Mexican Het Dance*, ending with this stanza:

> We danced, we danced, we danced
> Our feet didn't miss a beat.
> Our bodies were so close
> We were exchanging heat.
> My heart was beating fast,
> I could tell that Grace was my kind.
> I smiled 'cause I knew
> This was not what Miss Finch had in mind.
> OLE!

A personal word here from myself: as a lesbian feminist writer who wrote articles for the Australian lesbian magazines *Lesbian Newsletter*, *Lesbian News*, *Labrys*, *Lesbiana* and the *Lesbian Network*, 1976-2006, I can attest how thrilling as well as affirming if also slightly scary it must have been for all those lesbian writers, poets, and artists to see their work published in a lesbian periodical, especially if it was for the first time. In fact, many of the writers and artists in CL/LL went on to be or already were well-known and accomplished writers. It's possible CL/LL gave them the opportunity to reach a wider readership at a time when they needed it most.

So why did this successful lesbian magazine stop production at issue #56 dated 1995-1996? The editorial collective explained in Notes to Our Readers: "Last August our major distributor declared bankruptcy. They owed us $4,500—money we've lost for good."

That debt was the straw that broke the lesbian camel's back. On the whole, lesbians don't have a great deal of disposable income, and most of us, at some stage or other, have lived hand-to-mouth to survive. The wonder of the lesbian community, as shown by the on-going nature of the lesbian feminist revolution, is that we have such a belief in ourselves to exist, such a drive to produce our artistic vision and tell our never-ending stories and create our art in all its many forms, all of which is driven by a radical feminist vision to save ourselves and the planet, that we can't help but get out there and do all the things that need to be done if we are to do more than just survive.

And that's what the lesbians who produced all 56 issues of *Common Lives/Lesbian Lives* had—a belief in themselves, in the lesbian writers and artists and poets, in the lesbian readership, in the lesbian community, so that there was no way they were not going to fulfill that commitment to produce yet another edition no matter how tired or stressed they were till, like even the best of activist collectives, they had to fold. Mind you, those 56 issues of CL/LL from 1981 till 1996 was a mighty achievement and those of us who benefited from that labour of love still value you and the efforts you made on our behalf.

MELANIE DEMORE

Jean Weisinger

CELEBRATING JOAN NESTLE

The Collective

Joan Nestle is well known as an author, historian and creative visionary, as well as a champion of femme identity. In 1973, she cofounded the Lesbian Herstory Archives with Deborah Edel in Brooklyn. The archive is designed "to hold on to anything and everything that could tell a lesbian story," as described by Carolyn D'Cruz in Joan's newest book, *A Sturdy Yes of a People.*

In 1981, Joan took a chance on a new lesbian publication and submitted "Esther's Story, 1960," which was published as the first piece of writing in the very first issue of *Common Lives/Lesbian Lives*. Joan wrote, "I had heard of Esther. She was tough, a passing woman whose lover was a prostitute. Sea Colony talk. We all knew stories about each other like huge ice floes we would occupy the same ocean without touching. This night we touched."

In 1998, Joan returned to Esther's story, taking in other possibilities of her gender expression which she published in *A Fragile Union*. Since 2001, Joan has been living in Melbourne, Australia with her love, Di Otto. We celebrate Joan here, as she believed in *Common Lives/Lesbian Lives* from the start.

Jerre Kalbas and Joan Nestle reading the very first issue of *Common Lives/Lesbian Lives*.

Photo Credit: Deborah Edel

REMEMBERING ANNE LEE

Kim Painter

Anne Lee

In 1981, at the age of 34, Anne Lee died of cancer in Iowa City. Her work was not widely published, yet her local reputation was enduring. She was remembered at gatherings as her works were read and her story shared. Her words continue to compel because she was willing to look down the barrel of it all: mortality, the creative drive, love, and anger. Anne was always right there peeking at the unspeakable with a wry smile. She refused to succumb to the twin goblins of fear and vulnerability yet never denied their existence. Anne embraced the experiences of her life's numbered moments without reserve. Her unsparing eye produced literature of a rounded shape, just right for holding an abundance of human experience. Anne Lee's writing offers comfort even while it explores our nightmares.

REST CURE

Anne Lee

From Common Lives/Lesbian Lives, Issue 3, Spring 1982

This is how it was in Iowa. Or this is how she remembered it later, when it clung to her like bits of twine, when the memory was still so full and pungent that it woke her in the night and unwound her slowly in the darkness of her well-locked room.

That her bed was fairly empty, she was fairly sure, and she searched in vain for the sight and sound and smell of her lover, who was still, inexplicably, in that other place. The bed itself lay flat and smooth, implacable, and she felt it press against her skin.

In Iowa, when she had lived there, when she had lived there for that one week, it had been the reality which had awakened her, the fact of her lover, the fact of Outside. She would reach, in her sleep, for her lover, would open her eyes and her mouth and her hands and her ears to the night and would pull it inside her and draw in her breath that so much was allowed.

It was as though her feeling for this place was the product not only of this life but of others. There was the current peace produced by the visit itself, by the contact with what was best and most alive, and there was the deep and odd subliminal peace produced by memories of things she'd never seen. There were objects and places, intersections of the mind which she remembered, and unknown corners turned in the knowledge of what she'd find, and women who she knew would be her lovers, and women who she knew would be her friends. And all of that, knowledge and memory and sensate peace, was wrapped around the moment.

She saw precision everywhere, the motion of the inevitable and true, and she accepted it, and watched, as in a dream, as her own movements echoed what she saw. It had surprised her, at first, as she watched her hands, to see this new precision, this sense of purposefulness she had sometimes glimpsed in others. It was a symptom, she supposed, a symptom of the fact that all seemed possible here. Possible, and worth doing. A function of hope, perhaps, or a function of time, which had slowed perceptibly as she stepped from the plane, so that the smallest motion caught and held her and time expanded, exacting homage for what was good.

If there was death here, it did not grin at her from corners. If there was violence, it had not sought her out, and when she woke, it was not in terror, but in astonishment of open windows, of air and moon and fireflies and stars. She was awakened by happiness and the physical sensations which it produced. The reverse of nightmare. The opposite of fear.

She reached, in the night, for her lover, and her lover was there, and she felt the curve of ass and thigh and murmured in her sleep and drew her lover closer, and walked enough to look at her and saw her safe and shining, and said to herself, remember it, remember it.

In the morning, she would run the mile and a half to the mailbox and back again, meeting no one, rejoicing in the surface of the road, the soft, brown earth between the rows of trees. Remember it, she said to herself. I must remember it and make it last. This may be all I have. I must save it now, against that time when I have gone from here, when there is nothing but asphalt and concrete. I must save it now, against that time, when I have gone from here, and there is nothing but the agony of a revolution in which the only blood is ours, the only casualties are ours, when I must go back to my comrades and say what I have seen. We know of nothing else there, in our insular little lives. We have our work, which is revolution, and we think that it is all there is, and we are tied to our phones and our watches and our unspeakable knowledge, and we think that that is all there is.

So I must go back, and quickly too, to my comrades and lovers and friends, and tell them what I have seen. They won't believe it, of course, but it will be a happiness at least. They will see that I have believed it. They will see that I have seen.

Odd. Strange that they, who have seen so much in their work (which is revolution) that they who would believe anything, will not believe this. Will not believe me when I say what I have seen. My friends and I have seen terrible things, things so terrible that they are never mentioned, even to each other. We have seen things, and heard things still more terrible, and we have hardened ourselves until we can hear anything without retching or tears.

Well, that, at least, is a lie. Or not true. We do what we can. I, personally, have doubled over (and not in laughter) at the slightest provocation. I have wept at morning and the concept of another day. I have known women (soldiers) who have not cried in years, and whose pain comes out in needle point and insomnia, in migraine and nightmares and Valium and booze. I have seen women who run ten miles a day to keep from murdering their children or their landlords or themselves, and I have seen women who could feed themselves on nothing when hope was gone—seen them move through fear and pain and terror, beyond exhaustion and despair.

My friends and I have seen terrible things, but I have seen this, too, and I will tell them. There are squirrels, still, I will say. Not here, but elsewhere. There are squirrels, I will say, and fireflies leaping over the hedgerows, and there are flowers and crops and berries, and there is air, still, not here, but elsewhere. There is air, and there is one place, at least, where it is possible to look around you without screaming—where there is something to see besides violence and destruction and decay. Something to see besides death.

When I was there (I will say), I was able to look at things without screaming, and they entered me whole and I have preserved them and brought them back to you. They entered me whole, and I have them, and give them to you as best I can with all their colors, all their shape and size. I give you their movement and cycles and change. I give you out Outside, and Naked, and Alone, and Sky. I give you morning without watches, and night without fear.

When she left that place and returned to her work (which was revolution), she took her memories with her, and gave them to her friends. They did not, of course, believe her, or not entirely, but it gave them pleasure to see that she was pleased. She was different, now, in some way they could not readily define. She laughed more than usual, although she had always laughed, and she cried more than usual, and it seemed to them that all of her had not returned, and that her thoughts were far away. When she talked of that place, her eyes would burn, and she would nearly make them see, and they would smile and shake their heads as if to clear them.

It seemed to them that all of her had not returned, and they watched her come back a little at a time, clinging fiercely to her memories, drawing on them daily, sucking them dry. If she, herself, had returned slowly, her lover had not returned at all, so there was missing her lover and missing that other place, and she went on with her work and waited for her lover, and clung fiercely to her memories which had long since ceased to be a comfort, and she felt that the important parts of her had been torn away in leaving. Disemboweled is how she felt, and held herself and ached and moaned and would have wailed, but had not the strength for that. Disemboweled, and bereft, the longing constant and terrible and sure, she waited for her lover.

When her lover returned, they would talk about it, about going to live in that other place. Her lover said it wasn't perfect—was hot in the summer and cold in the winter. Had mosquitoes and chiggers and rodents and flies. Had rednecks and fascists and rapists and men. Had conflict and process and struggle, just like any place else. Her lover said it wasn't perfect, but the eagerness in her voice belied her words. It wasn't perfect (no ocean or mountains), but it was lovely; it was certainly worth a try.

The voice of her lover sang in her head, and she waited for her return, and thought of her there in the house with the sky, and thought: this is how it was in Iowa, this is how it will be. The voice of her lover sang in her head, and clung to her like bits of twine, and hope was so full and pungent that it woke her in the night, and unwound her slowly in the darkness of her well-locked room.

Anne Lee wrote this story in the Fall of 1980. She was 33, lived in Pasadena, CA, and worked at Haven House, a battered women's shelter. In 1981 Anne moved to Iowa City, where she died that summer of cancer. Anne was a founding member of the CL/LL collective. (1982)

CROSS

Canyon Sam

From *Common Lives/Lesbian Lives*, Issue 11, Spring 1984

My earliest memory of dealing with what I later learned was a conflict or crisis of cultural identity was when I was approximately ten. Perhaps I was nine. Pressure had been building for a long time. I felt pulled in two different directions. On one hand I was encouraged by my family to be close to the family, close to the Chinese values that my parents were raised by: to be studious and serious about my education; to fit in, go by the rules, not rock the boat; to relate to white people but not in a close or real way. To know that my calling place was not somewhere in the outside world, it was back to the family.

This made for yet another (as we were all being raised the same way out there in the Richmond District) Chinese schoolkid known for being quiet, hard-working and a good student though undistinguished in any other way.

***

Both my parents grew up in close-knit Chinese communities—my father in San Francisco Chinatown, my mother in the Chinese community in Fresno, California, where her family owned and operated the largest Chinese restaurant in town for 30 years. Her father and two of his brothers, their wives and families of several children each all lived under one roof and worked at the restaurant. The 16 children went to school together—the roll call for years being "Alice Jing, Alicia Jing, Arthur Jing…Caroline Jing, Fred Jing, Gilbert Jing, Hazel Jing…May Jing…" they never had to have outside friends my mother said, because they had each other. They slept head-to-toe, head-to-toe in bunk beds in upstairs bedrooms, the rumble and whistle of the train through the San Joaquin Valley as familiar and routine as their own lives. After school, all the children went to Chinese school together. After Chinese school and some dinner, they went to work at the restaurant...till 10 pm weeknights, till 2 in the morning on weekends. They began at seven years old washing tumblers; as they got older, they did plates, cups, pots and pans. At junior high school age, they bussed tables; when they in high school they waited on tables, first the lunch shift then the dinner shift. The boys who were high school and college age did the dinner shift.

Both my mother and father were raised by parents who had come from China and to whom they spoke in Chinese. Neither knew English when they entered kindergarten.

***

By the time they married and had children they were in their mid-to-late 30's, and by the time I grew up they had moved from the two-room apartment in Chinatown where I had spent the first 20 months of my life to the middle-class Richmond District. My father—the youngest of five boys—was the only one in his family to go to college, and my mother one of four daughters who did, studying nursing at the community college while living at home. (Her brother, like most Number One sons, was pushed to become a doctor.) My parents had big dreams for us—realistic dreams: we would all go to college, all enter respectable professions, live good lives. Raise our own families.

I was given dictionaries, study lamps, wristwatches for Christmas. My friends received dolls, clothes, bikes, toys, and games. The neighborhood and my school were a combination of kids from working class, lower middle-class and middle-class families. Maybe a third or a quarter was Asian—mostly Chinese and Japanese. The rest Italian, Irish, Armenian, Jewish, WASPs. A sprinkling of Filipinos.

From what I observed, Oriental kids did not question. We did as we were told and did it well. From what I saw around me in the classes, the schoolyard, the steady diet of TV and media, the rest of society was another way altogether. They questioned, they participated, they broke rules, were livelier, freer, more articulate, enjoyed themselves more, as well as were more confident and had a stronger sense of themselves. And if doing well at school was what counted—and it did—they were able to do that as well.

I looked down on my father for not being able to pronounce his r's and l's: "Your Uncle Peter and Aunt Purr are coming this weekend." "People in other countries of the world are starving." Reading and writing were basic skills my parents had but did not have any real interest in or particular passion for.

***

I thought as a group, though there were individual exceptions of course, that Asians were timid, hesitant, inarticulate. I found Chinese school irrelevant and did not intend to do well. I went obediently every day after school for three years, giving up my precious playtime because my parents wanted us to go so badly. They had tried to teach us at home, and when that failed ("Don't turn it off now, Dad! It's prime time; we'll miss "Gilligan's Island *and* "Lost in Space.'" "This book is written backward, y'know.") they pleaded, cajoled, and bribed us to go to Chinese school at a little church a few blocks away. I went because they wanted me to; my older brother who never responded to any kind of pressure refused to go, and my younger brother agreed to go if he was paid for every day he attended.

I became somewhat of a class clown. On the other hand, I was taken under the wing of the young Chinese associate pastor who, recognizing speaking and leadership qualities, gave me my first taste of life behind the podium. After a while, I was given the responsibility of leading the student worship service upstairs in the chapel every Thursday afternoon.

***

Asians, especially girls, were sheltered and kept on a short leash. My mother was bitter and angry and hurt about my spending time with other friends outside the family. "You're spending too much time with your friends; you're not spending enough time at home. You should spend more time with your family. They are the most important people in your life; they will always be there, your friends will not. Your family will come through for you for the rest of your life; friends come and go. Your family is what is important: Your dad and I and your brothers."

***

At one point, it came to a head.

I felt dull and heavy, as if a thick grey mass was knotted up inside my brain slowing my thinking, my acting, my judgements. I took long walks along the eucalyptus-lined roads in Golden Gate Park three blocks south of my house. I was nine years old and feeling pulled in two directions. I felt there were two different ways I was being brought up and they at many points contradicted each other. Each inhibited the other. I felt pressed to choose one or the other because I could not go on being so painfully conflicted and confused. I had to choose which voices to listen to. Choose between two different ways of being. One was going to allow me to be more of who I was: I *was* more outspoken, more outgoing. I could be shy…and certainly was for whole years of my life, but I was not a dull-witted, nodding "nice-little-Chinese-girl."

I was sitting on the fence looking out at one side where it looked to me like learning could go further, social interactions could be richer, and where there was more room to be me. On the other side, when I looked out, I saw there were places I didn't fit, boxes too small for me, there were restrictions, limitations that would hold me back. The emotional pressure weighed in the balance. If

I stayed with "the Chinese side" I would keep close to the family, stay protected, be assured of their approval and love. If I chose "the white side"—the values of the outside society—I would risk and probably lose some or all of that protection, approval and love.

***

I took walks to a big cross in the park. Climbing its granite base some fifteen feet to a ledge right below the white cross statue whose upper tip poked out through the trees on top, I sat there for hours when I needed to think. There was never anyone else there and I could be completely alone with my thoughts. (In hindsight, I believe this was a spiritual power point for me; I found uncommon clarity, wisdom, and strength there.)

I remember when it happened. It must have been a summer because when I walked home, it was late but still very light out. When I walked home afterwards, I felt light, like a huge weight had been lifted from me; the bounce had returned to my step as I went springing across the meadows, through forests, along pathways home.

This one day I had been on a long walk and then sat at "my spot" in the afternoon, early evening. It was summer, I was about nine or ten. I finally decided. It was decided for me. I accepted it. I jumped.

I chose white.

***

Looking back, I was not choosing *being* white over *being* Chinese. Obviously, I was Chinese, was raised in a Chinese family, with Chinese-American values, so I could never come out being anything but. More, I was seeing that some of those traditional values and family pressures stood in the way of my being myself. I decided I would not be adhering to those values in toto. It was not an egotistical or selfish rebellious decision, for I loved my parents and had a strong desire to make them happy. It was just that I couldn't be something I wasn't; it was impossible for me to hide and hinder so much of who I was. When I "chose white" I saw in the white world much more latitude in who I could be. As well I saw the inevitable disapproval ahead from those closest to me, though I was never prepared for it. What I didn't see was that this choice would make me different not just from white people, but from my own people.

Author's Notes, 2023:

Golden Gate Park had little signage when I grew up in the 60's, so I may not have known this sixty-foot tall monument, located east of Lloyd Lake, was called the Prayerbook Cross.

SF Chinatown: Chinese in America when I grew up were Cantonese and spoke dialects of Cantonese. They had begun to immigrate to California in the mid-1800's because of the Gold Rush. Later, starting in the mid-20th century Mandarin-speaking Chinese from other places like Taiwan, the P.R.C. and Singapore started immigrating to the U.S.

Actually, both my grandfathers, I've confirmed since the time this piece was published, were born in California. Both my grandmothers were born in China.

I'm startled by the use of the word *Oriental* now, but I guess the term was in use then.

"Steady diet of TV and media": In the early days of television, shows had all-white casts. We watched several hours a day of programming (!), shows such as My Three Sons, Leave It to Beaver, Ozzie and Harriet, Gunsmoke, Bonanza.

UNTITLED

Diana Miller

Art Credit: Diana Miller

THE DISHWASHER

Joanna Brown

Metal insides gleam like knives, like the steel surface of a pond or the clean expanse of my confidence when the world is sparkling. First it was installed badly and the shelves slipped out. Now it's fixed, and you think we have to run this thing every night because it's so small. I think it's wasteful. You ran it when I'd decided not to. And I love you like a whirlpool, but not in any way that is energy efficient. No, my love spins and throws circular sluices in unpredictable spirals. And my fury is greater than a rapid cycle, my wounds deeper than the cavernous depths of any appliance. Yet in the end there is solace in your arms that circle 'round me and touch my empty pockets and corners, wash out my crumbs.

AIRPORT

Tamara Hollins

We sit side by side in rocking chairs
Cheap wood shows though the scratched paint
Day light wanes into evening as airplanes come and go
Distance is between us—
a dictate that keeps us in bounds except in the small
    moments when you look at me
In that way we are silent,
scratching at the surface of division

FOR PAT PARKER

Jan Hardy

From *Common Lives/Lesbian Lives*, Issue 35, Summer 1990

I can see you now,
with your rich voice
and dry wit, gently
poking fun at us
for thinking you are gone

smiling and shaking your head a little
at the tributes
the tears

wishing we would all just dance
raise our voices together
take better care of each other
help the children grow

and if we really want to honor you,
we should honor ourselves enough
to do what you did:
speak out
speak out against bigotry
speak out against hatred
listen again to your beautiful
Black lesbian wisdom
and learn from your life

we are tempted by sadness
we are used to mourning

but we have no martyr here
we have your life, your words
a wealth of women's strength here
and you will love on

Photo by Linda Koolish

Pat Parker

GIRLS LIKE ME

Aischa Daughtery

born on a friday night / libra sun / i have always been a femme / femme like a cast-iron labrys / perfectly resilient & charming as hell / as in i've shaved more heads than i've cooked dinners & wear *woman* on my sleeve like it fits / femme as in lesbian / as in of course it would be my name that got twisted by the masses / universalised in some cheap bid to realign me with the men i pay no mind to / femme as in under / devoted to / in accordance with: butch / *that femme dyke* before any other label you could stomach / as in you'll try but there is nothing to fix / femme in every word that i speak & deed i carry out / where i fit & where i don't / when i pick up a pencil & cry & vote & make love i am a / powder-puff femme / no-games femme / i-love-the-sensuality-of-lipstick-names femme / as in the opposite of apolitical / as in i wear it too tight / too short / i kissed you in a bar last night & jogged past you this morning / femme like a safe-house / a scholarship / a chainsaw draped in mulberry silk / femme as in you knew exactly what you were getting yourself into / as in my pussy is not passive it is vagina dentata / i still have dreams about him breaking through the window and killing me / femme in the places women die / femme as in i call my lovers *Miss or Sir* & capitalise their pronouns out of respect or they do mine / i think i could love any woman if i were to spend enough time with her / as in you want to get to know the girls like me / as in you want my hair seeping through your knuckles / my bite shattering your shoulder blades / you think you love me because i'm good at pretending to listen as in my three favourite things are pasta & sex & being handpicked by history to hold the title / femme as in you say my name like an emergency / like a breaking news article for venus exploding / femme as in your girlfriend's muse / the fucking sun / survivor of it all / in mourning / as in i'll grant my own citizenship / take the freedom i am sold & *pretty* as a compliment / DYKE PRINCESS / THUNDER BITCH / i invented myself from scratch

Common Lives/Lesbian Lives, Issue 12, Summer 1984

HYPER-POP APOCALYPSE, OR, NONBINARY LESBIAN BLUES
THE WAREHOUSE ON WATTS, PHILADELPHIA PA

Alison Lubar

We sip warm canned water
while the boys in straps striptease
their fishnet shirts and stash them
on black pleather barstools.
By the bathroom, they apply
shamrock salicylic acne patches
under each eye, like tears.

Seasonal depression hovers
neon from the fog machine. These twinks
ignore our polyester slip-dresses. You would turn
their pulsing swaying thrusting
into a circle pit, take a baby gay for a spin
as your mace.

I curl around myself like the singular calla lily petal,
press against the basecoat painted backdrop; the press-
wood snags satin like a cat's tongue. I would let it rough me up,
more than any of these cissies [with the sea]. The old men
will still tell me to smile, no matter if the night
transformed them to a queen. I do not exist
to impress them. I dance to the half-beat,
slow it down, rooted as a solar powered
dashboard daisy. All of this feigned nature
is made from plastic. All of the green turned
to unbiodegradable glitter. Even the windows
are blackout-curtained, as streetlights shine

like sun. And in the morning, we can't believe
that Spring still comes,
with her tepid, wet tongue.

DO YOU CONSIDER THIS BLUE?

Mel Connelly

I thought maybe we could go to the '90s
Trade Beanie Babies, adjust the antenna on the T.V.

Thought for a moment we could go back in time,
put us on equal footing, close the distance between us

I thought it would be easier by now
to love someone so much like yourself

I remind you of your body, or
it's something like "I'm not good enough"

Really, it's me
I am not original (see above)

I despair success
I am sick of writing in male language

But every empty house I see
I imagine us moving in

I'm carrying the most boxes
You're getting more "womanly"

I'll give a while, continue
to wonder as I tend to do

I'll stop checking myself out in the mirror
and quit contemplating paint colors

But before I go
how does a yellow door

with matching shutters
sound to you?

COMMON LIVES
LESBIAN LIVES
a lesbian quarterly

SPECIAL LESBIAN PHOTO ISSUE

number twelve

RAIN

Mistinguette Smith

From *Common Lives/Lesbian Lives*, Issue 38, Spring 1991

It's easy for people to talk about violence if they haven't done any of it. I keep thinking about my friend who says that if men won't voluntarily reduce themselves to ten percent of the population, that we should do it for them. She also thinks that batterers and rapists should be killed. I mostly agree with her until I think about what it felt like to hold my newborn baby brother in my arms, who doesn't know what he'll be forced to grow up to be. Or think about the suddenness of give when bone snaps free beneath the weight of my foot.

I know a lot of women who talk like that. Some of them are even my friends. They loan me books and magazines and talk about the gynocidal plot to kill us all off, as if the world could go on without us. Sometimes I think they're just leftovers from the seventies who love a good conspiracy, and there don't seem to be any better ones around these days. What else is there to do when you spend your time doing things like chaperoning me at Take Back the Night marches and passionately reading the works of Andrea Dworkin and Mary Daly as if they were god?

Of course, you can't go around thinking about this kind of stuff all of the time. Some nights the silver film of rain is just too inviting and I can't help but want to be part of the wet kisses it leaves on the street. Even though it's summer, this block is awful quiet, like rain is whispering "hush, hushhh" through the streets. If I hold my breath, I can hear the neighbors' T.V. turned to the eleven o'clock news. They leave that T.V. on all the time, like it keeps them company or something. Probably don't ever get to hear the lonely sound of the occasional car whooshing up the street.

I love to walk in the rain in the summertime. When it's been hot like today, the first drops almost sizzle and make steam when they hit the baking concrete. Then everybody grabs something to put over their heads, so the rain won't mess up they two- hour trip to the beauty shop, and snatch the little kids inside, like a few drops of wetness is gonna melt them.

I feel bad for the little kids, but I like having the streets to myself. I can go walking for miles and miles, looking in on other people's windows like little snapshot postcards of life. I once walked all the way downtown without even noticing it, looking at the different lives through those big glass picture windows that all the old houses in this part of town have. I like the feeling of being on the outside looking in. Sometimes I write stories about what I imagine goes on in there, making up some kind of real life for the people on the insides.

It's kinda hard though, cuz almost every house has the blue glow of a television shining out, so I can't even make up any good dialogue. I mean, what could people possibly have to say to each other if they would give up a good thunderstorm to watch T.V.?

So I just couldn't resist going out tonight. Maybe I shoulda rode my bike, but you go too fast to really notice what's around you unless you walk. Besides, this is my neighborhood, I know almost everybody here, even though I wouldn't speak to half of 'em if you paid me. Anyway, I put on my old beat-up tennis shoes that I don't care if get all wet, and snuck out the side door without my brother seeing me. I eased the door closed so my mom wouldn't hear me leave. If I can get out the house, I'm pretty much free: everybody is always dead sleep by the time I get home, so nobody even knows I'm going if I'm quiet coming in. It felt so good to be outside in the wind and wet that I ran the first six blocks. Everything was all closed up, this being Sunday and all. I didn't stop running till I got up to the neon sign in the window of Three Star Beauty salon, then my glasses were all fogged up, so I stopped to rest.

That's when I noticed the worms. Now this may sound funny, but I like living in the city because there aren't any animals, except for dogs and cats, which don't count. But every time I go out in the rain I forget about the worms. Big, fat slimy earthworms, swimming across the sidewalks. The kind that gush when you step on them, and make you slide and fall down. Goddam earthworms all over the sidewalks, so I had to run with my head down so I could see them and not step on them. I didn't even have time to look in the basement window to see what people who didn't watch T.V. did.

I was making a quick mental note to ask my friend who thinks we should kill men if she gets queasy at killing earthworms too, when I heard somebody walking up behind me. I was out of breath, so I slowed down, and put my glasses back on so I could see. By the time I stopped panting, he was right up next to me.

Now, I can usually tell a lot about a person right off when I meet them, before they even say a word. I pay attention to the little details, like how he was carrying this big yellow and blue umbrella advertising Wilson tennis balls. I knew he wasn't from around here because nobody in this neighborhood knows anything about tennis, they just watch football or shoot hoops all day in the kids' playground. He looked kinda young, so when he said hi, I said hi back. I figure he must be lost, carrying around a tennis ball umbrella and speaking to strangers in this neighborhood, so when he offered to share his umbrella I said okay. He told me he was trying to find the bus station, and since I was going that way I told him I'd walk part way with him, and show him where to go.

We were laughing about the earthworms, cuz he was dodging them too, when we got to the turnoff for the station. I said I'd see him around, and kept walking. All of a sudden I felt him grab my arm from behind, real hard. Before I could even think anything the world started spinning around, and my head hit the wall of the bus shelter behind me. I don't remember that it hurt, but I'm sure that it had to. I just felt dizzy, and for a moment couldn't believe that this was the same guy I had been laughing with a minute ago. I tried to push him off of me, but he hit me so hard that my ears began to ring, and then I couldn't hear nothing. It was like a movie with no sound. I watched his face screw up in anger, and his mouth opening and closing like a fish, but nothing came out. It woulda been funny if I wasn't so scared.

Suddenly I felt real calm. Seconds dragged out while I thought "this man is going to rape me." Real clear, just like that. Not all hysterical like you'd expect it to be. For a minute I panicked, I'd lost my glasses and I can't see a thing without them. Then, the next thought came, just as serene and clear as the first: "You know how to take care of yourself."

Now, I don't want you to think I was having visions or hearing voices or nothing. I'm not crazy, but for once I was grateful for my crazy friends. See, last summer they made me take this self-defense course for women with them. I got my mom to pay for it because she is so worried about my strange habits, like walking around alone late at night. Even though I'm not real strong or anything, I could do all of the stuff that the instructor taught us, and my "diploma" was the board I broke the last session of the class.

I was so calm that I didn't even think to worry about whether I would remember all that stuff we learned. I just took a deep breath and let out one of those powerful yells that I like to practice at the beginning of class. The rain had started to come down really hard, and I couldn't see for real now. Then I swung my arms up and out (*pull away toward the thumb* I hear the instructor say) and for a minute my hands are free, but he leans toward me and pins my shoulders against the wall. Shit. Now what am I gonna do? And I hear this voice, just like she was standing beside me, saying *knees bend in only one direction.*

So, blind as a bat, and deaf to boot, I pushed as hard and as fast as I could in the direction of what I hoped was his knee, and felt the most awful sound. Something went *snap!* like a sapling breaking, and a shudder went down my spine. We hadn't practiced this part in class. From somewhere far away, a voice that sounded like mine started screaming NO! I wanted to throw up, but kept screaming NO! No! no...It's not supposed to be this way! I'm supposed to feel like a woman of power, defending my right to walk safely down my streets! You didn't tell me it meant hurting somebody! And all I could think about was the sound of something fragile forever breaking, and trying to convince myself I had no choice, had done the right thing.

I don't remember how I got here to the hospital. I guess I realized I was hurt and I walked. I don't know what happened to the guy either. He dropped his umbrella and hobbled off, probably scared to death by all my screaming, thinking he found a crazy one. The doctor wanted to give me some valium, but I said no thanks. I've seen what they do to women with that stuff, turn 'em into zombies. One of the nurses let me use the staff bathroom so I could throw up and scream and cry in private. He seems like he understood, even if he is a man. He even let me keep on my own clothes instead of one of those ugly little hospital gowns, until they come in to examine me.

The doctor hasn't seen me yet, even though I've been here for half an hour, and the whole emergency room is empty. They're waiting for my mom to get here. I keep telling them that I don't need her, she'll just be upset, and she *will* need the valium, but they say they can't see me without her permission because I'm underage. I'll be sixteen in two more weeks. I wish I'd thought to lie about my birthdate.

I tried to call some of my friends, but no one was home. Probably at one of their never-ending meetings, trying to reach consensus about who makes the banner for the next march. I can hear the cops coming in, asking to talk to me about what happened. I hope I'm not in trouble for hurting that creep. I decided to write all of this down, so if I have to go to court I can be a good witness. Or at least I won't be so nervous when I have to talk to the police. I know they won't care about the stuff like how free it feels to walk at night in the rain. My friends would, though. Maybe when this is all over, I'll tell this story to them.

SELF-PORTRAIT

Chris Cinque

QUEEN CLUCK

Randa Downs

Nine years after a contentious breakup, it was August 2011 when I went to California to visit that ex-partner. She'd called to say she wanted to be friends again—put the past behind us. When I returned to my little Bainbridge Island cottage, my answering machine blinked franticly. Still another ex-partner, Chris Cinque, was wondering how I was. "Give me a call," she said. Well, I thought—if this isn't old girlfriend week. I waited two weeks to call her back.

The last time I'd seen Chris was in 2003 in Minneapolis. After breakfast, she invited me to her house to see her artwork. Her partner—in the kitchen cooking something—wordlessly glanced my way. When I heard Chris's message on my machine, I knew she and the stony woman had broken up, but something had kept me from reaching out.

This time I called her, and over the next nine months, we had long distance conversations about our lives—hers as a teacher and visual artist and mine as a child welfare specialist. We talked of our past theater careers and loved the synchronicity of having done solo performance work at the same time.

After months of flirting over the phone—something I thought would come to nothing—I said, "I've never told you this, but I saw you on stage three decades ago—before I met you. That was the beginning of everything, wasn't it?"

***

The first time I laid eyes on Chris, it was 1980. She was dressed as a chicken, a royal chicken at that. She walked onto the stage squawking, "A ball. A great ball. How wonderful! What will I wear?" She was strutting and fluttering around the stage ordering her minions to do her bidding. I could not take my eyes off her. Other actors became mere props. As her hilarious chicken mannerisms embraced the absurdity of her character, I could see the smart decisions she made playing a dumb chicken.

Then I became apprehensive—butterflies in the stomach. Sitting in the audience, next to my husband, I had the alarming sense of my attraction to this woman—a woman I did not know playing a chicken. I didn't wait around after the show to meet her, to tell her how delightful and funny she was. I couldn't have sputtered out the words. Good at compartmentalizing, I tucked the experience away.

Two years after Chris played Queen Cluck, I was in rehearsals for a new play with the acting company At the Foot of the Mountain Theatre. One morning, the artistic director strolled into our warmup session to announce the hiring of a new actor. When she mentioned the actor was Chris Cinque, my heart began pounding. How many Chris Cinques could there be? I had the same reaction as seeing her on stage—the fluttering butterflies and anxiety akin to panic. Only this time my sense of trepidation told me I was going to have to face something difficult.

I got to know Chris after she joined the ensemble. She was funny, immensely talented, whip smart and Italian. When we rehearsed a play about women who grew up in the Catholic church, the sexual energy became unmistakable.

One morning, our director handed us an apple and asked us to improvise the fall of Eve as part of the creation myth in the Book of Genesis. As the five of us tossed the apple around, each actor took a turn exploring Eve's relationship to the fruit—shame, ravenous delight, fear of the wrath of god. When it landed in Chris's hands, from 20 feet she tossed it to me overhanded like a baseball. She didn't see where it landed. That damn apple slammed into my mons veneris. It was painful and I felt as bruised as the apple. It took everything I had in me to keep from bursting into tears. I realized I was in love.

***

Our affair started months later in Philadelphia where we performed at the wonderful old Wilma Theatre. One night some of the other actors and I decided to go dancing. We set out for the nearest gay bar to relax and avoid men hitting on us. My courage in that bar still amazes me. I could blame it on the booze, but I knew what I was doing when I walked up behind Chris standing at the jukebox. She wore a black vest over a black shirt. I slipped my hand under her vest and did a slow slide up her back. Turning, she looked at me and smiled. We began to dance and when she kissed me the axis of my world shifted.

This should have been a happy story except for a couple of details. Chris was in a relationship with another woman and I was married. But there was no denying we had an intense attraction to each other. One night in bed, we smelled smoke and then saw a bright flame. During our lustful desire for each other, my bedside candle had ignited the edge of a pillowcase.

I was heartbroken when I realized Chris had no plans to leave her partner, and being the other woman was not a role I savored. We both were filled with guilt and remorse, and yet, she kept showing up at my door. The push/pull dynamic was demoralizing. One afternoon, a terrible fight ended as I threw lawn chairs over her second-floor balcony.

By that time, I had left my marriage and announced to all who cared that I was a lesbian. The chaotic affair with Chris lasted for over a year before I ended it. I moved away from the city where I'd fallen in love with her and went on with my life.

***

Here we were decades later. We described dreams about the other, disclosing the small notations we wrote in our journals that now held prophetic meaning. Had we subconsciously kept each other close all those years until we would meet again?

In June 2012, I was assigned work in St. Paul. I told Chris I would love to visit—maybe go to dinner or the theater. We did both. At a café we ordered the same meal—shrimp and polenta—which arrived in circles of whole shrimp ringing our bowls. Chris's eyes widened as the crustaceans stared dead-eyed back at her. "I need to go to the restroom," she whispered. "Yes, go!" I said, then gingerly pulled off the heads of my shrimp and switched our bowls. Chris was relieved when she found her shrimp pleasantly decapitated.

Our conversation that evening was a blur, though I recall gently brushing against each other as we strolled on a walkway overlooking the Mississippi River.

While arranging my trip to Minnesota, I took a few extra days to go up north for a respite. When I asked Chris where I should go, she liked the idea so much she said, "Maybe I'll go, too. School will be out by then. I'll look for a place for us to stay."

The next day Chris drove behind the wheel of my rental car to Betty's Cabins somewhere north of Duluth. When I casually put my hand on the back of her neck like it was the most natural thing in the world, she gave me a huge smile. Later, she confided she had sensed the electricity in that gesture just like the time I put my hand under her vest in that gay bar in Philadelphia.

My attraction to Chris and all the desire I had for her 30 years ago came rushing back. As we drove, I looked out at the grandeur of Lake Superior and smiled to myself.

When we walked into Betty's front office, she was listening to the radio—something religious, I think, because a man was talking about sin and the devil and the mark of the beast. Turning around, she stared at us for a moment before making her way to the counter. Was she sizing us up? Could she see the dyke in us? Did she think of sin and damnation? Betty was not warm and welcoming.

Later in our cabin, as Chris looked into my eyes I pulled her in and kissed her.

***

Chris and I ended up in a year-long, long-distance relationship that allowed us to meet each other again. One night we made love for six hours—a marathon of orgasms—a kind of sexual endurance test. I was thrilled to be so in love again—something I thought was over for me during my nine years of being single. We were in our early 60s and had lived full lives. Chris hadn't had a drink in over 30 years and was diligently working her program. She had received a master's in linguistics and was teaching—a job she loved. As a survivor of father-daughter incest myself, I had done a lot of healing and recovery. My 20 years in child welfare helped me better understand trauma and the role it played in my childhood and in my life as an adult survivor. I saw myself as the child I had been every day in my work.

Chris discovered her own early childhood abuse that we suspected had played a huge role in our troubled relationship so many years before. She was battling demons that neither of us were ever aware of. Chris first knew me as a recently out incest survivor and we wondered if this was subconsciously triggering for her. We admitted that neither one of us was healthy enough to be with the other back then. Now we were both ready and capable of making a commitment to each other—something that wasn't possible in 1984.

I retired in the summer of 2013 and moved back to Minneapolis. On June 10, 2014, we married before a judge. In her vows Chris said, "I feel like we met in broad daylight this time around. We saw each other's true selves and we trusted we could make it work this time." I said in my vows, "The fact that we were lovers so long ago provides a depth that wouldn't be possible without that shared history. The past and the present have folded into each other."

I love my wife deeply. In our passion, we are a perfect fit for each other. And yet, sometimes our abuse histories come roaring back in our need for each other, our wanting each other. Our shame begins small, then burrows its way, separating us from the present and demanding we return to the past and old trauma and fear. We hold onto each other like a life raft waiting for the wave of the flashback to pass. It breaks my heart, but now we both understand what is happening. We both know that the abuse we endured as children will always be with us. There is great comfort in being survivors together, in being old women together.

THE YEAR 2068, AGE 71

Ananya Garg

I finally got that butch haircut
It looked fine

Everybody loved me the same,
However a new motorcycle did appear
In my garage the very next day
Oh, I laughed, put the dog in the sidecar
And drove to the beach,

The sea air healed my breath almost
As well as the sand healed my stubbed toe

Last night I dreamt a beautiful dream
And this morning remembered

Started the day with a smile on my face
Knowing I, from somewhere in there,
Had put it on my self

That night, I read a book that moved me to tears
And read aloud the passage that did for my
beloved, and we wept silently
Together

I've nearly read all the books on my shelf now
It took nearly a lifetime

For life kept throwing new books my way
And you simply can't refuse
A gift of life

CANZONE

Amy Spade

We are moving too slowly, you and I,
a skittish, past-love fed adagio,
bass notes sometimes clear, sometimes jumbled,
sometimes too low to make out, must I
keep going home, feeling alone, jumbled,
what was Lucy's word? *Muddled*. Adagios
playing aloud, but my heart all allegro,
my hands all flutter, nervous allegro.

You are learning to play me, becoming
adept, your hands accustomed to finding
the melodic tones, hums and moans of voice
giving way to wonder, but my true voice
eludes you, the secret *I love you* bound
up in my throat speechless, artless, finding
itself stuck there, waiting for a sign, bound
by your metronome set at slow, becoming

pianissimo. It hurts to hold back
my heart, impulse reined in, tick-tock faster
than your metronome's knocking, you afraid
of hitting the wrong notes. Because I'm afraid
too, I sing above and below, around
what is between us. Don't want to take back
signs I've left in the music—look around
to see when I've tried to love you faster.

The light in my eyes betrays me, singing
a song I can't control, singing to you.

Don't pianists know they've struck the right note
by sensation of hand, arm, finger, eye
before the sound of keys?
Yet here I
sit, wanting to play you con brio, the notes
between us almost right, Lulu singing,
I've never seen such a woman as you.

OTHER HALF

Eve Jasper

I need more than the seat next to you.
Space, words, touch is not enough.
I want to grab your soul
and crush it into mine.
I want to hold your forehead
until all your thoughts,
however rough,
come crashing into my brain.
I want to drive myself under
your skin until
nothing between us remains.
No atom, no cell.
It will be our living heaven,
and our living hell.

I MET AN IMAGINED WOMAN

Diamond Marie Pedroza

and fell in love with her right away
"Romance" played while our smiles widened beyond
    our masks
Kuramoto never intended to produce such a serenade
but then again neither did Connie Converse whose waltz
    now permeates my formerly hardened heart
if I could be any more than what I am I would coil myself
    around the freedom you possess
because there is no greater fear than living my life the same
    as I always have

as I watch these lavender feelings seep into my skin,
    all I want to do is live infinitely in this moment
with you
when
we move
closer
so close I can see the different hues of blue in your eyes
then you
slowly
take off your mask under this fading sky
only to realize
you are someone I have always wanted to know
more than Therese when she first saw Carol
more than Carol when she resigned her life to be with Therese
even more than Abby when she kept on loving Carol anyways

there is enough of you to keep me intoxicated beyond the belief
    that we are magnets that won't ever detach from one another

my only desire is to crystallize this feeling
or somehow memorialize the speed at which love envelops us
      and renders us wanting more
I think about how lucky we must be not to have to share this scene
      with a screen
I think about time and how we won't ever have enough of it
I tell you, "I think this is the end"
you tell me, "this feels like a beginning"

Three Woman Moon by Rachel Feury

STRAIGHT SCHOOL FOR DYKES

C. Elliot Mullins

In straight dyke school, I learned
to wear my hair long and say "my husband" as if
    it didn't scrape across my tongue
to believe myself when I began sentences
    with "I decided..."
to organize my psyche into alphabetized bins –
    D denial
    F field trip
    L Little League
    M Meal Train
    P patriarchy, permission slip, parent-teacher
        conference
    T things we don't say

In straight dyke school, I learned
  not to tally how often people say fag or retarded
    or slut without looking around first
that a cost/benefit analysis of the closet pairs best
    with canned wine
      to center on mothering with its places to go
        and things to do and forms to fill out
        and dreams to
    twist into reasonable college majors

In straight dyke school, I learned
  that sex is bad and so am I
  to paper the closet, add built-ins, and never
    try the door
  to tell myself the story, again and again,
    of a good enough life

In straight dyke school,
    eventually my grades started to slip
    butches appeared everywhere to distract me
        from my studies with their chin-up-nods
    and t-shirted shoulders and thick thighs
        and brown eyes and nails to the quick
    good enough became impossible
    I started cutting class

In straight dyke school,
    No one warned me about the softness of woman-skin
        on woman-skin
    I stopped training up future capitalists
    stopped claiming what wasn't mine
    and dropped out

we don't care if we do, 1920 from *Common Lives/Lesbian Lives*, Issue 1, Fall 1981

DYKES LIKE ME

Rowan Harvey

Everyone in the world has to make decisions, no matter how upsetting. It's just a fact of life. As of current writing, I am the only butch lesbian I know. I wear steel-toed shit-kickers, heavy denim pants and leather jackets, and have hair shorn to an eighth of an inch. I wake up and do my best to look every letter the word "dyke."

At sixteen, when I first shaved my head, I was dating a person I thought I loved. We eventually parted on amicable terms when he realized he was a man and I was still a lesbian, but sometimes I selfishly wish he was still a lesbian. He understood me in ways no one else has since.

The first time I had sex was with him. We watched *But I'm a Cheerleader* in my bedroom at my grandparents' house and tried not to look at each other during the love-making scene. Then, once the TV screen was black and a wax-melter defusing soft vanilla into the room was our only illumination, I turned to him.

I smiled softly, hesitantly, and leaned into his shoulder. He petted my head before I rose and kissed him. Recoiling slightly, he returned my affection with little gusto. He never liked kissing.

When I finally reached for his panties, he stopped me. Said he was nervous. I told him I was, too. He said he wanted it, but wasn't sure how to start. I kissed his cheek and told him to let me take the lead. He did.

I was gentle, trailing my hand across his body and kissing as I went. I reached his breasts and he stopped me again, this time laughing lightly.

"Do you want to touch them?" he asked. I nodded. He huffed. "You shouldn't. They're not very sensitive."

I shrugged, disappointed, and slid to the end of the bed.

My fingers toyed at the outside of his panties for a while, warming him up to me. After a while, he nodded to a question I hadn't asked and, with one last look into his eyes, I slid his underwear off.

When I first tasted him, I could hardly believe it was happening. It felt surreal. Low lights, conflicting sweet and sweaty smells, and a lover who hardly wanted to be touched.

Regardless of how real it was or wasn't, I soon had him biting his knuckles, scratching at my new sheets and clenching his thighs. I pulled up to say, "if you need something to hold onto, you can grab my hair."

It was a silly statement. My head had been shorn consistently for months to mirror the porn I'd watched in the days before, but he reached to try. I could feel his fingers desperately, futilely, clutching at my scalp, digging and flexing only to find nothing useful. He gave up and went back to pulling at my bedspread.

Something in me felt disappointed, pained, lonely despite the body underneath me. I couldn't put a name to the feeling, but it was there nonetheless.

After he came, I stood up, swiped my hand across my mouth, and started cleaning us up. Staring at me, he asked, "do you want me to..." and gestured to my partially naked form. I shook my head. Smiled. Told him that eating him out was enough for me. For that, I received a nonchalant shrug. At least he wasn't complaining.

Days later, I picked him up at his house to go to PrideFest Milwaukee. As he got dressed, I sat in the kitchen with his mother. She watched me closely and I sweated. I had recently fucked her child, after all, so my nerves were high.

After minutes of agonizing silence, she turned to me, made a show of looking me up and down, and laughed.

"Why would you shave your head?" she asked without preamble. "My kid might as well date a man now!"

I chuckled along, gave some vague answer about the hot weather, and we returned to silence. When my partner arrived I quickly led him outside and we left.

Those two instances, my lover unable to grab my hair and his parent unable to see the woman under it, stuck with me long after they happened. Even after he and I went our separate ways, I thought about him and his mother. I still do.

Oftentimes, when I think of my ex-lover and his mother, I'm reminded of my own mother. When I first came out to her at age fourteen, she made a request as we drove to Menards to pick up an order of lumber she had waiting.

"Rowan," she said, "I want just one thing: don't shave your head, don't even cut your hair, and *please* don't be the man in the relationship."

I nodded along to her plea. Why would I ever want to be a manish woman? I was a lesbian, not a *filthy dyke.*

I like telling that little story. It always makes people laugh. I never tell the follow-up where my mother explains herself.

Driving to Menards for that order of lumber she said, "Rowan, I love you. I love you so much that I just want to hold you and keep you safe for the rest of your life. But I can't. So I want you to do everything you can to keep yourself safe. I never want to stifle you. I'm just scared that if you cut your hair, if you wear men's clothing, you'll get hurt. I don't want anyone to hurt you."

I don't tell the important part of that story because it would force my audience to face the fact that dykes like me aren't often safe in public. We get stares that make us wonder if we're going to become the next hate crime statistic. We get glares that make us *sure* we're about to become victims.

I'm lucky that I've never been attacked for my sexuality. I'm not looking forward to the day it happens, but I hope I'm prepared for it.

I've always been the type to scare easily. A symptom of my childhood which has followed me into my adult life. There are very few places I feel safe. I feel safe in my mother's arms. I feel safe alone with my best friend. One time, a very long while ago, I felt safe walking down the hallway of my school behind the dyke janitor.

I went to a privileged high school. The walls were a soft white, much like most of the people within them, and the furniture was always new. The exterior was constantly under summer renovation to make it look fresh. The last time I was there, it was red brick with yellow and blue banners. The school's colors.

I was similar enough to others at the school that I didn't get bullied, but people certainly considered me a freak. I was the only manish girl that I knew of. There were plenty of trans folks, but everyone I remember passed pretty well. Or they were quiet about it and never corrected a misused "miss" or "mister."

I never felt safe with people who were too scared to stand up for themselves. I don't begrudge them that, not a bit, but it always made me a different sort of afraid. Like I'd end up too quiet to talk, too.

Then, one early morning, I got my first glimpse of the dyke janitor. Now, I can't say for sure that she was a dyke, but she always gave me a big grin and "the butch nod" (if you know, you know) when we saw one another.

Her hair was gray, short, and spiked. Her clothing was loose, her face wrinkled, and her build stocky. She looked exactly how I imagined a middle-aged dyke to look.

Upon that first, silent meeting, I stared as long as I could. I wanted to follow her down the hallway, accompany her on her cleaning route and learn everything she had to share about her work and the world she lived in.

But I couldn't. I was going to grow up into a famous writer, not a janitor, and there was no way I could ever be like her.

Still, nothing brightened my day like seeing the dyke janitor. A word never passed between us, yet I felt a kinship with her. I wish I could see her again someday, just to thank her.

The dyke janitor, like my mother and my ex-lover, lives loudly in my memories. She might even be a bit louder than the others.

Regardless, I get sad when I think about her. I wish I could see people like her, like *me*, every day. But I can't. I go to a nice Iowa college, talk almost exclusively to other academically trained writers, and everyone knows that the corporate world has no room for manish dykes.

In my first semester of college, I took a creative writing class. It was in the basement of the old, history-rich writers' building. The walls were a bit grimy, but the chairs were new. It was nice, sort of.

Most of my peers in that class were women, as seems to happen in every writing class. Just as in the rest of my life, I was the only butch dyke. The semester progressed with weekly classes of student-submitted experimental fantasy and realistic fiction, with the odd piece of science fiction from the men, and I enjoyed it. More than my high school writing classes, anyway.

It never failed to surprise me, though, when a lady wrote about two women in love. It happened a handful of times, but it still felt significant. It was also bittersweet.

Every lady who wrote such stories looked like a *lady*. It was revolutionary when they wrote about women in love—who could have guessed they were gay! Look at them, breaking stereotypes by dressing according to their gender!

When I wrote about a lesbian in love, though, I'm sure it surprised no one. I'm a *dyke*, not a lady, and stereotypes are where I fit best.

I couldn't help but feel alien to my peers. I was appreciative of their lesbianism, but it was different from mine. Prettier than mine. I don't know when I started feeling this way, but once I noticed it, I never stopped.

Now, I'm almost twenty years old, I just signed the lease for my first apartment, I'm quitting school to go into landscaping, and I think about everything that has led me here.

My pain when I couldn't be a proper woman for my lover. My mother's plea for me to be safe. My lesbian classmates' prettiness.

All of it grapples daily with the elation and comfort I felt around the dyke janitor.

Because of that dyke janitor, because of every old dyke photograph I saw in my formative years, because of the dyke writers I've seen online, I exist as I am.

I want to give every baby dyke, the ones who don't know yet and the ones who do but don't want to, the same feeling butch dykes give me: comfort, safety, love, and *hope*.

If I can give even one little lesbian hope for the future, then I'll have done my job well. I don't care that it will get me in trouble someday. I want the future generation of lesbians to grow healthy and whole and, Sappho help me, I want to help plant those seeds.

BUTCH COLOGNE

Merril Mushroom

When I came out butch in the 1950's, the cologne we wore was an essential part of our butch image. The cologne of choice among my peers was Old Spice After Shave. Because lesbians all were women, we needed some way of differentiating among ourselves so that we would know whom we could go with, so butch-femme roles in lesbian society were very important and clear-cut. Butches didn't go with butches unless one of them was willing to "flip femme" and bear the ridicule that came from doing so—a fact which sometimes prevented women from getting together even when they really wanted to. There also was a label for women who claimed to be neither butch nor femme or either butch or femme—we called them "ki-ki."

Ki-ki lesbians went with whomever they wanted. They were permitted to "be butch" or "go femme" without being derided for it, but they were looked upon with some disdain by those of us butches whose role behavior never wavered.

The problem was that back then, the only models we had for our relationships were those of the traditional 1950's female/male heterosexual couple, and we were too busy trying to survive as lesbians in the very hostile world of heteropatriarchy to have time to create new roles for ourselves. Besides the ever-present threat of violence from straight men, we were felons under the law because of whom we loved. We could be arrested, charged with "crimes against nature" and incarcerated in prisons or mental hospitals for being a lesbian.

I always was a strict butch and I sometimes was a drag butch: I led when we danced, lit the cigarette, asked for the date. If I was in the mood, especially when doing the bar scene, I'd go in full drag. I usually wore men's pants and shirts anyhow, because I was tall and they fit me better. I'd wear a jacket to hide my breasts, since unlike some drag butches, I did not bind them. I'd slick my hair down into a duck's ass with wing sides and a pompadour or waterfall front, 1950's biker style, with one casual curl hanging just-so over my forehead. I was not trying to BE a man, just to PASS as one. The whole point to doing drag was in the passing, in being able to fool the straight public into thinking we were men while we all were in on the secret that we were in fact women. Also, it was safer to go out in the world on a date with a femme if we could pass. Straight men would beat up butches sounding the battle cry, "So you wanna be a man? Let's see you fight like a man… "

Most of the drag butches I knew, although we dressed and acted according to the male model, did not think we were REALLY men, nor did we want to BE men. We liked being women, although we were not necessarily proud of being women. What we REALLY wanted were the "goodies" which men had—the freedom, the power, the paycheck, and the legitimacy to be seen openly with the women we loved. We gave little, if any, thought to the contradiction that, although most of us did not like men at all, we accepted the role models which they provided for us.

Women in the 1950's were considered to be dependent and inferior. They were supposed to be chaste, faithful, and devoted to serving husbands, children, and community. They definitely were not supposed to express independence or sexuality. As lesbians, we dared to go against all that and were despised for it by the straight majority. Because we had no strong lesbian role models, we patterned our behaviors and our relationships after that which was available to us. Since maleness was equated with power, strength, pride, and freedom, we as butches took on the male persona in dress and manner. We might indulge in a good bit of drama and theatrics around this as well. This was the way we gave voice to our butch identity. Our butch persona was the way we presented to the rest of the world—the posing, the rituals, the choreography of being butch as we moved through life.

The word "butch" can be either adjective or noun. It can be a label describing a particular set of behaviors or characteristics, or it can be a statement of identity. Our butch self is something we are born with, a sense of being that really can't be described using the inadequate vocabulary of our language; but we know, we recognize, what butch is when we see one or when we are one. (I could compare this to other qualities, for instance colors: take the color green—I couldn't describe exactly what it is except to say it's green, but we all recognize green as green when we see it.). Characteristics and qualities of butch identity cannot truly be explained in terms of heteropatriarchal descriptions like "masculine" or "feminine," but must be seen from within the paradigm of the complimentary opposites of butch and femme, like the two sides of a coin.

But butch is more than that. On a deeper, more intimate level, closer to the core of real butch-femme distinction, the dynamics go beyond simple roles and social conformity. Because butch and femme are complementary opposites, they must be defined only in terms of one another. Ordinary words sometimes used to describe butch and femme are inaccurate. Butch is that which is not femme, and femme is that which is not butch, but they both imply and contain each other. They are reciprocal expressions of those qualities of being a woman that are found in all of us. There are common manifestations of power, protectiveness, dependence, and independence, but each role has its own expression of all characteristics.

As the years passed, I grew out my hair and became a long-haired, necktie-wearing, stylish butch, and Old Spice After Shave gave way to Canoe Cologne. During the 1960's, I became a hippie butch and scented myself with lavender oil and sandalwood. By the time I had become a feminist in the 1970's, I had grown proud of being a woman and no longer wanted to engage in male theatrics. I tried on the lets-not-claim-the-butch-femme labels' way of being a dyke, and I stopped using colognes altogether. Now, in my 8th decade of life, I am a somewhat worn old country dyke, and I really don't care how I smell. Through the years and behind different aromas, I have worn different labels and taken different images, and by now I can take them or leave them. But throughout, and even to this very day, I know that from deep in my heart of hearts and all the way through my being...

I am still the butch.

Merril Mushroom from *Common Lives/Lesbian Lives*, Issue 9, Fall 1983

FORGET ME NOT

Tanya Olson

Let me not Let me not
be the last lesbian who
remembers our bars
Our smoky bars Everyone
smoking Serious smokers
Cocktail smokers People
smoking outside People
smoking in Smoking Marlboro
Reds and Golds Smoking
Camel Blues Smoking American
Spirit Smoking cigarillos
and cloves Waking to the reek
of stale smoke the first reminder
you had gone out the night
before Let us remember
these sticky bars For we
drank and drank and drinking
spilled Spilled Budweiser
Spilled Zima Spilled Jaeger
Spilled Slippery Nipples Spilled
Sex on the Beach Spilled bottom
shelf tequila Spilled every
rum and coke I ever ordered
Spilled them on ourselves
Spilled them on each other
Fought about the spilling
Forgave each other for
spilling Drank because
bars were the place to look

Bars the place a trueself
shown Bars one place
the trueself seen Straight
people seldom in our bars
back then Straight people
had better options than
our bars with latenight
stickyfloor pushyshovey
fights Fights over love
Love real Love imagined
Bouncer inbetween
to breakup the fight
Bouncer a bulldyke
in boots hat and tie
Hurrah hurrah for
these bars and dykes
Remember them
both forever

Let me not be the last
lesbian who found her
people on a screen Not
the last to recognize
herself in the light butches
of TV Tatum Kristy Jodie Jo
Let me not be the last who
learned to crush through
the screen MaryAnn Lori Kelly
No one knows who you look
at when you watch TV No one
knows how it is you look
Let every lesbian always
remember our long promised
Dusty Springfield biopic

Let us count the number
of gay boy biopics made
over those same years
We must make them make
our movies Remember
the annual rumor of who
this time would play her
KD Melissa Adele Nicole
Also remember Whitney
and Robyn We must never
forget their love Remember
how we watched Cissy
and the brothers try to
make them hide their love
We heard words that screened
their love We saw through
love's tuneful disguise
I get so emotional baby
Whitney confesses *everytime*
I think of you and we knew
who she meant Whitney
reminds us *Ain't it shocking
what* and sits for a moment
on that beat before she pivots
and drops the line back in
its track *love can do* Whitney
dead now Dusty dead now
May we always hear the love
in their soar Let me not be
the final lesbian to believe
Dolly and Ann Richards
were a thing Not the last
to see that photo of them
together and recognize love

Dolly so sturdy in her polkadots
and sequins Ann permanently
handsome in her Rose of Texas
boots Hurrah hurrah
for these stars and dykes
Stars and dykes forever

Let me not be the last butch
stranded on Last Butch Island
Let me not be the culminating
bulldagger Not the terminal
stud Not the concluding soft
butch Not the ultimate stone
Somebody has to bring an end
to the diesel dykes Someone
will be the final Butchie
McShorthair in town Surely
I can't be the last to wear
my hair like Elvis Not the
closing flattop Not the crowning
pompadour Let mine not be
the finale of the high and tights
If I am let me say I am sorry
Butches had a real chance for
change and we blew it We lived
so far out we thought getting in
equaled change We lived so far
beyond we felt both diseased
and immune When they opened
the door right in the middle
of our kicking it down we thought
that meant we had won And let's
put an end to this story while
we are here Butches aren't

being erased Butches aren't
being replaced It has simply
become our time to go extinct
Extinct only means swallowed
by the earth Extinct another
stage of the world's endless
change Extinct means someday
diggers will uncover our bones
Turn up the buckles of our belts
Find the last scraps of our boots
As they dig and sift someone
makes a sign to honor the site
Somebody later will graffiti it
Artists will sketch us and hum
a tune Theorists will speculate
about how we lived Historians
will argue over whether we were
imagined or true The exhibit
designer will build a dummy
butch Too wide Too tall Place
her in a diorama propped
against the bar It is shocking
future scientists will conclude
Simply shocking what
love can do

A PANDEMIC DEATH

Tamara Hollins

she already was shrouded by the hospital sheet
only her death remained, lingering at her bedside
there was no last breath rattling in her ribcage
only the thought that this was her life
and somehow it had concluded
without the shine of greatness

LOVELESS LOVE

Papusa Molina

From *Common Lives/Lesbian Lives*, Issue 23, Summer 1987

Because love is absent...absent
   - written in blood and torture –
reason enough for reminiscences...
collected in bitter drops
of anxiety and scattered dreams.

Because time is not mine anymore,
nor the hour,
   or the minute,
and even if the hands on the clock-face keep spinning
It will never be the time of your arrival...

The night turns long and lonely
   - dark circle of absolute absorbed moment –
ill-fated glance longing for closeness,
needing to remember,
   to talk about you,
     to save the event.

I am responsible for the love, the hope,
   and the loving memories of your existence.

Why, negative word,
the flower began to wither?
   Or is... perhaps that death has always infiltrated
step by step into everything?
   Or maybe love has its limited life, its time,
its ways, its own eyes closing by the minute?

Because if love was the only reason for my existence
I'd be touching it on my face, my body,
   holding it in my hands,
     - ill-fated wings –
       my mouth...And even in God
         who always sleeps here in my chest.

I would raise the dream
   like a morning emerging in splendor,
     like a rose in its secluded garden,
       like a kiss from her sensuous lips.
I would magically bring this love back into life saying:
   "Here it is"
     shining as a morning star,
       soft and warm as a fragile nest.

My beloved: "Here it is..."
And I would start filling the emptiness, the absence,
   with all the beautiful things I possess,
     with every thing I nest in my innermost recess,
       and what is left...
With a thousand stars, suns, silent nights,
   words, whispers, kisses, tears...
And I'd be so close
   that there would not be any space left between us two.
And on the infinite pillow,
two static heads would face the sky
   until dreams inhabit their awakeness
     or death encloses their lives.

Sometimes when I find myself enclosed
   - next to your panting chest –
giving you arboreal names,

water, salt,
    wind entangled in the darkness of your crown,
shaping your mouth, parting away your sands,
leaving you like a fish,
    like marine bird, white seagull,
your mossy bark,
    your perfect caress,
        your being…
I simply pronounce: "I love you."
    And the words become river, metaphor,
        poem, lullaby…

Words were emerging
    and sketching your presence,
words were mine
    and I had them on my fingertips,
        in the center of my eyes…
Words were touch you, drowning you,
    exquisitely soft words were yours…
I wanted to say, I said:
    - on quiet nights –
grape-words, peach-words,
    bird-words, poem words
        love words.
I don't remember them,
    I repeat them,
        I keep repeating them,
and I shape them ripe on the most desirable forms,
    more intimate, more ours,
        more love, far away love,
            tall love, grown-up love.
I don't memorize you,
    I live you in elegant flame,
        in water,

in swinging blood,
    in slowly turbulent blood
        which quiets and awakens me.
I have your immortal signs on my throat,
    my feet, knees, entrails.

I open my eyes
    and I come from you;
I close my eyes
    and I go to you.
And your prodigious force attracts me…
I am in your touch, your kiss,
    scattered in the circle of love,
yours in your warm universe,
    yours in your being,
        in the home of your dreams.

I am remembering, not loving,
coloring minuscule things,
    rebuilding piece by piece
        stone by stone,
this ocean-home dressed of sand,
    foam, beaches and waves;
this destroyed home of my entrails,
which you have
    – bit by bit –
inhabited with your presence.

Remembering
    – rose by rose –
sleeping or awake,
with the humble opulence of loving,
    simply loving you,
holy in my arms,

    absolute in your body,
my homeland, sweet earth,
   warm heaven.

Let me be your flower,
    your exact dimension,
       your intimate corner,
          your life, your being...
Duplicate in my eyes,
    embrace yourself in my arms,
       shape yourself in my shape,
          be immortal in my blood,
Because love is just Love
    when it is love
       love,
          love.

Love is just love
    because of love, love, love.
It is there and it's there for nothing...
  Because it is fragrance, tender name,
    suddenly awake, trench of my body,
       of this grown-up body of yours.
It is where you left it;
in shadows or light,
    in your surroundings.
Or perhaps walking the empty space from me to you
without purpose but the walk in itself,
with its indelible blood.
    with its tattooed blood which registers your presence.

Without forgetting you
    entirely forgetting you,
every day, year,

each season with the name given by you,
winter, summer,
or walking dressed or naked in the bedroom.
From the farthest star you look upon me,
giving me the air of your lungs,
sleeping with your presence,
with your sleepless dreams.

If I still speak it is through you,
if pleasure overwhelms me it is yours,
if pain breaks me down
let it come from you.
I want to forget you in the oblivion of love,
silence carpeted with your memories,
robe of stars with which you dress me,
to call me,
- in the middle of the silence –
your beloved.

I am filled with you,
warmth of you,
trembling of you...
I had wanted to leave you in my past
but you penetrated the present and my future.
My self had been adjusted more to you
with an incredible contained tenderness,
with a muteness which bites my lips
to drown your name in my entrails.

ENTWINED

Cindy Cleary

18x16, charcoal and walnut ink on paper

POEMAS DEL AMOR, amor

Papusa Molina

Porque el amor está ausente...ausente...
escrito en sangre y tormento,
es que puedo hacer reminiscencias,
recogerlo en gotas amargas
de ansiedad y sueño disperso.

Porque ya no es mío el tiempo, ni la hora,
ni el minuto...
Y aunque gire la aguja del reloj
nunca será la hora de tu llegada...

Es que la noche es larga y sola,
circulo negro que totalmente me absorve...
Intemporal hora aciaga,
mi despavorida mirada a ti se alarga.

Necesito recordar, hablar de ti...
salvar el acontecimiento.
Soy responsable del amor, de la esperanza
y del amoroso recuerdo que cultivo.

¿Por qué, negativa palabra,
se empezó a marchitar la flor?
¿O es acaso que siempre la muerte
poco a poco tiene que infiltrarse en todo?
O que el amor tiene su limitada vida, su tiempo,
su tránsito, sus ojos que se cierran...

Porque si sólo por el amor fuera
yo lo tocara en mi cara, en mi cuerpo,

en mis manos – alas despavoridas -
en mi boca...Y hasta en Dios
dormido aquí en mi pecho.

Yo levantaría el sueño
como una mañana que surge esplendorosa,
como una rosa en su jardín,
como un beso en su boca.
Mágicamente lo levantaría y podría decir:
"Agui está; luminoso como estrella,
suave como nido."

"Querida, aquí esta..."
Y empezaría a llenar el huerco, la ausencia,
con lo que hermosamente tengo,
con lo que anido en mí misma,
con lo que no se ha ido...

...con millones de estrellas, soles, noches
palabra, arrullo, besos, lágrimas...
Y estaría tan cerca,
que no habría espacio entre las dos;
y en la inmensa almohada de mi lecho,
dos inmóviles cabezas mirarían al cielo
hasta quedarse poco a poco dormidas
o tal vez muertas.

Algunas veces abrazándote más,
cerca del jadeo de tu pecho,
dándote nombres de árboles,
agua, sol, viento enmarañado en tu pelo...
Dibujando tu boca, apartando en tu arena...
dejándote como pez, como pájaro marino...

Cosechando tu fragancia, tu seda,
tu corteza, tu musgo,
tu cumplida caricia, tu ser...
Puedo decir: "Te quiero..."

Y la palabra era rio, metáfora,
verso, arrullo...

Nacía la palabra y te enmielaba;
era mía la palabra y la tenia
en la punta de los dedos, de los ojos...
Te palpaba la palabra, te inundaba,
exquisitamente tierna
era tuya la palabra.

Quiero decir...te dije
en sosegadas noches,
palabras uvas, palabras duraznos,
palabras pájaros, palabras versos,
palabras amor.

No las recuerdo, las repito.
Las sigo repitiendo
y las moldeo en las formas más deseables,
más mías, más tuyas,
más amor.

Lejano amor, cercano amor,
alto amor, crecido amor...

Yo no te memorizo,
te vivo en elocuente llama, en agua,
en mecida sangre

que me sosiega o enerva.
Tengo tus inmortales señas en la garganta,
los pies,
en las rodillas, el vientre.

Abro los ojos y vengo de ti;
cierro los ojos y voy a ti.
Y tu prodigiosa fuerza me atrae,
me recoge...
Estoy en tu tacto, tu beso...
Tuya en tu tibio mundo,
tuya en tu ser,
en tu hogar de sueño

Estoy recordando, no amando...
Coloreando minúsculas cosas
que voy ordenando en la casa,
en la marinera casa vestida de playa,
espuma y arena...
reconstruyendo paso a paso,
piedra a piedra,
este hogar en ruinas que llevo dentro,
pero que poco a poco
se ha habitado de tu presencia.

Recordando...Rosa a rosa,
despierta o dormida,
con la humildad de quererte,
simplemente quererte.
Bendita entre mis brazos,
absoluta en tu cuerpo...

Déjame ser tu flor, tu exacta dimensión,
tu intimo hueco, tu vivir, tu estar...

Duplícate en mis ojos,
envuélvete en mis brazos,
modélate en mi forma,
inmortalízate en mi sangre...

Porque el querer solo es Amor
cuando es amor, amor, amor...
Y amor, solo es Amor
por amor, amor, amor...
Está y está por nada;
porque es fragancia, tierno nombre tuyo,
súbito despertar, trinchera en mi cuerpo,
de mi crecido cuerpo tuyo.

Déjame hablar a través de ti.
Que si la dicha agobia mi cuerpo,
Sea también la dicha tuya.
Que si el dólar me agobia,
sea también el dolor tuyo...

Quiero olvidarte en olvido del amor,
silencio alfombrado de recuerdos tuyos,
túnica de estrellas con que me vistes
para llamarme en silencio tu amada...
Tu única amada...

Pero esta donde tú lo dejaste,
en sombra o luz, en torno tuyo.
O caminando el vacío que hay de ti a mí,
sin más propósito que el de recorrerlo
con su indeleble sangre,
con su tatuada sangre
que registra los sentidos
con súbita y erguida pena inusitada.

Sin olvidarte, enteramente sin olvidarte...
Cada día, cada año, cada estación
tiene el nombre que tú le pusiste...
Sea invierno, o sea verano,
o caminase vestida o esté desnuda en la alcoba.
Arrebatada de estrellas tú me estás mirando,
viviendo, dándome el aire de tus pulmones,
durmiéndome con dulzura tuya,
con sueño tuyo.

Estoy llena de ti, tibia de ti,
temblorosa de ti...

Te he querido olvidar
en el olvido del amor...
Pero no he logrado más
que penetrarte mucho más en mí,
ajustarme más a ti
con terrible ternura contenida,
con mudez de mordaza
que se muerde los labios
para no pronunciar tu nombre...

WHAT IT TAKES!!!
(AKA BILLY IN THE FIRST PERSON)

Cherry Muhanji

Ms. Holiday's hangout was no more than a basement done up to get the most from the very best. The underground room "jes" was. It wasn't meant to rival the smart rooms on 52nd street but "jes" did. Anybody might drop in—downstairs. The Duke, although Billie wasn't much to his liking, Helen Humes, Sweet Mama String Bean, Louis, if he was in town, and Lil on occasion. When some yokel just up from the South in high water pants and a short jacket with shorter sleeves asked (and they always do), *why's this the best place to jam in?* everybody said, it "jes" was. It was dark and dirty and had a layer of grease on everything in the kitchen. Southern emigrants had already heard that the white folks were paying good money—so much so that a Negro with thrift could afford Minnie Waddles once a week and eat deep dark greens laced with spinach, hot water corn bread, summer squash with the hooked necks, candied yams, red pepper sausages, ribs, chicken, and chitt'lings in due season. Not only did the room cater to the palette so, too, the eye. It was laid out in a sea of red-checkered tablecloths, convenient in the day time, I suppose, with a menu of fried potatoes, bacon 'n' biscuits, grits 'n' gravy, with the smell of strong black fragrant coffee. But when the naked red and blue light bulbs were switched on at night, and each table was covered by a white tablecloth and littered with half-empty Mason jars of recent gin, crumbled napkins and spilled beer, the room changed. Add the hum of the late crowd—time to jam!

Kitchen, lip, hip, and groin smells held sway. The scent of Blue Gardenia slashed across the throats, inside the thighs and on the wrists of ladies-of-the-evening made them strut, and me dizzy as it strummed the nose, but slowed their gait if their johns were fast and the money easy. Later queens and sugar mommas, usually upstairs, made their way on down their faces sliced in half-shadow. Smoke from thin cigars billowing from beneath the stairs caught the moving eye like a camera. Ringed fingers and glossy nails, suddenly out of the shadow (click) made your eye wander; catch a muffled cough, a sigh, focus in on Humphry Bogart big picture hats, and Zoot Suits. (click) Everybody's on the make for the same thing, but differently. (double click) Mostly, this was a place where the cats could play, not for white folks—like on 52nd street—but plaay!

    From that sort of thing that happens in a place like this whenever jazz musicians get together—cats shooting the breeze, you know, like that—telling lies and kicking butt, I learned that Billie was in early. Roaring in, just out of a big yellow taxi cab. Kicking off her wet shoes at the door. Tossing her cape at the hatcheck girl before descending the stairs in her stocking feet. Glad to be out of the way and out from in front of white folks, I bet, who didn't know what she was doing, but knew that whatever it was, they wanted *in* and they wanted *it*.

    Seems she suddenly got quiet. In a groove from her last "hit"? Still caught in the frost from downtown where she'd "entertained" white folks up close and "personal"? In here connecting nods—talking heads from one table to another—buzzed; person to persons at the bar answering the unasked question, *Is she here yet?* Pressing her knees together swaying them to the music, eyes closed, heart slow and steady, the moving camera clicks whiting out the darkened room filled up with eyes that asked, *is she, ah... gonna swing tonight, or what?* After two takes of "Tea For Two," and several disruptive chords of "Mean To Me," The Prez, Mr. Easy Street, his tenor sax playful, making everybody feel young, skipping, (in this case, riffing), 'cross the meadow picking up lots of forget-me-nots,' knew without looking at her make several sluggish attempts to reach into all that billowing organdy cascading across her bosom and pull out the words to a song she had written, low in that hoarse and behind the beat way she had, "Ahhh I wrote it, Prez, after The Duchess did me wrong. Help me with it some, later, huh? Maybe?"

Oh! But when Lady Day was setting in—high as a Georgia Pine, like all the cats say—with thickly arched eyebrows and red/rose lips—everybody got the message. Tonight she had a rope of hair hanging down the middle of her back that jumped when she jerked herself "awake" on a phrase she liked. Then she'd mellow. Even in this room you could see the big jeweled earrings, meant for catching whatever light there was in the smoky blue rooms she worked in. Her arms, still clothed to the elbows in fingerless opera gloves, moved to an internal rhythm while the fingers of her left hand tapped out a muffled sound on the sides of a white satiny clutch bag resting unsteadily in her lap, as it rode wave after wave of cream-colored organdy. Her dress, not at all ladylike, hung off the sides of her chair. The Lady was skewed all right—sitting outside the circle of jazz cats—and the Lady right now was low.

Of course, she hadn't directed that piece of paper, wet at the edges, to anybody but The Prez. Father/lover/brother/son turned, because she was sitting behind him, lifting her face and with his eyes asked, "Lady?"

"Get that fuckin' cheerleader bitch outta here, you hear me?" The band moved toward silence. Each eye followed Billie's gaze, which was falling on me like tumbling dominoes. Not all at once but each body that was tethered to a horn signaled to another body, and to another, and to another, finally ending when the bass player said, "Time out, my man. Lady Day's got somethin' on her mind."

All eyes on Billie, then me. I was just in, but out of the circle myself, struggling to get my horn out of the case (my fingers still stiff from the cold), bending down in front of the Men's Room because there were no more chairs and no more free tables. (No hat check girl for me. And I kept my shoes on.) But I *was* thinking, had been all day, about what The Prez and all the rest of the cats would play. I wondered—had been for days. Could I? Would I? Dare?

Momma had always said colored folks make do, and she did. But they, like her, knew that life, our lives, were all about tomorrow. That today was about white folks. Tomorrow, someday, over there, in the sweet bye and bye, in that great gettin' up mornin', was about being Colored and Colored was about tomorrow. So when had I decided to up the ante and do it today? Was it in watching her? Those rare times she'd let me sit in? No. Hearing her make sounds that startled at first, signal to the horn players then over to Big Bill Booser who'd move in—adding the guitar, knowing what she meant if no one else did? I did. Always. High, she'd ramble on about her circus days when she blew real sweet anytime she wanted under the big top? Circus days? Big top? Or when she'd be traveling light with Ma Rainey's group, backing Bessie on a tune or two? (stop, smile, camera, click). Pops Armstrong she'd add, *yeah, all that came after he hit high "C" and shatter the world.*

Could? Would? The Prez do it for me? Bring both of us on line? More important than that, would he? Times before he'd heard me, seen me—knew how when opening my mouth just so—tightening, tasting, tonguing the mouthpiece—how I felt. Yeah, he knew, when my horn made that turn, lit one more candle in the world.

The Prez, Billie Holiday's main man, a magic cat, had to know when something was about to go down, right? How could he play like that if he didn't know, huh? He had the benefit of Pops sound and all that, right?

How is it that this set of cats didn't? Why was that? I guess the logos hadn't swept over them yet, and The Prez was slow to state—explain in the way he could. I was anxious. He was not, and there you have it.

I'd walked from the subway to the club. Getting off two stops before I needed buzzing with something new just under the surface, like the bottoms of my ears, the collar of my coat ignoring the tops. No matter. The bottoms warmed in anticipation. The tops on a different track. I'd liked to think that my feet were making new grooves in the snow, but it had been coming down for hours and people had left their own. All I could let myself think, *I'm just pressin' and reshapin', ya' dig?* Then I felt the weight of my horns, and wondered as I always do, even while my feet were shaping and reshaping footprints in the snow, *what is this thing that drives me so?*

This session like all the rest would be noisy, mixed. The men would challenge. Cut. Challenge. Cut. Like that. All I wanted ever to do was to play with these cats, and back Lady Day. They respected her, and that was cool, because she was with The Prez and fast becoming Miss Holiday to you. And that was cool, too. But I was a nobody and had nobody. I needed somebody to let me stay.

If any of these cats held the music close in the way The Prez did they had to let me in. Hair laid or not, lipstick on straight, or the seams in my stockings, right? If he thought this chick could groove, then so be it. I was in. But holding on to that one shining moment when they all opened up to me was hard. The piano, the bass, the drum, their horns in mid-air—something in them, a thing they didn't know, forgotten even, bowed. Always. Always unable to hold that... what? Trust? Hope? Sight of a woman standing alongside them tuning up her horn in the way they did, readying to blow—ready to get the job done. They backed off and went into massaging their manhood before my first note ever hit the air. *"How that little thang thank she gon' drive the bone home, man?"* their eyes asked each other. Leaving me to wander around, ya' dig, like a sheep looking for a shepherd.

But if, and god this was a big if, I/me/horn/self was about to break—delicately like the girl I was then or, crack wide open like the woman, I was becoming, something... whatever... got caught as they say, on up, I swear, coming outta me, staring at the tip of my toes traveling on up through the top of my head... have mercy! Funny, then and only then whenever I am drivin' the bone home becomes a smile of watermelon, just so... pink, heavy with black seeds, bursting with juice, resting on the slick surface of that oil blue table cloth covering the kitchen table, yellow with noon.

Don't get me wrong. There were lost dreams in that kitchen—Momma at the sink straining spaghetti, saving the starch to do Mr. Morgan's, our boarder's shirts; late evening in the pantry beneath the steps her blowing gradually stopped. The ocean blue of that oil cloth under the green, green, watermelon rind, the white meat of the rind meeting the pink, set me at age six and at eye level on fire. Brushing my pigtails out of the way, I entered all that mystery, color, texture but told myself in no language that I even knew at the time, that out of that "Still Life" I could and would make music.

Momma knew what was happening to me, and wanted for me *not* to settle for who she'd settled for. Jesus. She'd rise to the occasion, but only in church. It was all so bittersweet for her now, but if, and even then it was a big if, those kitchen colors could speak, what would they say? Greet me with what I already knew? Had heard on John R street...

"Gimme a pig foot and a bottle of beer?"

Say wha-a-atttt? I say. "Gimme a pigfoot and a bottle of beer."

Say wha-a-atttt?

"Daddy, I say daddy, daddy, daddy where'd you sleep last night?"

"Say wha-a-atttt?

"I say, I say, I say, Daddy, I say Daddy where'd you sleep last night?"

From that time till now I knew if I was standing by the gate I was gonna ring the bell and "Sweet Home" would be in sight. I'd make ready, somehow, to drive the bone home.

When cats get together we... ah... well, my own dreams go something like this:

The Prez looks up when I come in... No, when I fly in cause he'd announce, "Here comes Hummingbird, bringing pretty little rainbows." The Prez, the magician made up worlds as it suits him. He'd learn to do that when being who he wanted to be meant making it all up. Like the way he blew. Or like I do-horn-player-jazz musician—female. Sad, though, the only use Hummingbirds have to the Prez is that they hover. I could walk through any door any place at any time in the world and he wouldn't care to notice, but he'd move over because that's the kind of godly cat he was. There was always the chance, when he blew supplications to the Logus that the Rapture might happen. And he expected to be there. He was, after all, a pilgrim looking for a shrine, a mystic looking for God, making up sounds that were looking for somewhere to move into. He had the best cats in the business working with him and he had Lady. See why I hovered?

In my dream sometime Jesus, for whatever reason didn't bring the Rapture, and a given set was ho-hum, he'd make himself forget about Him. Cause when the Lord didn't come through in that set, or appear all evening he'd be blue, move into forgetfulness.

The Prez was polite even though whiskey had been moving through his veins, a long time now, exiting through black holes that were beginning to show themselves as blackouts. When the Lord was a no show he'd think, not tonight, but Hummingbird is here.

He'd explain to the cats this way.

"You, me, God don't matter, but pray for Hummingbird. Forget about Him."

And he would. Next time he'd forget, again, his expectation lost somewhere between the silver flask he kept tucked in the pocket of his jacket that he emptied between sets, and the House filled while he was laying out. Forgetting was easy like Uncle Sam, who he was always a few steps ahead of, to recording sessions with white guys who could hear the Music but couldn't play it and got paid twice what he did.

But oh! With Hummingbird in the air and sweet promises. If the cats hesitated even a little he'd move in the middle, lay his horn to the side—riff a little here and there—coax my wings to ease up, settle down. In my dream his attention on me brought the cats to attention, having whispered to each other that a chick in the mix brought bad luck. No matter. Just when what The Prez had forgot to remember was about to be remembered, the Music would move into the "holy" place. I'd hit an odd Bud Powell note, spray a barrage of Bettys—and then *one will be taken and one will be left*, take off on a Monk lick—*two women will be grinding at the hand mill, and one will be taken one will be left*, or erupt after a time into a Margo licking—*and at an unexpected hour*, when my Muse became the fuse that took everybody to the stars, *the Son of Man* cometh. That's when it got great!

Usually later women came in on the arm of some smooth cat, but really to hear Billy. Their movements—dancing or not, sipping cocktails or drinking beer—brought to my mind the loop of neverending circles within circles within circles. Getting tangled was nothing new. One slip—POW! You're hooked on rainbow loops. I could see them around dancers, Billie, the room, and the muffled laugh of them at the bar. Suddenly I'd think of ice cream on the top of cones and how after licking, I ate the whole thing.

But it was the tappers that stopped my world and gave everybody a rush. No loops, but long generous legs leading to small ankles that wedged themselves into large loud tap shoes. Short skirts. A little lace. A little after thought, here and there. Why do they wear those lacy little things? Maybe because they're special, huh? Maybe it's because we were all there caught in an eternal moment.

(stop, smile, camera click)

Billie had just a few months before getting hold of *that* tune, *Strange Fruit*. It changed her life, and the writer. He came in, gave her the poem and she took a new direction, and so did he. Later, we heard he was raising the Rosenburg kids. That tune put her in a place that made reading comic books between sets while white girls sang her arrangements mean next to nothing. Sometimes, though, Billie couldn't suppress that deep laugh of hers. When it suddenly struck her, "Am I the only one that finds this funny?"

I heard one time she went into hysterics when asked about the state of her health, her habit, the world, Joe Louis, and the FBI. "Those boys?" she asked finally pulling herself together. "The ones in straw hats and cheap suits and double stitch shoes? I never worry 'bout those good ol' boys. They're doin' their best for God and country. Me? Have trouble with that? Naw." And with a nod to the reporter or interviewer she'd say, always sweetly, "Yeah, honey, you betcha, everything's just fine. Couldn't be better. How 'bout you, Sugar?"

God knows that Lady could be one thing one minute and another thing the next, but this? She was good at taking her audience out and leaving them strung out. Like pointing out to city kids where the outhouse was and when they began to smell the shit in their lives, she would introduce yet another song that made accepting the way it "jes is" impossible. Nobody after experiencing her could really go home again. But the whites kept her going because, she reasoned, "they think they got a right to keep on comin', and comin' and comin' in, night after night, stone faced, close up on me all the time. Yeah, Sugar, they got a right all right."

Well, all Blacks know about shit houses and that white folks build them. However, *these* white folks, who were into this hip Black thing, really thought she meant it. That they were gonna get away clean. Unfortunately, so did some Black folks.

There she was defying logic night after night after night. Glamorous, sassy, a woman in charge. (Now ain't that somethin' worth more than a nickel?) They kept on coming, Black, and white any old time. Black folks whistlin' and stompin', white folks clapping politely. Both takin', and takin', and takin', more, and more, and more. They truly expected her to keep doing what they had no intention of—finding a way to God through her music.

Too bad Lady Day never understood that she was the Passover Lamb for all the Jews and the Gentiles that came in nightly, and all the rest who couldn't. Maybe she did. She died, didn't she? And left everybody feeling what it feels like to have nobody.

In the meantime Late Night and Dawn had seeped in through the basement windows and spent their brief time together ignoring Evening. Evening, dressed in a black cutaway-tux with tails, top hat and cane, white silk scarf draped about her neck, had, like me, been unabashedly watching mostly the tappers, drawn as we always were, despite Evening's appearance, to the funk and lavish promises of their bodies. Evening was starting to sulk—knees high with her arms around them, rocking back on her haunches—not ready to leave just yet. But as Dawn moved toward Late Night feeling her thighs under the table, Evening fading fast slipped past them yet once again, unable to watch first, their coupling, then their birthing of electric blue in that time of magic.

The set was hot. The men dog tired. Me? It was hard to say. Lady? Harder still. The Prez—the best of the lot—was content to place his pork pie hat on his immaculate butter and move toward me in that steady arrangement he had of exiting a place. First his hat in place, his horn in the case, his suit jacket on, a hit from a flask now in his hand, and a cigarette lit. Leaning over, his face just above my ear, whispered, "Sorry Sugar, it's like this, ya' dig? For women it don't mean a thing if it ain't got that swing."

I was placing the bone back inside the case when Billie finally clear spoke loud enough for me to hear, "And the bitch plays two horns!" Then from across the room and across now empty chairs called, "Tell me, tell me, tell me how'd you learn to play like that? I say tell me, tell me, tell me how'd you learn to play?"

"Say, ah Hummingbird can't you hear Lady?" The drummer asked.

I didn't answer. Not that I wouldn't. I couldn't. I'd been inside Billie's clothes all evening—silently undressing her—never missing a beat that was pointed out to me, while playing behind her. The full mouth I knew. The near plump body swallowed tonight in organdy I hated. Wondering all evening what simpler clothes on her might look like. I imagined the sepia-colored stockings. Take them off, Billie. Panties and bra take them off, Billie—but slowly. You can leave your slip on, but drop—one strap at a time.

"Tell me. Tell me. Tell me, ain't it so? Them that's got shall get. Them that's not shall lose, so the Bible says, and it still ain't news. Momma may have…"

"That's what I miss," I suddenly blurted out. "I've missed you. Just like I missed the sound of Pops' horn the first time I heard it."

"Hey! Did Pops teach you to blow? My man."

"No, my Momma did."

"So you got Momma problems too, huh? It's awful when your own Momma won't give you no money. Talked to me like I was in knee pants."

"Yo Momma done told you, when you was in knee pants. A woman's a two-face, oh." Joe Beady blew a quick riff of the melody through his alto sax in notes so low and forlorn that Billie's eyes teared over and moved toward their corners. But before her face masked over she said, "Yeah, Prez, The Duchess a worrisome thing…"

When Billie lays her head back earlier that evening The Prez, with his tenor almost horizontal and Billie feeling for the words, drawing the Music in, the muscles in her neck taut, holding her hands just so, snapping her fingers, everybody in that room knew that she was singing to Sadie with a sadness that they knew, too, the kind that if you ain't careful can take you take yourself on up outta here.

Later, when we would be alone boozing it up among other things she said in one of those Billie moments, "Sweetie, so you like riffin' the Scotch too." I frowned not understanding.

"Like when The Prez invites you in. I like your mute, takes us all in, ya' dig? Your moves are smooth, Sugar. Like taking candy from a baby. I hear the way The Prez's horn smiles and I like the way it carries on in its own sweet way, never crowdin' you, never anxious. Nice, Sugar, real nice…"

"Them that's got his own...I'm gonna ride on the Super chief straight out to Hollywood. I got me a movie to be in."

"Lady," The Prez said to Billie while looking directly at me and over at her in that way he had with her, warm and stern like a father/brother/lover this time.

"She'll make you feel there are songs to be sung, Sugar, bells to be rung." There it was again, the Prez's way of speaking—sometimes in song lyrics. It was simple. If you didn't know the words, you had little to say to him. He needed the words to make sense of the world and the Music. That's who Ms. Holiday was—teacher to his horn—that's why it spoke in poems. Without her, he drank himself to death.

Drifting back to the song she continued, "Papa may have, God bless the child."

Words again. Billie could coax feeling, deep feeling from anything—me, old songs, songs that didn't even have any feeling—riffing them with a sadness that could rock the world.

The Prez, the super cat—makin' a horn do things—well, he was there when I'd introduced that tune that had me buzzin'. He knew what some tunes can do. How they won't leave you alone—make you forget to put on a hat—like tonight. (What was my hair gonna look like when the snow melted in it?) He'd heard me making my move, watched my descent many times before dropping slowly to earth (never overstating the obvious), after takin' my horn to places even he ain't never been. And it frightened and fascinated him in ways that few men ever get to and fewer women still. And Oh! I knew it was beautiful, can ya' dig? Like the covered heads of bowed women praying at a shrine.

During my descent I caught The Prez deep in thought not knowing then or now what had happened. And in an instant of time, I saw all the doorways of my life with men just like him standing in them smoking hard, trying to quell the jitters.

Notes:

Minnie B Waddles was born about 1898. In 1940, she was 42 years old and lived in Shreveport, Louisiana, with her husband, Clarence.

Abel Meeropol was an American songwriter and poet whose works were published under his pseudonym, Lewis Allan. He wrote "*Strange Fruit*," which was recorded by Billie Holiday. Meeropol was a member of the American Communist Party, but later quit.

Angela Wellman and India Cooke

JULY JOY: 1775

Abby Lynn Bogomolny

everyone
loves my husband,
but I married him for his sister.
we tend the garden together
as our strength and youth are equals.
most long and dusty mornings
we move in harmony,
through the rows
lilt and limb,
step and lift,
her long wavy hair tied,
until a need draws us to the creek
whereupon we splash, laugh, and float
as her hair, a freshwater fan,
envelops me in its lively joy.
my mother knows
as she prepares meals at our hearth
that my husband labors far from here
to earn the land that feeds the family,
and as a son of liberty, he will be
the first to fight for the colonies.
I suppose he is kind, compared to most men,
who swear, drink, and treat us roughly.
every few months he returns for a spell,
hoping to leave me with child.
while it's not proper to speak of such,
his sister never leaves me weak or sore.
if I do not look forward to this chore,

it is not that I am ungrateful:
we would not have this home without him,
but without his sister,
there would be no *joy*.

Photo Credit: Rainbow

Common Lives/Lesbian Lives, Issue 36, Fall 1990

NACIYE

Leonore Wilson

Come to my house early and I will feed you
    olives and cheese, yogurt bread and dates, lamb and honey,

I will fill your pockets with handmade baklava
    like long ago secrets,

and together we will worship the sun at daybreak
    and stoke the wood fire,
and I will tell you about my homeland,
    and the thousands of Kurdish women resisters

murdered by Turkish forces, women fleeing Isis,
    so many with babies and so many rebelling saying:

you will not attack our cities and kill our brothers and our sisters.

See I dress in camouflage for I am still a warrior,
    a strong warrior, not a matron, an old matron.

I am a young daughter, mother, wife.

I will protect my village, I will die freely to protect it,
    I will be   a martyr...

Here in California, see I have a graveyard;
    come I will show you tombstones

with no bodies,   where I kneel to the spirits of those
    who have died in the struggle for a just independence;

martyrs, *so many martyrs*...

I have a museum, too,   come I will show you my cavern
    of books   and books,   iron pots

and copper lamps, and the old sitar over there
    I sometimes play on the stairs under the turning stars

near the pastures of goats sheep and llamas,
    and brass oil lamps to light the way...

Come I will show you   how to pick olives, how to
    thumb and phew them tender one by one

in the wicker basket with straps of red leather
    I will tie   around your waist.

And together we will wonder if rain beats on roofs
    in the old country gentle as a baby's marbles

or if the rain has turned to bullets.

Come and hold my hands that have clipped
    umbilici   as well as lavender rosemary,

wild onions, garlic clusters;
    and see the flesh lovely as Niceye,

this good name my mother gave me like sweet water purling
    in a creek bed in June;

a stream where we will place our bare worn feet
    and you and I will smile girlish smiles

like hammocks swaying   and we will know the love
    between women, not old matrons

but young sisters singing, for there is always a reason
    for ripening, and we will be wild doves among mint and laurel,

gold bees among blossoms, and there will be *sustenance*
    always *sustenance* remaining for our journey...

CADET CAP

Margarita Meklina

In one sweep, music sheets with *Saint-Saëns* swirled up and landed. Jasmine kicked the pedal attached to her Kurzweil and abruptly stood up. She pulled two yoga mats and one carpet runner under the instrument and the keyboard almost toppled over but then, inch by inch, crept towards the radiator. Jasmine's weight was only fifty-one kilos and, when the Irish cold crippled her heart and froze her fingers in flight over the keys, she had to wear a hat and Russian snow boots inside her bedsit. Looking disheveled with only one tassel on her orangey Peruvian hat and with balls of sleep in her eyes, Jasmine kicked the mats that were there to guard her music, not letting it spill over to the flat downstairs. But the neighbor "down below" still banged on the ceiling each time Jasmine would just look at a clef or play in headphones only with clicking.

"I'm so sick of this bullying!" Jasmine was raging. "And of sockets falling into our soup! And of the mouse disco and poo! They happily dance and indulge despite these flashing ultrasonic devices! Can't the landlord do something?"

Jade, Jasmine's partner, shoving into her backpack a five-liter Drumlin Hills water bottle, was too busy to answer. No moment could be wasted before she'd start jumping with all her weight next to the Kurzweil. An eye for an eye. A jump for a thump. The sound war was waged four years ago by their ground floor neighbor, a stout woman in a cadet cap, when Jasmine and Jade moved into this former nursing home converted into a badly functioning dwelling with extortionately high rent. Not blinking an eye, Cadet Cap told Jasmine, during their random encounter at the Newsagents, that a wooden broom handle was applied to the ceiling to produce the thunderous sound. "You're not going to force your lifestyle on me," Cadet Cap warned her.

Jasmine gathered the music sheets (multitudes of small black birds sitting on staves), put on her reading glasses and gave *Saint-Saëns* one more chance. The music soared and Jade, in her stone-washed overalls, paused to admire the geometry of soundscapes, breathing heavily after three dozen jumps. Jasmine, her hair long, flowing, kept lyrical lines, a tender reminiscing elegy. Jade felt vulnerable when a nocturne was played on her body at night. The same hands, the same chromatic scales brushing her spine, chords pressed on her lips. The heart was pumping heavily, Jade's head dizzy from an impossibility of divine music mixed with domineering broom rhythms from downstairs.

Jasmine was getting ready for her therapeutic triumph, a headliner at the Unitarian Church in a big concert. Now she stopped, figuring fingers... then, with her head attentively bent, gently swept the keyboard again with her elf-light hands and flowing hair. The famous pianist Vladimir Ashkenazy praised her evocative tone. His quote about Jasmine's sensitivity was on glossy flyers that Jade had to distribute.

An aggravated drum wave took center stage again. The cadet woman had blue, stone eyes, a face cemented with makeup, and a grenadier height, a perfect companion to her tenacious strength. Weak in her knees, big-boned but soft inside Jade couldn't compete. But jump for a thump, jump for a thump. With a backpack of Drumlin Hills on her shoulders, she began jumping up and down, putting all her determination and devotion to Jasmine into this task.

She invested so much time into Jasmine's comeback to piano playing that she was often frazzled. Did she feed the kefir grains today? Jade's baby face, framed by purple-coloured curls, frowned. Her colleague at work, a young but motherly helpful Croatian, brought her these grains in a Ziplock bag. Unfortunately, according to Jasmine, these were the wrong kefir grains. Jade started researching how to convert milk kefir to non-dairy. She wanted to do it for Jasmine who had all sorts of allergies and medical problems.

Three epileptic seizures in two months! One in Tesco when buying honey, another at home when hanging a thermal curtain, and the third at a charity shop ready to pay for an evening dress for an approaching concert. On top of it, Jasmine had an aversion to dairy, so Jade was doing her best.

"Do you remember if I added sugar and soymilk?" she asked Jasmine who usually managed a small talk over her *Saint-Saëns* and broom escapades. After the second brain surgery, nobody expected that Jasmine would continue playing and inspire parishioners in local churches with her angelic singing and hymns, but here she was, practicing despite her aversion to dairy and the adversary Cadet Cap!

"Sugar—yes, soymilk—we just ran out," Jasmine said and then shuddered: brutal broom banging resumed. Whenever she felt wronged, she started reminiscing about her surgeon who forgot to take out the metal staples from the back of her head.

"He comes in and says, how do you value your short-term memory, can you imagine? And I answer, I am a musician always learning new scores, what do you mean?"

"And he says, well, but some skills of yours will be gone once we do the procedure."

"So I complained to his superiors and they assured me that he is as gentle as a butterfly during surgeries, just insensitive talking."

"And I helped you to file the complaint, do you remember?" Jade prompted. They always played this game when invoking things from the past. To jolt Jasmine's memory and make it elastic. Just like a body oiled with an almond oil.

Almond oil... Jasmine used to rub it over Jade's naked shoulders and back and then cover her with her melodies... Now, after the second surgery, they were never relaxed; the tumour in Jasmine's brain was benign but it kept hemorrhaging without any warning.

"And do you remember my yellow coat that I wore to cheer you up in the hospital? I slept in it on the floor, next to a trolley bed, when the security guard came and told me to leave..."

"I even remember how we tried to figure out those pre-surgery compression stockings and burst out laughing when they tore in our hands…"

"Do you remember how I spent three nights in your bed, disobeying the guard and hiding under your blankets, making sure that I'm there when your turn for surgery comes?"

"Oh God, a medical team came on their regular morning round, and, averting their eyes from half-naked, half-asleep women, asked which one was the patient!"

"They didn't know indeed," Jade laughed. "Since we both were waiting in bed! What an improper, sexy infirmary!"

Energized by the memories, Jasmine started her Handel and the broom banging resumed. Handel, Haydn, Bach, then hymns. Besides a big concert later this month, there was a service on Sunday at a church nearby. Jade ran to the kitchen where they kept their five-liter bottles.

"Did you drink all the water? Just an hour ago, there was a full one. Once I start jumping, the thumping stops at least for a while because she feels intimidated by me. I wish we didn't have a rental crisis here in Dublin."

Nipping out, she came back with more "Drumlin Hills." Jasmine was learning hymns, Cadet Cap was banging. Jade suddenly realized something:

"Isn't Carmen coming? Shouldn't you learn her arias now, postponing your hymns for a couple of days?"

Even before the tumour was discovered, Jasmine was exasperated by "fiddly calendar apps" and social gatherings. Among voices, she couldn't distinguish which one was addressing her. The recovery period after the second surgery lengthened. Jasmine was still forgetful, and Jade had to work from home half of the week to assist her.

More than once Jasmine went for a nap when Don Juan or Pagliaccio were due for their rehearsals (she took several opera students). Jade had to let Don Juan in and rush to wake her. Usually Jade just hid in the bedroom with her laptop, but this time she had to make herself known. Oh, the look on that lad's face as he slowly realized that the partner of his drop-dead-gorgeous, but easily tired accompanist was a female! As for Pagliaccio, he just lost patience knocking and left.

Frequently Jasmine would learn the wrong score or have a schedule mix-up, so conversations like those below often took place.

"Let me remind you that in your calendar I see "Hansel and Gretel" at five! Is it Hansel or Gretel? How can you handle them with Tsar's Bride at six? You shouldn't do so much work… Bride was all by herself the last time, when you excused yourself to go to the bathroom to puke."

"And what about Eugene Onegin? Did you prepare his piece?"

"Tosca and Electra share the same time slot, was it because one of them didn't fit?"

"I don't think that Don Juan is coming this Friday. Do you remember that he is already touring in the U.S.?"

"Do you remember that Christ gave his life for us?"

Carmen forgot the money, Tosca got a cold and cancelled two times, Onegin suggested to his teacher that they get some beers, distrustful Pagliaccio started spreading rumors that his former music teacher was not right in the head, and finally the Sunday service came. They sat in the church, Jasmine at the piano and Jade on a bench, with a bottle of hot water to warm Jasmine's hands.

"We remember that Jesus Christ gave his life for us."

All parishioners echoed, "We remember that Jesus Christ gave his life for us."

The regular jovial and thoughtful priest, a former social worker, and an invited priest read their sermons. Besides them, there was only an older man in thick-lensed glasses, hard of hearing, and a young mother with a baby with golden earrings. No one else.

Jasmine's voice soared up and the warm shower of harmonies descended on Jade. Breathing in the full, meaningful air of this empty church, she thought that without this music mission, she would be just a middle-aged woman who didn't remember if she'd fed the kefir grains.

All of this was a miracle.

"We remember that Jesus was created in his likeness and we are his creatures."

When they prayed, Jasmine closed her eyes praying with everyone else. The pressure in her head was so strong that she often got nauseous, but she loved this small church and wanted to provide the free service.

"Didn't I do grand, didn't miss any note and memorized the order of the hymns?" Jasmine smiled.

"Do you remember about Jesus's deeds?" Jade joked.

"I worry about my short-term memory," Jasmine joked in response, "not about long-term memory. Things with Jesus happened a long time ago."

The priests called everyone to taste the bread and the wine, but Jade stayed in her seat. Any taste of alcohol would remind her of her sore state just years ago. She quit drinking when she met Jasmine. Now she felt a sudden urge to get drunk. At least this long day was almost over! She had printed out for Jasmine "The King of Love, My Shepherd Is." Made sure that Elektra was taken care of. Jumped at least forty times. Stayed with Jasmine during the service and saw that some people still believed in the existence of Jesus!

She brushed Jasmine's soft cheek. Encouraged by the priests, they started greeting each other and she held Jasmine's finely tuned, sensuous hand. Another parishioner came in late, in an inappropriately short skirt, just off a bike, like a gladiator with thick, sport-hungry calves, and the priests looked away so as not to see the edge of her bum.

This tender temple... touching and flying... caring crescendo... Jade kissed Jasmine on the cheek. Jasmine whispered, "It's not the right place." Jade shuddered, her heart hammered by her neighbour's thumps. God, was her stint as someone else's portable memory being dragged out unnecessarily? Jasmine is so demanding and fussy. Jade couldn't recount the last time they had made love.

Photo Credit: Morgan Gwenwald

J.P./Port Jefferson from *Common Lives/Lesbian Lives*, Issue 15/16, Summer 1985

MARGARET'S DEATH AND THE PLUNDER

Mary Aviyah Farkas

Driving home that cold dark winter evening the third day of January 2006, I knew deep in my bones that something was profoundly wrong. I found my wife much as I had left her that morning, still on the bed, but slumped over, blue and stone cold. She had died sometime that morning, before or after I checked on her, I'll never know. My habit was to tiptoe into her bedroom, shut off the incessant TV and the pellet stove, and blow her a kiss. She'd trained me not to wake her, as she often didn't get to sleep before three in the morning. So I was quiet, and my kiss landed in the stuffy air of her 80-degree room. She liked to sleep above the covers, and the heat was always cranked too high. I went to work that morning having performed this morning habit, and noticed she was on top of the covers, half sitting, leaning against the firm pillow shams. Her days began a good hour or two after mine. Let her sleep. She had an 11 o'clock appointment at the office, I knew I'd see her later.

But she didn't keep that appointment, nor two others that afternoon. I was worried, but she was often called into court on short notice, to provide expert testimony as a court mediator. She was sought after for child custody cases. The lawyers loved her as an expert witness. She had excellent credentials, dressed smartly, always spoke calmly, professionally, and oh so intelligently. She knew kids and she knew the laws. Was always able to peg the alcoholic, abusive fathers. Always tried to be fair, but the safety of the kids came first.

All day my gut told me that something wasn't right. She didn't answer our home phone, and I had my own full schedule to deal with, so I put my worry out of my head, as best I could. It was the first day back at work after the long Christmas, New year holidays.

Cell phone service was extremely spotty in rural Mendocino County and I just figured she hadn't been able to reach me.

It was already dark, early winter dark when I pulled into our steep curved driveway. Her car was in the driveway, her bedroom light was still on, just as I had left it. I raced up the entry stairs, could barely insert my key fast enough, and started yelling her name, MARGARET, MARGARET as I went from room to room till finally I got to her bedroom at the far end of the house. There she was, slumped over, one foot dangling off her bed, blue and ice cold.

Cardiac arrhythmia. Everyone assured me that it had been sudden, nothing could have been done. She'd never gotten out of bed. She'd been dead all day. All day. I had no idea. And I never said goodbye.

Each long unending day after her death I felt as if I was being dragged through Hell, inch by tortuous inch, each horrible second leading to each gruesome minute of sheer torture. Night fell bringing no relief. No sleep, just more Hell. I was in total shock at the loss of the woman I loved, my wife of 18 years. This unspeakable excursion into Hell bore no comparison to any physical pain I'd ever felt.

We held her Memorial Service less than two weeks later, over 200 family, friends, and colleagues in attendance. After the long Service, after testimony upon testimony of her love, kindness, intelligence and profound skill; and after the long receiving line, holding people as they vented their shock and disbelief, my brother and his wife drove me home. I just wanted to collapse. It was a frigid, dark January evening. I sat in the back seat waiting for the heat to come on, miserable and longing for bed.

We drove the 30 miles home in silence. I was completely spent. All I wanted was to have a bite to eat and go to bed. When I finally thawed enough to ask for scrambled eggs, my tongue tasted salt. Stranger snot, my snot, my tears, their tears all crusted my face. I never felt so tired and despondent.

Before my brother had finished cooking the eggs, before the toast had popped, before I was able to get a bite of this bland, stomach-soothing meal, suddenly, with no warning, Margaret's family descended. Her daughter, the doe eyed physician son-in-law and their three children were staying in the guest room; I'd forgotten they'd be here yet another night. But it wasn't just they who arrived. Margaret's sisters, all five of them with their husbands. And her one brother and his son. Suddenly an uninvited horde was in my home, and I couldn't, could not cope.

This horde roamed about the house, remarking on the Beauty of This; How Exquisite Is That; Boy Look What's In Here; Oh Joan! She has a Baseball collection; Look, a signed Mickey Mantle at bat; A Steve Young signed Helmet; Oh, come take a look! Michael Jordan and all the Bulls. They roamed from room to room, with Cash Register Eyes; with Envy Eyes; with We Can Take Whatever We Want Eyes; with She Doesn't Have A Husband To Stop Us Eyes. They opened every door, they looked and took what they wanted. And no one stopped them.

They'd known that their oldest sister was the most educated of them all, knew that her doctorate brought in good money, and Hell, her two kids were grown and gone. And her partner did OK too. Hell, good enough to afford this house, her suits, her shoes; Hell, good enough for ALL her collections. Aren't we the rightful heirs?

I stood mute in the kitchen. My brother and his wife, Margaret's daughter and the doe eyed physician just sat in the living room. Watching, not saying a word. Making no attempt to stop them. My oldest brother, nearly 15 years my senior, did nothing, did not protect me. And I couldn't. I was totally spent. Dumbfounded at this theft. In disbelief at their brazen cruel audacity.

I should have called the Police, but I could not muster the energy to deal with the law. I was drained of all will to act. I didn't have the strength, inside I was dead. Because I wanted to die, a piece of me just didn't care. I had been living each day, feeling dragged through Hell, inch by horrible inch. I wanted to join Margaret in death. I had barely made it through the hours long Memorial Service and greeting line. I was like the widow in Zorba the Greek, unable to move, watching as the black clad Harpies rob her of everything valuable.

As if this weren't enough, as if these Zorba the Greek Harpies weren't satisfied with the things they could easily pocket, the portable things, as if their greed wasn't slackened...then the Moving Van appeared in the driveway.

Yes. Margaret's ex-husband had left the Service early, drove 60 miles to Santa Rosa and arranged to pick up a 30-foot moving van. He then drove it the 90 miles to Willits, now in the dark, snaked up our narrow hillside driveway, and positioned this monster van to receive her bedroom and other furniture.

Who was I? We'd only been together 18 years, we'd built a loving life, a beautiful home and office, we'd celebrated marriages, births, we grieved her parents' death. We were part and parcel of each other's lives and large families.

None of this counted. We were just Lesbians, Queer; our relationship didn't really count, didn't matter. She wasn't "Really" married. What belonged to her was now "Rightfully" theirs. They were her "Real Kin."

With this haul, and not a word to me, the Harpies, the Rapists finally left.

SHE SAID

windflower

Stubborn child.
Defiant child. Defiant as a hurricane
wind. Sitting on a cold
linoleum floor
refusing.

My mother told me what
matters. Best not to wear that
skirt too short. Get that hair
out of your eyes. Keep your opinions
to yourself. Men don't like
smart women.

She said it would kill
my grandma. Loving another
woman. She
told me it was the best
thing that ever
happened.

A BEGINNING WITH NO END

windflower

I left the ice hanging from branches
like the crawling creaking
of reclaimed barn board in the wind
freezing the locks of cars.
The home where we began to make a life
together that frigid first winter
with its Plexiglas windows and hollow core door
our coats frozen statues on hooks
against its flimsy back,
our dogs bounding out the door
into the full force of February
returning with eyelashes glistening like diamonds.
Stars leaning into dawn
our waterbed a boat in its own warm harbor
our crisp breath against the bedroom air
our flushed breath against each other's bodies.
eight years later

These same bodies thirty eight years later
living on the Mendocino Coast, cliffs
painted with purple ice plants
tidal pools of sun drenched sea stars,
still remember all the love held
in eleven hundred square feet where
we first plumbed the depths of our desires
kisses that melted glaciers
kisses that know neither season nor coast.

CHAMA NOTES—AUGUST 1989
Rebecca Henderson

In my awareness of the natural world, I started out by being in it—on the farm and fields and pastures. I got separated from that world, physically and psychically, in college study. Biology meant classification, analysis, naming of separations, capturing living plants and drying them, capturing and raising animals to manipulate or dissect them. Traditional scientific analysis is what I learned.

Then I added the manipulative perspective of engineers and planners in order to become a landscape architect and planner. At work I sat in my office researching in books and writing reports or had meetings to talk about nature and what was about to happen to a particular piece of it. As early as 1973 I was reading about acid rain and depletion of the ozone and the greenhouse effect. And my work was helping the process continue. My job was to provide a better fit of power generation projects into the landscape. My work minimized initial local environmental damage and helped tone down the opposition to the projects.

During this time, while working on these projects, I met three things. One was the concept (and observable facts) of the interrelatedness of everything. The ecological studies left no doubt that things were intricately, delicately, and continually connected with each other. The second was the awareness that we could *not* accurately predict the outcome of most of our actions in nature. Thirdly, evidence mounted that our past actions were causing great damage to the environment, to the whole earth, in fact.

Attention to these three things propelled me out of the technological/analytical work of manipulating the environment. And it propelled me into seclusion. I found that if I was powerful enough to be part of the solution to environmental damage, it meant that I was close enough to be part of the problem. There was not a technological way to fix things or to prevent environmental damage resulting from the existence of our highly technological, petroleum-based society. Eventually I quit my job and went into despair, which is about as effective a method of seclusion as any. I withdrew in pain and sorrow and anger, to the numb comfort of that despair.

For a time, my conscience as an environmental activist yelped in protest. I should be out *doing* something. I couldn't. I didn't make connections with either the activists or with the naturalists who simply went out to enjoy the natural world. I just had to sit still and feel how bad it all felt.

Three Mile Island happened, and then Chernobyl. In this whole long period, I would hear things on the nightly news, and let the tears run down my face. I would read the paper, lay it down quietly, and sorrowfully go back to work. At the time, I was doing bookbinding – a kind of work which was as far away from petroleum or electricity or real estate and land management and recreation as I could find.

I think, in terms of body illnesses and trauma, this period represents the time from the onset of shock to the point where one begins to feel things again, if ever so slightly. I was numb – and just had to sit through that time. But through my tears, the healing continued. I began creating a different space—through working with my hands as a bookbinder and by paying attention to the women in my life. I began to care more for my own self and learned to be more kind to me.

My experience as a lesbian had often made me feel like an outsider, that I didn't belong. The lie is that "The world is set up thus and so, with married people, husband and wife who have children, and these family units constitute the building blocks—the heart and core of our great society and the Church." Demographers will tell you this is no longer true, if it ever was, but the lie lives on.

Quakers I grew up with were not so strict and closed about non-married people, but shied and skittered, then became very silent, about things having sexual connotations. Talking about such things as being a lesbian made them uncomfortable. I had a pride about being a lesbian even before Stonewall, but kept it hidden, keeping my "private" life entirely to myself.

Even though I could do my work as a landscape architect and environmental analyst without it remotely including my private life, I was outside the usual social patterns. To advance on into management, I would need a wife to help me, and that, at the time, required that I be a man. I was "outside" on that one just by being a woman, not necessarily a lesbian.

Primarily, there was a separation of self and work, of the personal and the political. Separation as a lesbian, separation as a Quaker. Exclusion is the principle, and the "in's" change the criteria to make *sure* others are out. It is the principle that fuels both racism and sexism. And the fear of exclusion is what makes the whole thing work.

So, the lesbian part of my life was separate from my environmental work. It was "outside" of my work. In contrast was my thorough intertwining of falling in love with a woman for the first time (Ann), and poetry about nature, adventures together outdoors, and being in the wilderness together. Camp provided a whole summer in the wilderness with women! It was quite, quite close to heaven, I thought. My poetry to Ann was stock full of references to the natural things I knew.

So was my poetry of despair after she got married to a man. I not only lost the woman I loved, but nature as well. I had lost the connections that had given me joy. And because all this was secret, I suffered alone. There was no one to understand the importance of what happened to me, or to help me put it in the context of grief and mourning.

In the next few years, I found joy again being outdoors with other women, but could never quite look at the natural world without the old wounds opening. This too, was part of the despair I withdrew into in the bookbinding days—outside of even the world of plants and animals and earth and sky. A spaceship existence.

"Hello out there!" "Me?" "Yes, you." I was called back and it was lesbians, my friends, who kept saying, "Yoo-hoo, we're here!" This was during the despair time in Iowa City. My friends went cross-country skiing and backpacking and mountain climbing and canoeing. Some lived in houses out in the country with animals and gardens. I worked part-time at the women's bookstore where I had access to the lesbians' books about nature and politics and spirituality. I was in the thick of discussions of lesbian separatist politics. I was in love with women. These were all immensely important in thawing my shock about environmental concerns. It made it possible for me to feel things again. I was accepted, for the first time, it felt like, as a woman among women. I found a home. We were *all* outside the mainstream culture and hallelujah for that. The farther away, the better.

Over time, I became sick from carbon monoxide exposure from a faulty furnace in my workplace and the increasing air pollution, and several of my friends suffered likewise. The community around me helped out, with packing and moving and selling out from bookbinding and getting a new job and beginning to enjoy life.

In a clear sense, I became able to be in the natural world *because* I am a lesbian, because I shared with lesbians an ethic and a consciousness about nature that contrasted utterly with the mechanistic, technological approaches of mainstream culture. As part of a community of women, and in relationships with my lovers, I was not allowed to wallow in the despair. When lovers went off to love another, I had to squarely face the pain of it and emerge. I was jerked out of despair by other ways of seeing things, and by finding myself in clear opposition to the forces creating the environmental catastrophes. My old sense of nature returned and my old ways of looking at things were understood by the women around me.

The real test of this, however, was when Quinn and I first started walking. I was back outdoors with a woman I loved. (Eeeps, danger that she would go away!) I was back where someone asked me the names of flowers and trees. (Damn it, I can only remember their Latin names.) I was back where I could feel gleeful and exuberant. (My body still was thinking it was sick.) I was back where everything is alive. (But surely those rocks are inanimate objects.) And I was back where that old despair might lurk behind a sunset. (But it's beautiful!)

So, with lesbians I found a path back to nature. I had found a group of women near me who appreciated what I saw and knew deep within what I felt about the outdoors. Kindred spirits.

There is another key way that lesbian culture differs from the mainstream that has to do with fear. It is not that we're a fearless bunch, but rather, we have learned to move and do things and claim our freedom in spite of fear. Because we distance ourselves from men, we are less vulnerable. All ways that you rely on another person provide the means for them to have power over you via the threat of their withdrawing what you need from them. We cut down on what we needed from them. We faced up to them collectively where we individually could not (such as the shelters for abused and raped women that we set up). We found our own ways to keep healthy and relied less and less on men and doctors to heal us. We found our own economic base (until the whole scheme collapsed), and went our own ways.

As we distanced ourselves from men, we discovered that it was our *fear* that had allowed them to maintain power. If we were not afraid, their power evaporated (as per pacifist tradition). We practiced keeping our fear in check.

Men have had a hold on the wilderness, on the outdoors, that is glued together by fear-creating myths. Bears, wolves, mountain lions, rattlers – all of these are "valiantly" fought and killed by men who emerge triumphant as the protectors of the weak (women and children). It is all a ruse to keep women indoors and immobilized. Heroism is a mask for slaughter. In a similar way, rape keeps women indoors and immobilized. We don't discount or underestimate the danger, but have learned to diminish our fear. Men have managed to scare women witless about the out-of-doors, and women have internalized this thoroughly.

But, "Here come the lesbians!" In the first place, we have a new assessment of how dangerous it is, unbiased by men's need to scare us out of it and keep it for themselves. In the second place we have learned to go into the wilderness and be outdoors in spite of old fears and conditioning. We have learned how to use the fear reactions of alertness and adrenaline in our favor, instead of letting those, and our worry, immobilize us.

I would posit that lesbian experience of nature is very different from either men's experience or from straight women's, because of the lack of inhibition due to fear. And some women besides lesbians have learned to not be afraid of the outdoors, and have debunked the wilderness danger lie, and I count those women too as my kindred spirits. One is conservationist and author Margaret Murie who believed it best to raise children in the wilderness because it is safe.

I know my experience out-of-doors is different from many women's because I have been working on dissolving my fears. My inclination is also to share the wilderness, not to hoard it and keep people out. My inclination is to *be* there, not to *do* anything with it. And I want to be there as simply and easily as possible. (I don't want a stove, refrigerator, shower, and TV in my RV with a boat towed behind and a satellite dish on top. No kidding, I've seen all of these on one rig.) All of these attitudes have roots in the lesbian culture I have been part of.

Writing this is another step in the process of my return to the outdoors. First, I physically returned by walking long distances there and living there. I learned to simplify my needs and gear to a point that this is relatively easy to do. Then, each time I go out I have to shed the clutter of urban life. It takes about two weeks to get my body clear of all the pollution and muck. My head clears, my vision gets sharper, I hear better, and I begin to be lithe and supple. Each day I walk in this stage brings more energy. My mind needs to unclutter in a similar way. The chit-chat in my head as I verbalize things drops away a little and I have more attention for observing things. The next step is to allow spiritual perceptions to have a place and a focus in my daily pattern.

As I walk, I take heart from all the tiny brave things growing up through the asphalt. (Irises are particularly successful at this.) I notice the grass creeping around the edges of eroded places, like skin heals around a wound. Also, I now know that it is in the nature of high things to come down lower with the wind, water, and gravity. That is, erosion is not the evil I formerly thought it was. And similarly, I take heart every time I see or hear of people who reject the technological society and seek to simplify their lives. My work seems to be to notice these healings and to bring them to the larger consciousness.

Part of what happens in pain and despair is that I can't hear and see clearly. Colors are pale, things appear flat instead of three-dimensional, light is dim, and the edges of objects are not clear and sharp. Sounds are far away and muffled. So, each time color and clarity, depth and light and sound are comprehended, it provides a chance for healing. If I observe these, it heals me. If I can share them with others, it provides a connection for them to all that's there and may also help to heal them.

TRAPS IN WATER

Mi Ok Song

for Bernice

Common Lives/Lesbian Lives, Issue 37, Winter 1991

I see lobster pots—
trapped in water
with their delicate, but
deadly netting—

I, too, have been
caught

knew it was dangerous—
got involved anyway
because the heart doesn't think
about becoming trapped—
only in being
lifted and freed.

On the surface, everything is
calm, peaceful—while
down below
a struggle

thrash against
the wooden planks
hoping I'm not going down
for the last time.

Drawing by Mi Ok Song

MAYBE IT'S THE ONLY WAY

Stephanie Sauer

Most mornings now she rises with teeth sore and muscles clenched. It is not just the cyber-attacks on her press' website upon the announcement of new titles with names like *Heterossexualidade Compulsória* and *O Desejo Homossexual* and *O Corpo Lésbico*. But it is that. It is not just the times her career has been sidelined by misogyny, but it is that, too. It is not just this week's news that a trans woman was slaughtered, diced, and stewed by her lover, but it is also that. It was not just the Black family of five whose car was riddled with police bullets in Rio, leaving most of them dead. It is not just the Black men who will be killed at the hands of a police officer today nor the seven women who will be killed at the hands of their husbands, but it is that. It is not just the months spent at her grandmother's side as she relived, trapped inside Alzheimer's, her childhood rape every time the nurses changed her undergarments, but it is that. It is not just the children in cages along the U.S.-Mexican border being raped, beaten, and starved, or the generations of harm this will inflict, but it is that. It is not just the fascist presidents of both countries she inhabits, but it is that. It is not just that the earth would fare better without humans, but it is that, too.

Now, her nerve endings scream in chorus: *we can take nothing more*. They plead for song, and she turns to the music of her adolescence when a similar rage tore through her: early 90s country sung by women. She needs their gravely, guttural, loud refusals, the violence in their lyrics. She needs to see clenched jaws and non-smiling eyes locked on cameras, fires set to sites of pain. She needs to sing lyrics like, "I ain't saying it's right or it's wrong / but maybe it's the only way" and "it didn't take 'em long to decide / that Earl had to die." She needs these like she might die without them.

A girl some called *hick* in the rural 90s, you see, had little access to feminist theory unless it came on country radio or her mom's daily dose of Oprah. Yes, there was edgier pop on MTV, but only her rich friends had that channel and she couldn't always see her friends. Usually, this was because she was grounded. Usually, she was grounded for some sass or secrecy. But she had a radio and momma let her walk to her uncle's house to watch Country Music Television. Her uncle liked the way Jo Dee Messina's nostrils flared as she sang some squeeze goodbye. The niece also liked Jo Dee and Tanya, Pam and Reba, and secretly crushed on Terri. Her uncle liked to sing along too, especially to the songs where the man who beats the woman dies in the end because his daddy had beat his momma but she never got to do any killing. His momma only curled up with her granddaughters to watch *Fried Green Tomatoes* in the daytime after she retired. The uncle tried not to get weepy at lines like, "She tried to pretend he wasn't drinking again / but daddy left the proof on her cheek," so his niece pretended not to watch him out of the corner of her eye. They sang instead at the top of their breaths at the violent bits.

The niece did not know where her rage came from, exactly, but most folks told her it was probably just hormones. She figured it was her stepdaddy or how her momma shunned her first kids when he and the new baby were around. She figured it could have also been her grandma's sadness or the way the boys at school wouldn't let her play on their team anymore. She figured it could have been any number of things, but said probably it was just hormones.

So, the girl made friends with a neighbor her age who also found herself angry for no apparent reason. But the neighbor did have good reason. She was the dark adopted daughter of an otherwise pale family and her older sisters, who dressed like Beetlejuice if he'd joined Wilson Phillips, were especially mean, always calling her *monkey* and ganging up two against one. So, the neighbors played outside every day until it got too dark to see.

At ten, the girl some called *hick* moved into the unused half of her parents' cabinet shop. She was tired of her family and felt she was ready for some independence. The shop was especially cold in winter, but she liked better being by herself. Her stepdaddy seemed pleased, too. He had moved out at fourteen to work on a chicken farm and thought moving out early would grow her up good. She wasn't so sure, but her anger kept her warm enough and she could play the radio anytime. The songs taught her it was good to crave freedom and that anger was okay. Lorrie Morgan taught her to shout "no" when she meant it and Trisha Yearwood confirmed that she lived in a world that wasn't made for her. Pam Tillis insisted that women could be lustful too and Patty Loveless gave a man's gaslighting what for. Reba's Bobby Gentry cover taught her that even girls whose mothers turn them out could end up alright in the end, and Martina showed her that sometimes it's okay to burn it all down if things get too bad.

Most days, the girl sat on a granite boulder beside the shop with the blue belly lizard she'd caught under a manzanita bush and kept as a pet. She dreamt of a life beyond the pine-studded hills and rodeo roar. She wanted to be the girl in the Sarah Evans song who "growed up to be a woman / and now she'd gone in the blink of an eye," but not because of some boy. She wanted her own all-by-her-lonesome cowbo(d)y song.

The girl would learn decades later that her country radio then was not like all country radios all the time. In those decades, something had come out howling in the voices of rural women. In the years since, she heard less and less of the howling and of women. Now it was all honky men singing about how pretty their gal was or how sad they'd been when she done left because they'd been a dipshit and had to start drinking again. Or they'd sing how proud they was to be backwoods or how much they missed Mayberry. She didn't quite understand what they all had to be so upset about, so she didn't listen much.

The girl some called *hick* did end up living beyond the pine-studded hills and rodeo roar. She escaped first to southwestern Mexico to learn Spanish in a free high school exchange program and, after graduation, she scrubbed toilets in northern New Mexico where she marveled at the news that her lover sang backup vocals on a country album. She marveled even more at the news that the lead singer herself was a lesbian, even if not an out one. That summer she found the Indigo Girls and found out Melissa Etheridge was *family*. That summer she sang in front of others, accompanied by her girlfriend or her girl's guitar. A year later, she was in Madrid studying Iberian literature and frequenting dyke bars and writing poems in dark cafés. She ended up at the state college in Sacramento the next year when her loan money ran out. She never did pursue country singing like she'd dreamed, mostly because she didn't want to stay closeted, but she got good at memorizing the Spanish Romantics and liked the H.D. she was assigned, so she studied poetry and recited her own at open mics.

A decade later at a fancy artist colony, she met the woman who'd written the lyrics to one of her favorite songs. The woman spoke so highly of country music as poor folks' poetry, of its Afro-Celtic roots to the other fancy art colony folks that the woman's pride surprised the girl. The woman asked the girl to quote her favorite line and the girl cooed, "I might have been born just plain white trash / but Fancy was my name." That the woman who wrote the lyrics was Black did not surprise the girl so much as how proud she was to speak well of country music to fancy art colony folks, for the girl had long hid her own love of these poems.

The girl became a woman with the help of her rage and was now living most months in Brazil with a woman she called her *spouse* because neither of them much liked the words *wife* or *esposa*. They ran a publishing press together, first in Rio, then in a city where a lot of radios were tuned to sertanejo stations. She liked the sertanejo, with its familiar guitars and accordions and steady beats and melancholy wailing. She loved how her friends who grew up in the cerrado would stop everything to sing *Evidências* at the top of their breath whenever it came on the radio. She loved how it was a music born of storytelling. She even liked the plaid shirts with pearly snaps and the worn, dusty cowboy hats on the album covers. She found the prevalence of male duos with names like Tonico & Tinoco and Chitãozinho & Xororó to be funny in the way that the best backwoods things are funny, and suggested to her spouse that they form a duo themselves called Tantão & Muitão. They, too, would sport mullets and sing of failed dreams and bad crops and lost women and moving to the city. Neither of them played instruments, though, so Tantão & Muitão became performance art that they never performed.

By the late 2010s, she found that the sertanejo she liked was giving way to a sertanejo she did not. It smacked of US pop country's blandness and evangelical bent. She found this new sertanejo full of men singing about sex and god and saudade in a way she could not fathom the women they sang about honestly enjoyed.

So, the girl who turned woman with the help of her rage began to listen to more forró and chorrinho and MPB and the electronic *funk* some queer bands played at the city park one fall. She still marveled at the repentistas and danced during carnival, attended concerts and sang *Evidências* at the top of her breath whenever it came on the radio.

One night before the virus, when the cerrado smelled of dry iron, she rode with friends out past the Chinese embassy and down a dirt road. Grupo Seu Estrelo, Orquestra Alada, and other artists were protesting the new fascist government by providing live music, dancing, and theater-as-procession in the *caipira*—translation: *hick*—style. People trickled in, talked, laughed, ate, drank. A single drum beat boomed. Hush. Hand pounding hide. A call. A response. Another boom and a voice crying. More hands slapping more hides. The sounds hollowed the woman's insides. All the bodies around her becoming her body in their aching.

Pounding halts. A conch horn. A different drum, slow, steady. Rattles shake ankles into dust. Shakers rattle gourds. Masked dancers form a procession and a red-painted cangaceiro carrying a megaphone emerges, taunting the crowd with real dangers and absurdities, a trickster come to trip up Plano Piloto politics and our despair. A giant lizard of strings and sticks hovers shimmies on stilts, punctuating the cangaceiro's words. Drummers line the procession, pound bodies into moving. The pounded clay bodies inhabit one another, flesh absorbing us as we absorb drum, dirt swallowing us all whole. We are switching to first person plural because we are returned, each into each.

ALMOST EVERYTHING I KNOW ABOUT HEALTHY RELATIONSHIPS I LEARNED FROM MY CAT

Everlyn Hunter

"The best test of whether a couple still has a functioning fondness and admiration system is usually how they view their past."

John Gottman, Ph.D., and Nan Silver
"The Seven Principles for Making Marriage Work"

It had been exactly ten years since I last had a pet—a companion and best friend, eager for my return home. There was only one problem. Ten years ago, I discovered a severe allergy to cats and a milder allergy to dogs. I now had a great apartment with loads of light and windows for a cat to follow the arc of the sunlight and a huge backyard that was enclosed with trees to climb, birds to chase, and squirrels to taunt. I googled hypoallergenic breeds and settled on the loyal, intelligent Siamese breed.

A few weeks later, I found the perfect Siamese on the website of the Long Beach SPCA. I planned the acquisition meticulously. I would adopt on the Friday of a three-day weekend, so that we could bond before I had to go off to work. Off I went, only to arrive and find that the replacement for every pet I'd loved and lost had already been adopted. Listlessly, I combed the two cat buildings, passing by hopefully yapping dogs to the two remaining Siamese in the facility. In a cage, way in the back, lay a tiny five-pound, cream-colored, Seal Point Siamese. She didn't meow, nor did she look at me when I tapped on the bars. She had a fresh scar on her stomach and she wouldn't eat. When I asked about her I was told that she was a stray that they had picked up three days before. She had been pregnant and had been given an abortion and fixed at the same time. She had just been medically released for adoption within the hour that I showed up. I asked to see the second Siamese. In a back-room cage lounged a hairy beast who filled the inside of the regulation sized carrier with an angry, malevolent chocolate presence—pure feline evil. I hightailed it back to the sick Seal Point and said, "Gimme that one."

They brought her out in a cardboard carrier. I opened the top and she began to purr, a deep, rumbling motor of contentment. I was infatuated and did what infatuated people do—dropped a couple hundred dollars on necessary accessories, put her in the car, and headed for home. I opened the top of the box while she was in the car, she crawled around a bit, made it to my lap, crawled into the crook of my left arm and feel asleep, purring. When we got home, she ate, pooped, and fell asleep at the foot of the bed.

All was well...until...I noticed a slight cough that became worse over the next three days. Using the coupon for one vet's visit within five days of adopting, I took her to the pet hospital where they told me she was close to death—dehydrated with a respiratory infection she had probably picked up at the shelter. She needed to be injected with fluids and had to be on three different antibiotics for up to three weeks. And even then, it wasn't a given that she would survive. They asked what I wanted to do. I was pissed. The shelter had to have known that it wasn't just the surgery that had her being listless!

Returning her to the SPCA within the 15-day window was definitely on my to-do list: I had five days to make a decision knowing that a return was a death sentence. I gave her antibiotics three times per day and night with no guarantee of health or life. Each night as I contemplated her death, she continued to eat, poop, crawl to the foot of my bed and purr. That gave pause to my angry death-dealing mood. But the deeper question was, if I made a commitment of time, effort, love and money to the relationship knowing that she might die, would it be worth it?

The memory of friends and family who lived with or had died of AIDS resurfaced, and I asked myself the same question. If I had known that they were going to be sick and would die, would it have been worth it to have loved them in the first place knowing the pain I would feel when they died? We all die. Couldn't the same question refer to each of us regardless of health status? The answer became self-evident.

I have a cat. Her name is Gracie.

Marilyn and Marsha from *Common Lives/Lesbian Lives*, Issue 33, Winter 1990

DYKES OF THE SEVENTIES SEND A MESSAGE TO THE 2020's VIA VILLANELLE

Sandra Renew

We're lesbians, we're queer, we cause a storm
No need to take a position, an agenda
We're on the edge, we're defiantly the norm

It's not as though we care at all for form
For you, my feelings always verge on tender
We're lesbians, we're queer, we cause a storm

It's not as though our love is lorn
As lesbians we've no trouble with our gender
We're on the edge, we're defiantly the norm

Our finery is not what's normally worn
In jeans and boots we're sometimes the offender
We're lesbians, we're queer, we cause a storm

Your hatred of queers only makes us yawn
We don't need your hate-mail, just return to sender
We're on the edge, we're defiantly the norm

We break the mould, we break the form
The form of us, no masking render
We're lesbians, we're queer, we cause a storm
We're on the edge, we're defiantly the norm

COMMON LIVES/LESBIAN LIVES COVER #1
Lisa Schoenfielder

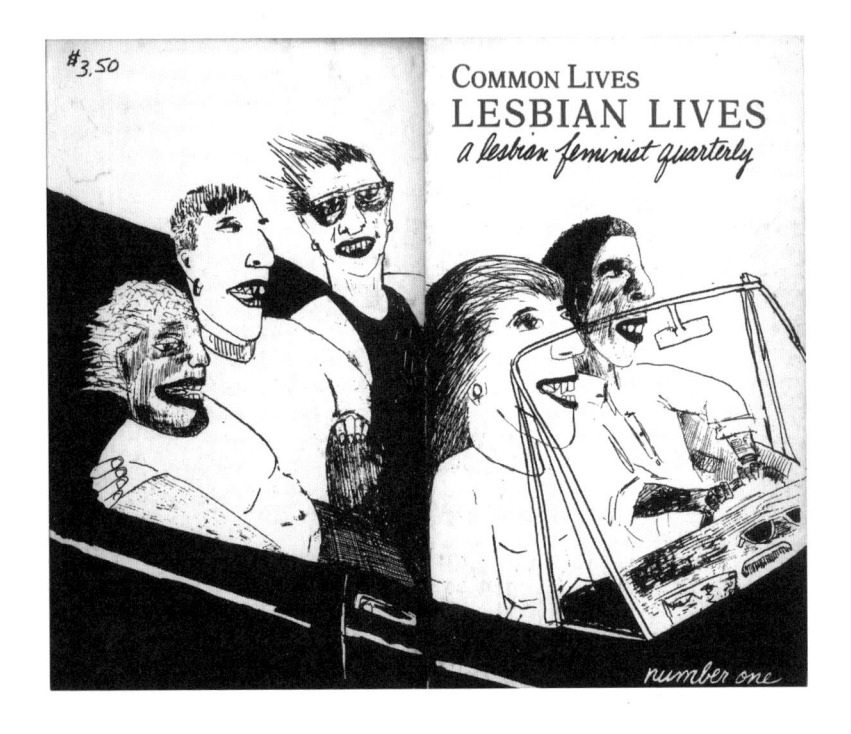

LITERARY DYKES TO WATCH OUT FOR
Alison Bechdel

From *Common Lives/Lesbian Lives*, Issue 18, Winter 1985

From *Common Lives/Lesbian Lives*, Issue 18, Winter 1985

LONG TIME LOVE (SONG, 2021)

Linda Shear

It was freezing
It was snowing
It was sticking to the ground
Two hearts starting out
In the middle of a winter storm
You brought your tooth brush
You brought your dog
I remember
That first kiss
Like a late January sunrise
Filled with every bead
Of morning light

> *Chorus*
> Such a long time love
> Two hearts wrapped in sleep
> Such a long time love
> Two hearts alone but never lonely

Is it early
In the morning
Or the middle of the night
Is it moon beams streaming in
Or the sunrise first light
Is it birds who
Call at night
Or the singing with the rise
With your arms and legs around me
Sipping breaths and rising hearts

> *Chorus*
> Such a long time love
> Two hearts wrapped in sleep
> Such a long time love
> Two hearts alone but never lonely

I let the dogs in
I let the dogs out
A hundred times yesterday
Now you and our girls are fast asleep
I'm on my first cup of green tea
I'm at our kitchen counter
I read the comics
I read Dear Abby
Waiting for our bedroom door to open
When you come back to me..........

> *Bridge*
> Time is taking hold of us
> Lifting us through dust
> And placing us gently back down

Is it early
In the morning
Or the middle of the night
Is it moon beams streaming in
Or the sunrise first light
Is it birds who
Call at night
Or the singing with the rise
With your arms and legs around me
Sipping breaths and rising hearts
Two lovers starting out - tonight
Such a long time love........

SANTA CRUZ SUNSET

Paloma Raffle

WOMAN IN ARMS (SONG)

Tess Catalano

Music and lyrics written and performed by Tess Catalano
Common Lives/Lesbian Lives, Issue 14, Winter 1984

The Woman in my arms is a revolutionary
Fighting for her country, Sandinista, Freedom Fighters
She has seen the government shoot her mother down.
Self-determination for the woman in my arms.
> *Chorus*
> We are fighting in every nation
> We are living in every cause
> We are everywhere, struggling, struggling
> Women in arms.

The woman in my arms is a historian
She fights the university uncovering their lies.
She can feel the heavy hand of a tenured position.
Truth in education for the woman in my arms.
> *Chorus*

The woman in my arms is a struggling mother.
She seeks an honest schooling for her daughter and her son
She can play that double role of secretary mother
Free day care for the woman in my arms.
> *Chorus*

The woman in my arms is a survivor.
She has fought the hands and minds of men
> who've tried to own her

She will see her woman friends, fight that battle once again
An end to the violence to the woman in my arms.

SUNFLOWERS

Lori Curry

Artwork by Lori Curry

MY ONE WILD LIFE: CLASS

Marie Cartier

> *Tell me, what is it you plan to do*
> *With your one wild and precious life?*
> *-Mary Oliver, 'The Summer Day'*

What did I do, the famous poet asks? Well, I survived, first of all, because that's first.

Then, I got to ask the question and give an answer.

Then, I wanted to do so much—be a famous poet, too. But, really, so, so few get to be that.

And after all, I needed money, so I was a waitress— breakfast, dinner, cocktails, diner, a short order cook, fry cook, a janitor, a secretary, a saleswoman… and all that time I was a student. I did theatre and one woman shows, and poetry slams and plays and I went to school and got degrees like other people get winter coats—just in case.

Because you never know how cold it will get.

I taught remedial English, traveled the country teaching speed reading. I got advance degrees and journeyed as far as I could from where I was born without drowning and I baptized myself in the waters of California over and over to be sure God saw me.

I'm here.
With my precious life: it's *mine* now. I chanted that over and over—the only mantra I needed in a land of soulful

reflection. My life. It's mine. I watched the sun dip into the Pacific like communion and swallowed it whole.
Here I am.
I was a teaching assistant, teacher's aide, tutor research assistant and then I taught at one, two, then three universities at the same time. The freeway flying beneath me. Driving a Chevy Nova with 300,000 miles on it until my mechanic said, "No mas," and would sell me a windshield wiper only for the driver's side. I used every tow, every year, that AAA gave me, and I never lagged in my Premiere membership. I took the 710 to the 405 to the 101 to the 210 and back to the 405 to the 10 to the 710 to the 73—and it was never a joke. The freeways were the grid of possibility, of *how to make it.*
I got a Ph.D., all the while teaching at two schools full time and traveling two hours in between each school and where I went to school—an Isosceles Triangle—the golden standard of *I can do this.*

Because, for me, there was always security in school. School being the first place that held me.

My first school. I couldn't go to the bathroom in the small room in the back of the classroom. I couldn't get up and go there.

Why? Was I afraid to pull down my pants? To be alone?

What happens to girls in small rooms alone with their pants down?
Well.

I sat in my classroom seat, attached to my desk in first grade, and let the urine run down the aisle and I didn't own it.

It wasn't mine.

The teacher stood next to me. "What are you doing?" she asked. But I didn't answer her.

I wasn't there.

She tried to adopt me out of my home but my mother argued for *me*, argued that I was mentally ill and didn't need to be in school, shouldn't be in school, that I would never learn. She wanted me at home making breakfast. Cooking for the 2, 3, 4, 5, kids she would have in a Catholic home, with no choice on the horizon. My father built a stool for me at seven so I could reach the stove.

When I hear today the words "home schooling" I freeze. Kids like me can disappear completely inside a "family" home like mine.

School for me was that line from *Hamilton*, "I'm not throwing away my shot."

Somehow, I snapped into place. That teacher—she did care.

Those six hours in school every day—were mine.

I learned to read, struggling out of silence so profound it did not include words, and the first one I learned: *dog*. Spelled backwards: *God*.

Help me, God, I learned to go to the bathroom and the first time there, inside the toilet paper dispenser, I found brown folded sheets of paper. It was miraculous and free.

I pulled several sheets out and out and out and I folded them together to make a book. I stuck them inside my shirt and took them home.

I was going to be something. I was going to be a writer.

I am not throwing away my shot.

And now, past sixty, I'm still going to school. And I am still teaching in several schools.

And I keep an eye out for those students who can't find the library. Or their story.

I teach students how to write their own story.

Our lives in the end, our precious lives, are only stories, aren't they?

Visit with the very old person, and all there is *are stories,* and the hope of more stories.
Visit with the very young person, and all there is *are stories,* and the hope of more stories.

What makes a life is the stories that go back and forth. Here and there and there and here, the hope I can make my story my own and that I will love it enough to read it again and again.

Work hard, I think. Play hard. Love hard.

I never got famous. I never got tenure. I never got time off to write, unless it was on unemployment (which I have been on several times).

I worked and I survived with my precious wild life, which
is so much more than so many people ever get. I know

that. And my wild life? What did I do with it?

I saved it. I held it. I loved it. I kicked open a door with it.
I let it breathe and go to the bathroom and sleep and eat
and I gave it a pen and paper and an *I am*.
In the end, what did I do with it? I am with it, my beating heart:

still here, still here, still here. Still with a pen. Still with a voice.

Those irrepressible words on a page: here I am, here I am
here I am.

THE SLOGAN FETISH

Sue Katz

Lena took pride in creating clever protest signs. At the start of women's liberation in the late 60s, her favorite was "If they can put one man on the moon, why not all of them?" Later, one of the outstanding achievements of her life was coming up with: "Anything you can do, I can do bleeding."

By the second Gay Pride March, Lena graduated from the rather vanilla "Two Four Six Eight. Gay is just as Good as Straight." While Lena was not the only one to sport "Dip me in Honey and Throw me to the Lesbians," she was the only one approached by a stranger who shamelessly tucked her arm into Lena's and whispered, "You sure give good sign." This woman was named Jeanette and she immediately fell for Lena. The feeling was mutual.

Jeanette became Lena's most ardent fan. When Lena carried a sign one year that said, "If lesbianism is a disorder, may I call in queer?" Jeanette nearly swooned. The next year was even more tantalizing: "Does this strap-on make me look dykey?"

It turned out that Jeanette *did* have a very particular fetish: she was sexually aroused by well-chosen words. There was even a name for this tendency: Narratophilia. Meanwhile, Lena's interest in the pithy saying was political, not erotic. Once she grasped the fact that slogans made Jeanette moist, she found her girlfriend's obsession disconcerting.

Jeanette usually went to bed before Lena, and would read until Lena's arrival. If it was a book with brilliant prose, she'd be all over Lena as soon as she joined her under the covers. At first Lena was thrilled to get such an eager reception, but when she realized it was the reading materials, not *her* presence, that made Jeanette hot, she began to freak out. Jeanette, though, was entirely unconscious that this was a kink. She assumed all readers felt sexually passionate about the words they encountered.

After the lethal explosion at the Boston Marathon, which provoked attacks around the city on people perceived to be Muslim, Lena attended a small demo with a sign saying, "Another Jewish Dyke Against Islamophobia." Many people came up and thanked her for her sign. She would have been more gratified if she wasn't distracted by Jeanette hanging on her and rubbing against her—in this entirely inappropriate setting.

The minute they returned to their apartment, Jeanette wanted to take her to bed. "I'm so wet," she whispered. For Lena, the coin finally dropped. After all, what if it had been a vibrator Jeanette was using before Lena came to bed, instead of a book by Jane Austen or Joan Nestle? The couple loved their sex toys: why not consider prose to be Jeanette's favored foreplay toy? In fact, on an intellectual level, it could well be considered an impressive, even poetic upgrade from a mere clit sucker or magic wand. With this spin on Jeanette's sexuality, Lena felt much better.

Years later, when the couple went to a reproductive rights demo, Jeanette was nearly overcome with the vapors. Her head swiveled as she tried to take in the signs. One said, "Restrict Dicks, not Janes." Another said, "Against Abortion? Have a vasectomy." When she saw a woman holding a big piece of cardboard that said "Public Cervix Announcement: Fuck You," she had to go sit down on the curb of the sidewalk to pull herself together.

Lena was marching with a few friends from her softball team and didn't notice Jeanette going to the side of the road. However, the woman with the "Public Cervix" sign *did* notice. She bent over Jeanette to see if she was okay. Aroused, Jeanette looked up into the eyes of this stranger, and forgot all about Lena.

UNTITLED

Sabrina McIntyre

THE WING OF FIRE

Sarah Walsh

At the hot wing eating contest my skin caught on fire. Bright orange sauce smeared around my mouth, cheeks, nose, and hands, burning a fiery, unyielding burn, but I knew I had to continue. No way was I going to give up the $200 prize for *Most Hot Wings Eaten in an Hour* just because my skin felt like I took a match to it.

The old capsaicin was doing its work. Out of the corner of my eye I saw a man giving up. Hot tears and snot ran down his face as a waiter rushed him a cold glass of milk.

No way was I going to let that be me. I had to keep chewing. The minutes ticked down like hours. One by one, people forfeited. In what felt like an eternity, only two of us remained. Now I had to make every second—no, every millisecond—count.

I began to notice a change creeping up on me. Fingers, face, mouth, tongue went numb. I couldn't even taste the wings. *Keep on chewing, keep on chewing,* I muttered, now my mantra.

Only one wing remained. Glancing at my opponent's plate I saw he also had only one wing. My heart skipped a beat. It was neck-n-neck, wing-n-wing. My fingers locked into position for chicken-wing-holding. As I struggled to pick up the last wing, my adversary glanced up, giving me a sly grin. He knew he had this in the bag.

Suddenly, my fingers unlocked and I grabbed the last wing like it was a dollar bill on the street. Every tooth in my mouth tore off the meat and skin, leaving nothing but bone.

"The winner of the annual chicken wing eating contest and of $200 is... MISS KATHY RAY!!" the announcer declared.

Wait a minute. That's my name. He called me!

"So that means...I WON?!" I shouted.

"Here's your trophy ma'am, along with $200!"

I sat dumbfounded, staring into space. This is real, this is *actually* happening to me.

Cameras flashed as people rushed up shouting *Congratulations!* Heck, I even signed a few autographs!

A glance revealed my opponents bitterly sulking at their luck.

"How in the Sam Hill does some little ol' gal like that beat all of us at somethin' we've been doing for years!" one grumbled.

The answer was simple.

I kept chewing.

Common Lives/Lesbian Lives, Issue 42, Spring 1992

Drawing by Sudie Rakusin

GAP

Dagmar Jill Spisak

Look, I want to be funny
and happy and whole heart-ed
here. I want to say she didn't
die and he didn't leave and you
aren't smoking cigarettes. And

all this gap,
this pause of silence waiting
to fill with meaning as it is lived,
as the next breath draws
the present moment into itself,

this potential scares me. I'm scared
of sunlight striking leaves
like snow, of a golden glow where
you have that disappointed
look on the page.
                But if you can't
be confident be brave. Sometimes
the moment between the out
and in breath is the exact moment
where things come clear. I'm told

to embrace it, the gap, the wave,
all the shadows, the uncertainty.

MOTH LIGHT

Dagmar Jill Spisak

Like a moth toward light
here I go despite the singed
wings. When I'm free, and a woman
walks in with little sparks flashing
around her I'm winging it
for home, she's the sun and compass
and the direction calls me with this
goal though it's pretty clear she's
too tall and too fem and too
young to be caught in my
six arms, too weighty for my flighty
intensity. But the heart is a wing
and it will move toward a flame
and if it flares in a blaze I will blame
only myself. So show me those sparks,
baby, show me what you can do
with a wide open heart pumping
hard getting up this hill of air.

ELDERS

Tamara Hollins

riding on the backs of those who came before
lifting me high during troubled times and leading me forth
singing songs of joy in my ear
making ways for me to jump as high as the sun

LAUNDRY

Maria Mínguez Arias

Inspired by Jacqueline Woodson's poem Limbo

Their soccer uniforms
size 6 and 9 year old
hang under the p g and e wires
where the mockingbird
mockingly shits

His soiling
a reminder
that there is no happy
ever
after
family selfie

Still
I smile
with a full heart

And a longing
right below my ribs

For when the laundry was just my lover's and mine

For when her white linen cropped top
swayed giving in to the Bay's warm breeze

For when my lips kissed the lace right above her collarbone

Before the children

LIMBO

Jacqueline Woodson

From *Common Lives/Lesbian Lives*, Issue 28, Fall 1988

Your blue and white dress hangs by the window
on a rusted hanger bent up at the sides.
When the wind blows, the dress blows
When the sun shines
it gets a little less blue
a little grayer along the seams.

I called you yesterday
Maybe it was the day before,
to tell you to come on over and pick it up
It doesn't look good hanging there
with no curtains to the window
Everybody knowing what I know.

I don't know who answered
but she told me to put it in the closet
that you'd be by to get it soon.

So I guess you're wondering why
I left it where it was
hanging by the window,
blowing in and out like a beer belly.

I guess I'm hoping you'll come by,
maybe catch a glimpse of it and
think enough to come on upstairs

. . . I guess.

SEEKING MY OWN VISION

Beth Brant

From *Common Lives/Lesbian Lives*, Issue 2, Winter 1981

MAKING FRY BREAD

Corn soup and fry bread! Living and growing up in a Mohawk home meant a dependence on these two staples. But to me they were special, unordinary gifts from Grandma's hands. The soup contained my favorite thing of all, hominy. Sometimes, there was rabbit meat in the pot. But usually, it just had bits and scraps of left-over meals.

On the days we had this bountiful supper, Grandma announced it to me in the morning, so I could look forward to the ritual we shared together. Around two o'clock in the afternoon, Grandma took her apron off the hook and tied the voluminous white cloth around her body. Then she tied a tea towel at my waist. We'd get out the flour, yeast, salt, and sugar. The yeast came wrapped in silver paper. The tiny squares were kept in the icebox. Grandma cut off a small chunk and dropped it into a bowl of warm water. Meanwhile, we were filling another bowl with the dry ingredients. We had a big blue pottery vessel that was used only for bread-making. Soon the yeast started bubbling, and it was added to the rest. Grandma stirred it all with a wooden spoon, sprinkled more flour in the batter, and like magic a fluffy dough emerged. Then came the best part. We divided the dough between us and began the kneading. Grandma pushed and slapped that dough until it had yielded to her hands and taken on a shape that was to her liking. It took me longer. Seven-year-old hands are not as skillful or strong. But I never heard a hurry-up tone to Grandma's voice.

Sometimes, this process had to be repeated. It depended on who was living with us at the time. The numbers could change weekly. Various aunts and uncles and cousins who were laid off from work, or relatives visiting from Canada, looking for work in the car factories. A lot of fry bread to make.

When the kneading was done, the dough was placed to rest in the blue bowl. A damp cloth was put over the top, and the whole thing set in a warm place to rise. Grandma instructed me to go outside and play, because it made the time pass faster.

I hauled out my coat, leggings, and boots. She helped me into these warm clothes, and I ran out to make angels in the snow. As I made scissors with my arms and legs, I kept glancing at the kitchen window, hoping to see Grandma's face beckoning me inside, her great silver braids swinging back and forth. I lay on the snow, half dreaming, aware only of the stillness surrounding me. A peaceful feeling hovered above me. I watched the chimney sending out smoke that rose heavy, then dissipated into the sky.

Grandma's smile appeared at the window. She waved and called to me. I ran to the door and entered the kitchen. The frying pan was spitting from the lard melting in it. The tea kettle whistled and clattered. In a hurry, I pulled off my snow-suit and sat down at the table. Grandma took hunks of dough in her hands and slapped them flat. Into the pan they'd go, sizzing and rising thickly. A few minutes more, and they were turned over to do the other side. She poured the boiling water over the tea leaves in the pot, then covered it with a cozy.

Two china cups were set out. Milk was transferred from a bottle to a tiny pitcher decorated with red cherries. It was real English china, a gift from Great-grandma Lydia. Taking the fry bread from the pan, Grandma set it on a pink plate. A slab of butter rested in its dish. Grandma believed in having a place and home for everything. So the cheese had a cheese dish, the preserves had a special jar, the mustard and horseradish never shared the same plate. When Grandma left the reserve in Canada and moved to Detroit, she gathered her possessions around her and gave them significance. There was a story to each piece of china, each quilt, each chair and table.

Everything was ready for tea. Grandma sat down, shook her napkin, and laid it across her knees. I did the same. She buttered a piece of fry bread and put it on my plate. Then she poured me half a cup of tea, filling the remainder of the cup with milk. I waited for her to fix her plate. She was a stickler for good manners. I bit into the fry bread. It was hot, with that yeasty, earthly taste that can't be compared to anything in this world. "Grandma, did you invent fry bread?" She laughed, "Child, no I didn't. It's as old as time, maybe older."

The kitchen windows had steamed over. The room was warm. The woodburner rumbled and popped in the corner. We sat at the oak table Grandpa had made, talking quietly and drinking tea. Gorging myself on fry bread, I finally became tired. Grandma's eyes followed my movements. Black eyes looked indulgently on my gluttony. Her eyes were large and luminous. I saw myself reflected in her. Dark mirrors where a small girl with blue eyes and blonde hair could see the other side to herself. A double-blood child. White mother, Indian father.

I pushed away from the table at last. I went to the window and started to draw on the steamy surface. I traced a big heart. "This is for you, Grandma."

MOCCASINS FROM HOME

When I was nine, my friends never quite believed that I was an Indian. In a family of black-haired, dark-skinned people, I seemed like a changeling. Blond hair, blue eyes, light skin. Later, I would lose some of my lightness. My eyes took on a grey tone. I mellowed a bit. But back then, I had trouble convincing some people. This was before I learned to hide my difference, to pretend I was just like every other white kid on the block.

When I was nine, I didn't wear buckskins or feathers, but I did wear moccasins that were sent to me and my sister from Uncle Tom, who lived on the reservation in Canada. Each year Mama made paper patterns of my sister's. Then, Mama mailed these to Uncle, along with a letter, updating family events. I was told that Uncle refused to learn English, and always asked a niece or great-nephew to translate the letters from Detroit. His replies were written in Mohawk, and Grandma or Grandpa read these out loud at dinnertime. When the package containing our shoes arrived, it became a holiday. Each time there was a surprise. Once, my moccasins were decorated with beaded turtles. Another time, Uncle had made a fringe around the edges and sewn little bones here and there. When I walked through the house, I clucked and clicked and made lovely sounds. The year Uncle lay so ill with pneumonia, we didn't receive our shoes. Instead, a parcel was sent that held in its wrappings of tissue paper and yellowing newsprint, treasures. Precious gifts that remail irreplaceable in my heart. A feather from a wild turkey, and the shell of a painted turtle.

Sister wore her shoes out right away. I saved mine for special occasions...like taking a warm bath on a cold night, getting dressed in a flannel nightgown that Grandma had made, putting on my moccasins, and going to the kitchen to drink hot tea and eat cinnamon toast. And always, in the kitchen, were the women of the family. My Mama was a white bird, darting around, lighting on a chair, pouring milk in my tea. I loved watching the women.

I never tired of them. They spoke about life and death and children. I knew that women held the answers of the universe, right there, in that old, worn kitchen. I felt charmed, proud, special. One day, I would grow up and be like the women I sat listening to. Their voices were beautiful, like notes blown through a reed. I often fell asleep hearing them discuss important things. Whether it had to do with food or family or piecing a quilt, each detail was talked over carefully, and full of care.

When I was nine, I loved women passionately. Being carried to my bed in strong, loving arms, I touched the women in my life. A face, lined and seamed. A strand of hair, black as bear fur. A breast that a cheek could rest itself on. This was real.

My moccasins rubbed softly on my ankles. I trembled.

BATH

Zöe Bracken

we read Sappho in the tub,
bathing one another in soft fragments and sudsy water.
so much lost miles beneath the ocean,
salt water greedily lapping up words.
legs messily entangled under the warmth
she pools bathwater between her long fingers,
lets some seep out through the cracks,
i face the faucet, back turned to her, tucked in folds
lean back, gently now, eyes instinctively shut,
breathe so careful-like, turn worlds behind eyelids
to a sea of blue, orange, green
it flows down from her palms, down ears, down hair, down back.
now baptized, she pulls me in close.

SOMEBODY'S CHILDHOOD

Anne Lee

From *Common Lives/Lesbian Lives*, Issue 1, Fall 1981

Anne Lee from *Common Lives/Lesbian Lives*, Issue 1, Fall 1981

What she knew about death, she had learned mostly from her cat and what she knew about death was no help to her now. As a child, she had known about funerals, and the murmurs of condolences had stayed on her lips for as long as she had believed them, which was considerably longer than she had had any right to expect. When she knew about death, as opposed to funerals, the murmurs no longer stretched to cover her rage, and the rage was left naked, revealed for what it was.

Her own death, or the prospect of it, or its accomplishments, toward which she had moved since infancy, was seen, not as deprivation, but as release. To let go. To stop breathing. To have nothing, ever, to do. Ever again. That, she could comprehend, could see in her mind's eye, could wish for with all her cells. She could remember, still, her first, careful attempts at dying, by the only method she knew or had at her disposal. She would stop breathing. It would be as simple as that. She would hold her breath in the darkness of her room, and one moment she would be there, and the next moment, she would be with Jesus. The beauty of those earliest attempts was that she was so entirely hopeful, so utterly without a sense of guilt. She wanted it, she prayed for it, and did what she could do to help it along. It was only a matter of time.

Sometimes she would hold her breath until she swam into unconsciousness, and sometimes she would smother herself with pillow and blankets (sometimes weighted, sometimes not), and sometimes she would try both at once, sometimes in despair that it would never work, that she would never get it right, and sometimes (less often), with a queer blend of exhilaration and triumph born of her great expectations.

When she gave up for the night, which was only after exhausting herself, she would be awake and listen, would look at the shadows in her room and examine them for signs of life. But staying awake, like holding one's breath, was less simple than it seemed. There was a moment after which it was impossible to go on, even with the best of intentions, even with the aid of the most fervent prayers.

Dear heavenly father, she prayed, dear heavenly father, let me die. Let me be dead now. Or soon. Let me be dead. She breathed the words and felt them push and strain and harden against her ribs. She could hold her breath for a very long time, which was good, and sometimes useful, and she never, ever cried.

When she cried, they hit her harder and her head flew back and forth and they would say cry dammit, cry, and she would not, and she would hold her breath and they would hit her harder and her head flew back and forth and they would say breathe, dammit, breathe, and eventually she would.

But sometimes it was good, and sometimes useful, as when her brother said he'd kill her if she made a sound. As when she sat in church beside her mother, her mother's nails imbedded in her arm, her mother's eyes uplifted in most perfect calm.

Because she could not wish them dead, she wished herself an orphan. She wished herself an orphan, and brotherless, with the same intensity with which she wished for death, and merged the wishes just in case, lest they follow her to heaven.

She was never alone, or almost never, so that she was forced to listen always. Mostly she listened for noises, for sudden moves, and when she had the chance, she watched, as well, but there were three of them and one of her, so that sometimes she had to whirl around and around in the middle of the room so she could see them all at the same time, and she would turn and turn until they made her stop, and then pretended it was a game.

She had lots of games. Or others, anyway.

Her favorites, her other favorites, were being invisible, which she mostly believed, and flying, which she knew for a fact was true. The flying was mostly difficult, and never quite got her where she wanted to go, which was down the front stairs (like Heidi) and out of the front door.

It was night when she flew, and she tried and tried and she would fly around the room a little first, for practice, and then down the stairs, and halfway down, the door would open and she'd be almost there, and then suddenly she'd be back in her bed and the house would be quiet and she would listen just in case. She knew, from her books, that flying was fun, but for her, it had long since become a chore, and she flapped her arms in terror, frightened of falling, and fearful of pursuit.

Her brother lay quiet (the sleeping dog) in his room across the hall. She longed to poke him with a stick and wake him and make him scream. Sometimes he screamed all by himself, and what he screamed was "no, no," and his eyes would be wide open, but he would be asleep. Mostly in this house, no one bothered to come up the stairs to see what was wrong, so he just screamed until he was finished, and then he would lie back down.

When her brother screamed, she hung onto the covers and waited for it to be over. It was worse when he screamed than when she screamed, because he was bigger and the noise was bigger, and when she screamed, the noise was little or not at all, and it mostly gave her something to do while she was being scared. It was bad when he screamed, because it was big, and a noise, and sometimes it took a long time, but as long as he was still screaming, she knew he was asleep. And that, of course, was something to be desired.

In the day, she played with her farm and read her books, or her mother's, when she could get them, and her father went to his study and her brother went to school. When her brother came home, he would make nooses with rope. She could never remember what he did after that, but sometimes he would set fires.

Her farm had two cows and a pig. It had other animals too, but she liked those best. She liked the animals one at a time, she did not like them together. They were made of rubber and were very hard, so you could squeeze them as hard as you could and nothing happened.

She liked it best when nothing happened. She would sit in the nursery with her back to the wall, and squeeze her cow as hard as she could for as long as she could, then she would be tired, and she would rest. Sometimes she squeezed the cow while she read her book, and it always made her feel better. Or she liked doing it anyway, she liked squeezing the cow, and she liked not squeezing the cow any more. It made her feel she had finished something. It gave her a sense of accomplishment.

Her mother liked for things to be finished. She, herself, liked well enough to finish things, but if a thing was finished (she had noticed), somehow the rest of it disappeared, and if it wasn't finished, then you still had it. It was a way that she was bad—that she started things instead of finishing them, and was never able to finish anything without starting it first.

She was careful to have no imaginary friends. She went into the book or the cow or the pig, and stayed there, (which was often dangerous enough), but she did not allow anyone to come out.

So she liked it best when nothing happened, when she sat in the nursery with her back to the wall and played with her farm and read.

She didn't like things to happen, and she didn't like cars. When she got into a car, it made her sick, even when the car was standing still. She sat in the front. Often when she got into a car (she had noticed) the door would shut on her hand, or sometimes a finger or two. It didn't matter where she tried to put her hands, somehow part of her always got shut in the door. It was not something you could cry about, either, because first there was the door on your hand then there was the hand over your mouth, and if you had tears in your nose, you couldn't breathe. So really, it wasn't anything you could cry about, but she didn't like cars, and they did make her sick.

Lots of things made her sick. She listened with her eyes and stomach, and she listened all the time. And watched. When she finally went to school, she watched and listened all the time, and nothing ever happened, but she watched and listened just the same, until it made her sick to go to school.

Sometimes when she was feeling better, she would bite her arm, and it was just like squeezing the cow. It made her feel good while she did it, and it made her feel good when she stopped. The other reason she liked it was because she could stop doing it whenever she wanted to, and seeing the teeth marks made her feel as if she had finished something. It gave her a sense of accomplishment. She could do it all by herself.

Sometimes she bit holes in her sleeves, by the shoulders, but that always made her mother mad, so she tried not to do it unless she really had to, and once she bit the nose off her Mary doll, but mostly she just bit herself because then nothing happened, and she liked it best when nothing happened at all.

Her mother liked things to be finished, but things seldom were. Biting herself (she had noticed) was a way of finishing, and so was screaming, and not breathing was best of all, but mostly, she had noticed, things never really did get finished. Mostly, things just went on and on.

NEW YORK POLITICS & FRIENDSHIP WITH BLUE LUNDEN

Quinn

In NYC in the 70s, I had some interesting times politically. I remember being at a city council committee meeting where we tried and failed to get a gay civil rights bill passed out of committee. The cynical politicians who defeated it had rounded up all sorts of people to testify against it. One man argued homosexuals should get the death penalty. After the hearing and negative result, a bunch of us occupied the city council chambers and ended up in jail. There we ran into Marsha Johnson, a trans woman we knew (thought to be a participant at Stonewall). On seeing us there she exclaimed, "Hey, what are you respectable queers doing here?" We all laughed along with Marsha about that.

Those were the days of a huge anti-nuke movement. I joined a group called DONT...Dykes Against Nuclear Technology. I remember attending a protest with a million people. They finally gave up even trying to arrest all of us.

Then there were the Women's Pentagon Actions. On two occasions women surrounded the Pentagon, and blocked doors with colorful webs that they'd spun of yarn and other materials. Most of us spent time in jail for this. I was in jail for a week after one of these actions, and fortunately had a cot next to my lover.

Getting to know Blue Lunden who was known as "the Mayor of New York City," was in itself an educational experience for me. She came out in the 40's in the New Orleans French Quarter as a teenager...told stories of being arrested time and time again, and spending time in jail for "wearing clothes of the opposite sex."

Through Blue I met Barbara Deming, a long-time lesbian and peace activist who wrote and taught about non-violence. She and her lover Jane Verlaine bought land in Sugarloaf Key, FL and started a lesbian land community there...one which is still in existence. Blue eventually lived and died there. I too would live there for several years.

Finally, I remember in 1983, walking a couple of hundred miles with Blue from NYC to the Seneca Women's Peace Camp. The camp was located right next to an arms depot storing nuclear weapons. With others we walked there, joining 125 women in what should have been a day-long walk beginning in Seneca Falls and heading down to the peace camp. As we got close, we were blocked by an angry mob. Though our walk was legal and peaceful, we were the ones who ended up in jail for a week. The story about that experience is available on the Internet, a 2008 interview with Rosalie and me. ("Quinn and Rosalie Regal re: Seneca Women's Peace Camp")

Blue is the subject of an award-winning Film, "Some Ground to Stand On", which can be obtained from Women Make Movies. And here is a story poem I wrote about her in 2009.

To Blue (1935-1999)

We call you the mayor
of New York City
fall in love
with your skinny frame
and boyish ways
your laughing blue eyes
and prominent teeth.

We fall in love
with the sheer density of you
the identity you've carved
from a hostile world.

Born Doris Dubois
in New Orleans
you decide in New York

as your hair turns white
to be "Blue" instead
but Doris lives on
in the stories you tell.

*We fall in love
with your stories.*

Of outcasts
from the stifling world
of Joseph McCarthy
where we had grown up
of refugees who
pour by the thousands
into the sector of
New Orleans that
you call home:
The French Quarter

Pregnant girls running
from scornful town
and scarlet letter

Children escaping
invisible violence in
righteous homes

Women purple with bruises
hiding from men
who want them dead

Multicolored couples
fleeing a world
where their love is illegal

Gay men and gay women
seeking the safety
to love who they love

Transsexuals, transvestites
fleeing the hatred that
crossing of boundaries inspires.

All refugees
in the land of jazz
together
in joyful dance
a celebration
of passion released
shattered spirits restored.

Yet even this riotous refuge
remains under threat
from vice squad raids
and nights in jail,
from repeated arrests
for "wearing clothes
of the opposite sex,"
from an endless parade
of salacious men
whose cravings provide
the jobs you take
in order to live
where you can be real.

We learn from your stories
what happened back then
to girls and boys
and men and women
who broke the rules.

With your life as a foil
we see more clearly
our own old fears of being cast out
from the uptight realm
that you and your friends
were calling back then
"The American Zone,"
see the masks we donned
so we could stay.
See too the rapture
we had swallowed
along with ourselves
rewards that could come
from hanging on tight
whoever we were
to our deepest selves
finding a way
to tell the truth.

We learn from your stories
to cherish our own.

Addendum:

I hear your voice, Blue,
from the other side
reminding me
you lost years of your life
to drugs and booze
were not after all
uniquely strong.

I know, dear friend,
but that is a story

for a different poem
the one where I stumble
broken
into your city
the one where you
and Rosalie
yourselves once broken
and nearly dead
now welcome me into the dignified warmth
of your sober lives.

Quinn, December 2013

RECOVERY

Everlyn Hunter

This is the first chapter of a forthcoming novel.

Her ritual is the same each time Crystal enters my office. She walks in ahead of me, goes to the chair facing the wall, and before she sits, reaches out and touches the whiteboard with the red writing—the five problem-solving steps to her improving her Math grade. It's hers, something that is uniquely her own and for a "garbage bag kid" in the foster care system, it's something worth lingering over. Then she sits and we begin the checking in. I'm behind my desk, computer screen open to the behavior reward system page, queued to Crystal's name and the week. "With two days to go you're at 80%."

"Could you plug in five's for the rest of the week to see if I'll make 90%?"

I do and the results come up short.

"If you do everything right for the next two days, you'll only make Level B not Level A."

"I'm okay with that."

"Bad week?"

"Yeah, I had a family visit."

"Wanna talk about it?"

"Nope."

"Okay, so then we'll just work on the problem with Math?"

"K."

Her teenage conversational stonewall is in full force but I try one more time to get her to open up.

"Crystal you do know that I'm not just blowing smoke here, right? I actually do believe everything I'm saying to you. If you can learn how to problem-solve, you can apply this to anything, big or small, problems with Math or family problems."

She's silent for a long time and I let the force of silence do its thing. I'm rewarded in ways I don't expect when she says,

"Dr. Willow, do you know what happened to me?"

I don't.

Now I have one more secondary trauma to add to my own.

#

Crystal's shared room holds two single beds with thin plastic covered mattresses, hand-drawn pictures and magazine cutouts fastened with scotch tape to the wall and little else. Zainab, her roommate, watches Crystal from the doorless open portal, as she creates a neat pile of her meagre belongings.

"Hey you in? The breakout's going down tonight at change of shift."

Zainab's excitement is almost as evident as the carpet burn scabs covering the left side of her face.

"I ain't a part of you shady bitches plan. I got one more day in this hell hole then I'm saying hello to a Level 12 placement."

Zainab advances into the room and perches on the empty bed. Crystal turns to survey Zainab's nervous, bouncy action on the not-so-bouncy mattress.

"Zee, do you feel like staying here...let me rephrase, going BACK to the Puff unit? Didn't they just let you out after that?"

She points to the nearly scabbed over carpet burn on Zainab's face, prompting Zee to duck and tilt her head in an effort to obscure the evidence of her latest self-harm attempt.

"Zee, don't get mixed up with them lifers' escape plan. They got nothing to lose, but you got so much going for you. You got book smarts, good grades and when you ain't skinning your face up against the carpet, you the prettiest girl in here. You off the Puff unit and you only got to stay straight for three months, then you out. Don't you want out of this prison?"

"Back to my family ?"

That's all Zee has to say for Crystal to have an answer to her question. She knows that after her Iranian Muslim tomboy roommate's family visits, Zee proceeds to rub her face against a rough surface repeatedly until she bleeds.

"Who's gonna look out for you when I'm gone, Zee?"

Crystal sits next to Zee and leans close enough to touch shoulders. A passing Aide stops, and yells, "No touching allowed!"

The girls reluctantly move apart.

#

The first fingers of light slip through the frosted glass of the bedroom window. The alarm clock has rung past two snooze cycles thirty minutes ago and Grace is dressed and ready for work except for her lucky Star of David necklace. She searches the elegantly appointed room in her simple black Armani silk t-shirt that blends well with casual blue jeans and black Brooks running shoes. With the addition of a navy collarless sweater, her California casual ensemble adapts well to either a professional meeting or a physical restraint hold on a suicidal student. She's ready for anything, except the woman in front of her.

June's gym-toned physique disappears from view as she pulls last night's blouse over her close-cropped hair and slips a toothbrush into her overnight bag.

"You don't trust me."

There is no slight upward lilt at the end of the sentence signaling that it's a question. Instead it's a bold statement delivered with a flat, harsh, abrupt tone—a statement of the obvious that prompts Grace's gaze and response.

"Would you like to know why?"

June's movements still and Grace continues.

"You've never spent a morning after the night before. You call only when in your car or at a weekend conference, and on one or two occasions, your phone suspiciously has connectivity issues when you're out of town. It doesn't take a rocket scientist to know you have something to hide. I don't know what and can only guess, but whatever it is, it doesn't put me front and center in your life."

"I didn't realize you were keeping track." June's incredulity is genuine.

"It's a curse, June, this hyper-vigilance. I can't look away. I notice everything and I have an overactive imagination that makes leaps of intuition after synthesizing all that input. I'm always keeping track."

The silent face off lasts for a tense few seconds before June brushes past and exits the bedroom. Grace follows through the living room towards the front door.

"Will I see you... later?"

The slight ache in Grace's voice belies her stoic demeanor and transforms the last "later" to "again." June pauses.

"Do you want to see me again?"

"Yes...No...I don't know."

Suddenly Grace is reduced once again, to the small girl watching her mother leave after a violent fight with her father, desperately wanting her to stay yet knowing that staying might mean serious injury or death. The responsibility overwhelms and leaves her frozen and confused. When she surfaces from her flashback, June has already left.

#

The scream explodes as I enter the building. It's a sound that pierces the heart like a fragmenting hollow point bullet, shattering into a million pieces. Each fragment traveling faster than the whole, tearing and ripping flesh, tearing and ripping flesh. The pain is never-ending, the wound has no cure. This scream damages forever. It goes on and on, stops everyone in their tracks—for only a second—before life goes on as if wounds such as these happen every day. Here at Bellevue Adolescent Center, they do.

I know I'm on time, but cannot tell once I enter the building because there are no clocks in the lobby and I wear no watch. The broken glass of a watch face could be used as implements of self-harm by the kids. The missing clock signals a more systemic problem. Clocks are the first clue to the level of chaos or order in an institutional setting. If the clocks all tell the same time throughout the physical space, it's guaranteed that someone in charge has ensured that everyone is coordinated with everyone else in the building. If the clocks tell different times, it's guaranteed that the environment is chaotic with everyone on their own schedule. At Bellevue Adolescent Center, there are no clocks…anywhere.

#

I walk to the second locked door, ten feet from the locked front door. I swipe my key card and listen for the faint click of the lock disengaging before pushing through the double doors into another hallway. Double doors to the right—locked—lead to the girls' residential unit. A locked door to the left leads to the cafeteria where the girls are in full-throated breakfast protest against what they call prison cooking and institutional food. Random snippets seep through the door jamb:

"Motherfucking Mario! I said I did not want no fucking oatmeal this morning. Can't you see I'm a delicate flower who needs her bacon and eggs!"

The kids swear that Mario, the cook, did time in the prison. Looking at bald-headed, six-foot, six-inch tattooed Mario and tasting his food, no staff is inclined to argue with this logic.

"Language Kiki. Please."

The tired voice of a unit aide at the end of her graveyard shift, makes a half-hearted attempt at keeping the peace.

"Fuck language! Where the fuck is my fucking bacon and muthafucking eggs!"

The other kids get mouthy on cue.

"Where you think you at Kiki, the Ritz Carlton?"

"Read the menu, nigga. Ain't no eggs here fo your ass!" Everyone laughs.

"Ain't nobody talking to all you. Mine your bizness."

Kiki screams at the sound of a bowl smashing against the wall, and a scuffle filters through the door. A glimpse through the bulletproof, shatter-proof, damn near black-box grade material window reveals Kiki, full makeup already impeccably done at this early morning hour, in a wall restraint against an oatmeal smeared wall—two Aides on either side hold his arms against the wall, bracing their knees behind his.

That's the first restraint of the day. There are at least five per day, sometimes more, rarely less, at Bellevue. This one ends a potential fight, no blood was drawn, no one hurt and Kiki calms down in seconds.

"Aight, no eggs, no bacon. I get it. Let me up, man. I'm good."

And he's released, goes back in line and tosses his hair in a final defiant swing. No one else breaks their stride and barely stop whatever they've been doing. They've seen this before. It happens every morning when Kiki's delusions get the better of him and he pitches a fit about his bacon and eggs.

#

I continue on past the offices of the therapists to the third locked door, swipe my key card a third time and look through the bulletproof, reinforced door window into my domain—the school hallway. Mr. Petty, an angular ectomorphic old man with a young man's stride, and Bruce, a short, furtive Cambodian, with a deferential air, lounge against the institutional puce blah hallway wall, carefully avoiding the chalk drawings celebrating Easter while Bruce explains the intricacies of picking just the right combination of three numbers in the Daily Lotto. He has a system that he swears works. Both men straighten up and hide their numbers as the door opens but ease back into a slouch when I enter. Mr. Pe[y greets me with his usual morning salutation,

"Hey what's up Doc. Want some tea?"

"Is it that same black crap you offered me yesterday that nearly burned a hole in the back of my throat while it was gagging me with its stench?"

"Yup. Same swill. Want some?"

"Sure. I'll take a cup if you squeeze some honey in it. Gotta keep the pipes limber for the kiddies."

Mr. Petty treats me like a visiting dignitary with small offers of kindness—his daily gifts. I'm his vision of Blackness made whole and racism cured, second only to the election of a Black president. I'm surprised he doesn't call me Michelle Obama. And being the well-brought up child that I am, I call him Mister, homage to his age and experience. He's the oldest and longest tenured staff member at Bellevue. And in this locked psychiatric center where staff are used and tossed like single-ply toilet paper, he's a fucking Methuselah.

"Is Dr. Spiteri in yet?"

"Course not. Think we'd be hanging in the hallway if she was?"

#

I turn left into the empty main school hallway and bring out my ring of keys to do the morning ritual of unlocking my office door before the rest of the staff arrives and before the kids are released into the school section of the psychiatric facility. I wrestle with the top deadbolt and then the bottom. Julio the head custodian gave me two keys to everyone else's one with a subtle warning,

"Lock the top and bottom locks on your office door. Around here you never know."

"Know what, Julio?"

He glances from side to side before saying,

"Only you have a key to the top lock besides me."

I thought then, three weeks before, that he spoke about kids being locked in the building 24 hours per day and sometimes getting into places where they weren't allowed. But the vision that meets my eyes as I open the door casts his caution in a different light. Crystal's body lies splayed across my desk, face up, sightless eyes and mouth locked in a wordless scream. There is no blood. In her hand, clutched in still rigid fingers, is my silver Star of David.

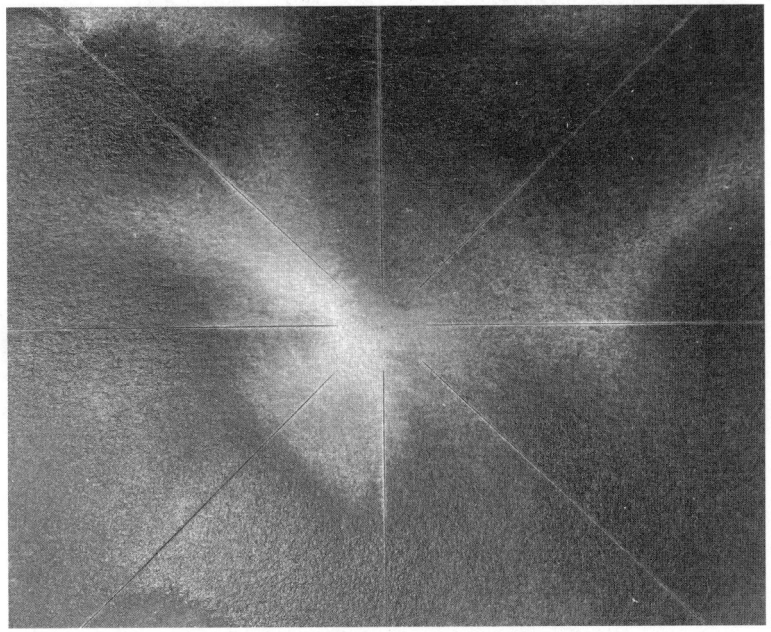

Untitled, Elements series by Britta Kathmeyer

GOODBYE TO(MORROW)

Olivia Loscavio

What do I do
When your name is more common in my phone
    than the word 'tomorrow'?
I cried in the bookstore while smooth jazz played
    over the speakers.
A granola dyke next to me talked about Kamala Harris's
    new book.
I wonder if she goes home to her
Granola
Dyke
Girlfriend
And they lie in bed together
Legs unshaved, no bra
Feminist literature on the bookshelf?
You didn't like to wear bras.
You thought you were a stud
But really you were soft.
You were my color purple.
I've always cartwheeled through the world
    bright pink
But being with you
Meant keeping my feet on the ground,
I think the grey from the pavement made me
    mauve.
I'm not sure what color you are anymore,
    Because you wouldn't say anything on our last phone call.
I talked to the wall so somebody would listen to me
    as I said goodbye.

A DYKE TO WATCH OUT FOR: IOWA DYKE MARCH, JUNE 2018

Aaron Silander

A friend introduced me to one of the organizers of this march. She said, "we're looking for an old dyke to speak." I said, "why don't *you* speak?" She said, "well *you're* older."

That's how I ended up here tonight. My name is Aaron. I'm old and I am a Dyke to Watch Out For! I moved to Iowa City in the spring of 1970 to be part of a women's living collective. Our intent was to make a revolution. A couple of us had good jobs, a couple had crappy jobs. We shared everything, from living space to meals, from clothing to cars. We pooled our resources so we could do the maximum amount of political work possible.

Some of us started a radical feminist newspaper; others organized childcare cooperatives. We worked on reproductive rights and formed a speakers bureau. Some participated in the Red Star Rising Art Collective and a guerilla theater group. We formed consciousness raising groups of all kinds and helped set up a Free University with classes for women including writing and healthcare; auto mechanics and carpentry; sex, race, and class under capitalism—and more.

We were a part of an umbrella group of two to four hundred women—the Iowa City Women's Liberation Front. Can you imagine? As many as four hundred women meeting in one big circle, at least once a week? We created new services and institutions to meet women's needs, to meet *our* needs. We occupied buildings and blocked doorways until we got funding for the Women's Resource and Action Center, the Rape Victim Advocacy Program, and later for Women Against Racism Committee, a group that came out of the Women's Center.

There is much to say and many stories along the way. But what I will offer on this occasion is that, in pretty short order, most of us came out—that is, those of us who weren't already out. The feminist newspaper became a radical lesbian separatist paper, "Ain't I A Woman," mailed from an undisclosed location somewhere in the Midwest. The Iowa City Women's Press became the only full-service gay women's press in the country including publishing, type setting and graphics, printing, and book binding. The women's restaurant Grace and Ruby's was a restaurant by day and a gay women's bar by night.

In Iowa City at the time, we didn't have much to do with planning Pride Marches. We didn't take part. The dykes remained separate; we had our pride after all.

In the summer of 1970, as many women as possible piled into a Volkswagen bug and drove east to the first—or maybe second—New York City Pride March after the Stonewall riots. The women I traveled with weren't quite out yet so, when we arrived, I hit the street looking for a meeting at the "Lesbian Loft." I wasn't going to let my sisters hold me back.

It was my first time in the city. My newfound confidence was short lived. With no clear idea where I was going and no landmarks in sight, I had a sinking feeling that I was lost. As I turned to look back, I saw two tall women approaching—one wearing a Wonder Woman tank top. You'd think I could relate, but for some reason I froze and looking straight ahead, kept right on walking. It wasn't long before they caught up. Sidling up on either side one turned to say, "Hey, I think we might be headed in the same direction." The woman in the tank top passed me a joint. That was it! I'd found my people. I went to the meeting and spent the night with a Central Park carriage driver.

At the New York Pride March the next day, I walked with 100,000 people, probably more. What an amazing experience—joyful and humbling. The Stonewall Riots and early Pride Marches were led by transgender women of color. I got lost in the sea of us and became aware of just how good it felt to lose myself, to be a part of a large, diverse and vibrant community. To be a part of...

that is what I'd wished for all along and was looking for in my community of lesbian separatists.

Today I work with 100Grannies for a fossil free future. I'm not a grandmother. You don't have to be. I work with the Mississippi Stand Solidarity Network, a wild and lovely coalition of young and indigenous people, Catholic Workers, anarchists and farmers, trying to stop the Dakota Access Pipeline from coming through Iowa. I volunteer at the Center for Worker Justice and visit ICE detainees held in Iowa county jails. I'm a part of the new Lambda coed softball league—we're looking for players, score keepers, and coaches. And I'm a part of an LGBTQ Twelve Step group that meets on Sunday nights.

These days I'm scrambling, as you may be, to figure out ways to stop the homophobic, fascist, shitstorm coming out of Washington and Des Moines. It is frightening. It can be hard to maintain a positive outlook and spiritual approach, but today we March. Dykes: take back the night—safely! Tomorrow we will join with others, and together I'm hopeful we will find a way forward!

***

This talk was given at a rally following a Dyke picnic and March on the eve of the Iowa City Pride Parade 2018. The content shared below was a part of a beautiful flyer for the event.

"Herstory: The Dyke March began in Washington, D.C., San Francisco, and NYC for visibility for lesbian, gay, queer, bi-dyke women to take power, in the face of the first white gay male dominated Pride Parades."

"Our March: Dykes march for our particular strength and ferocity in the political and social struggles we face as women, as lesbians, queers, studs, butches, femmes/fems, andros, bois, and as Women of Color, as older women, differently abled women, and as female people defying patriarchy! Anyone who identifies as a dyke, or whose story this speaks to, including trans women, Two-Spirit, enbies/nonbinaries, genderqueers, transmasc afab folk, and allies are welcome!"

"We're distinctly a MARCH, not a parade!"

RAINBOW FLAGS: A SPEECH

Rabbi Lisa Edwards

Beth Chayim Chadashim Synagogue (BCC), Los Angeles, California

Invited to represent the LA-area queer clergy, Rabbi Edwards gave a version of this speech at West Hollywood Park on June 26, 2015 during a rally in celebration of the 2015 U.S. Supreme Court marriage equality decision.

Good afternoon! The Bible Says, "sound the trumpets on your joyous occasions!" A shofar sounds to loud applause. *[A shofar is a ram's horn, the customary Jewish instrument used to fulfill this instruction.]*

Rabbi Lisa Edwards

Raise your rainbow flags high!

In the Bible's Book of Genesis, God placed a rainbow in the sky as a reminder after the flood, a promise never again to destroy the world because of bad behavior by humans. In Jewish tradition we take the rainbow as a reminder—in Hebrew an *ot habrit*—"a sign of the covenant" between God and humans: it is up to us, working in partnership, to make the world a better place.

Raise your rainbows!

Today, working in partnership the world became a better place! Some people think voices of faith have no place at a celebration of marriage equality. Some think voices of faith have no place here because of the many religious groups that have spoken so loudly *against* our right to civil marriage. But if you think faith voices have not been by our side in this struggle, think again!

In 1968 Reverend Troy Perry founded MCC—the Metropolitan Community Church—the world's first gay and lesbian church, right here in Los Angeles. In 1972 Rev. Perry helped a handful of gay Jews start the first gay and lesbian synagogue—*Beth Chayim Chadashim*, meaning "House of New Life," often called BCC.

In those years, no one was thinking we needed queer houses of worship so that we'd have somewhere to get married. Yet soon after their founding, religious weddings were taking place within their walls. Forty-four years ago, in 1971, a Methodist pastor officiated at a ceremony that set in motion one of the legal cases that resulted in today's Supreme Court Decision. Rev. Perry, and many other ministers along the way, brought the issue of same gender marriage *directly* to the courts.

The liberal movements of Judaism, the Reform and Reconstructionist, have publicly advocated for marriage equality since the 1990's, and rabbis in those movements have been marrying same-gender couples in Jewish ceremonies long before it became a matter of public discourse.

If you think religion and faith deserve no credit for what happened today, ask our friends Rabbi Denise Eger and Rev. Neil Thomas. They helped found California Faith for Equality in 2005, and have worked tirelessly for marriage equality. They send their regards to us tonight from Jerusalem and from Dallas.

If you think religion and faith deserve no credit for what happened today ask any of the clergy standing here with me today. Many of us are a part of the Los Angeles Queer Interfaith Clergy Council, others are straight allies—all of us are clergy ordained by our varied faith traditions.

Ask us about the couples we helped join together many years before any state said okay to same gender marriage. Ask us what our wedding calendars looked like in 2008, during that first short window of legal marriage in California, and in 2013 when it became legal here again.

Ask yourselves why it matters to thousands of couples and their families that their *civil* wedding be witnessed and declared legal by a clergyperson from their own faith traditions.

Marriage—that peculiar and particular joining of human hearts and souls—is high on the list of what serves *some* human needs, and the reason it has become a cause worldwide. It is why we are here tonight—in such variety of human experience—to celebrate this hard-won victory of the human heart. But "voices of faith" are also here tonight to say we know there is more to be done.

Today President Obama went from the Rose Garden, where he said that the Supreme Court just made our Union a little more perfect, to Charleston, S.C. to deliver a stirring eulogy for Rev. Clementa Pinckney, one of the nine Charleston AME voices of faith killed by the disease of racism and violence still running rampant in our country.

We know marriage is not the be all and end all of civil rights. We know that marriage is not for everyone, nor is it bliss for all who enter it.

And we know many battles remain—for transgender rights, health care rights (including mental health), rights to living wages, to shelter, to food, to legal immigration, to gun control, to an end to global warming, and an end to bullying and discrimination and prejudice and injustice in all its many forms.

As a religious community, today we celebrate how far we have come. But we don't rest yet. We know there is a long road ahead until the day when we can say that all people, all genders, all colors, all configurations of families, may truly rest secure, knowing that the law is there to protect us, so that *all* human hearts may open wide and let love in.

Mazel tov to us all! Let us bless each other as we move forward in our struggles and in our celebrations!

LOVE POEM WITH OLD THERMOMETER
Kate Leah Hewett

Includes words from E. M. Forster's "Howards End"

In the box of things from her house

is the wood worn temperature check
that I remember

its silver thread
that says don't get too comfortable,
tomorrow may be different.

In my pocket, the weather app
has all the same stuff and then some
but here we fall between two town lines
so we have to flick between both
to get something like accuracy

and this is better anyway because we
can run our finger along it, keep
a log in our head and track
how much warmer/colder this time around.

Let's try if we can to call it what it is,
unsteady ache for what our rattled minds
tell us was once true.

In the book I'm reading the writer says how
real life is full of false clues and sign posts
that lead nowhere.

But anyway I'm going to nail it to the wall outside
and we can check it most days til we start to see a pattern.

Is it ok? To be included in
what we're talking around
when we say look how much has changed.

Deb, Joan and Denver the dog, New Hampshire, 1984

Common Lives/Lesbian Lives, Issue #15/16, Summer 1985

AFTER 911

Melinda Goodman

I came back to you
in my forties
wearing overalls, Brenda
I stayed in your room
because you didn't trust
the rest of your house
But now you're gone, Brenda
Your house is gone now too

Brenda,
It's not that I hate my life it's just I can't bear
not getting so much of what I wanted

Losing the rest
of everything I ever loved.

Now we're planning
a Lesbian Widows Night Poetry Reading
February 17th
the day before the anniversary
of Audre Lorde's birthday.

She only lived, like you, to be 59 years old.

Audre said she was gonna "go out like a fucking meteor."
You went out like a lonely planet
destroyed by the ones who thought they owned
the right
to frack you
distract you

extract you from your wealth of tender joy
the dancing beat of your heart, the rhythm-ing
content of your valleys of emerald shadows
the hand sewn seams of your extreme awakenings
Your peaceable sleepen-ings
Your Coney Island amusement park purple icies
Your whirling teacups
Your gummy coke bottles
Your candy sweets
Black eyed peas
Morning coffee
local newspaper
Your serious midnight blue
car radio

(Your diamonds,
Brenda
Your diamonds)

All your big and little
cultured and un-cultured
raw black pearls

Video cassette tapes
Piled high unwatched unread hardback paperback histories
Pocketbook novels stacked against your collapsing walls
Your crumbling closet

Nodded out in your chair of endless low paid work
free domestic family labor
Beds made
Unmade
Tossed
Turned
Asleep in your clothes atop your fuzzy green and white

blanket left by someone...Someone...
who must've liked the NY Jets.

Your many many
Unknown
unknowable
secret passions
The whispers of your unblocked Middle
Passages.

It's not that I hate living, Brenda, I just can't stand not getting so much of what I wanted and the dissipation of everything else dear to me everything I didn't even know
how much I—
How much I—
How much I could have loved
How much I had
How much I could have done
with what I already
Had
How much I regret
not knowing
how much I could have done
How much I can
and could've
done
Without

I came back to you in my forties Brenda
Covered in white ash
Wearing a pair of black overalls
like Janie at the end of Zora's
Eyes were Watching God
testifying to her old best friend Phoebe,
"Yuh gotta go there to know there."

But all I know now
is
you gotta start from where you're at, Bren.
Stop where you're not
Then keep going...
even if you're not
sure

you can

keep on

Breathing.

Drawing by Jean Weisinger

From *Common Lives/Lesbian Lives*,
Issue 32, Fall 1989

PERPETUAL EMOTION NOVITIATE TRAINING, 1968

Jan Phillips

I went into the convent in 1967 because a nun saved my life when I was 12 and suicidal about being queer. I only lasted 2 years before they kicked me out for kissing novices.

The metaphors Sister Mary Matilda used to cut us down annoyed me. I hated being minimized. What pride I had I earned the hard way: my badge of honor.

As a Postulant, I resisted. But required humility wasn't enough to make me want to leave the convent—I'd been called to this life since 6th grade.

So when Mary Matilda drilled at our pride to get rid of our city-girl ideas and attitudes, I held fast. She'd smirk: "Each one of you used to be a big frog in a small pond, but now you're nothing but a small frog in a big pond." We had to obey rules handed down by one Superior or another, like Sister Mary Matilda—boss of the Postulants.

"You all think of yourselves as important, unique candles—but not anymore. We're going to melt you down, get rid of that 'uniqueness' that fills you with pride, and make one big candle from all that wax. You won't think so much of yourselves then."

I didn't appreciate her wry smirk one bit. I decided I'd go along as long as I could be true to myself. In one ear and out the other.

I ignored rules if they didn't match up with what I wanted. It didn't take long to figure out how to get the Pepsi machine to work when it wasn't visiting day. Plug it in. I collected quarters from my parents to get Pepsis for my friends. And we noticed our chaplain Father Battaglia's freezer was filled with a ton of goodies, so I pilfered his treasure chest and thawed them in my room. On holy days I had shrimp, coconut cream pie, Eskimo pies, and Sara Lee desserts.

One rule I didn't mess with was Grand Silence. We'd hear legends about people being sent home for uttering one word during that time, so I followed that one religiously.

Until they made obeying impossible.

It started during lunch recreation. After we did our kitchen charges, we had "outdoor time," 40 minutes to "recreate," when we could talk out loud, walk around St. Ann's Circle, play tennis, walk through the woods. Mondays, Wednesdays and Fridays we were allowed to mingle with the Novices—a big deal because Novices had their own meeting rooms, their own Superiors, and we hardly ever got to be with them.

During the first few weeks, after our joint recreations, I made friends with a second-year Novice, Sister Marie Catherine. Tall, freckled, funny, in chapel she sat right behind me; I could tell she was there by the scent of her Jean Naté. We both were reading Teilhard de Chardinand and kept our copies of Divine Milieu in our pews. When I'd stop to read after class or charges, she'd be in her pew doing the same. That's why I wanted to talk with her, to see what she thought about his huge ideas.

Concepts of a paleontologist and mystic were new to me. He invented words and entered the universe like a miner with a headlamp, burrowing into the heart of matter until he saw God looking right back. I'd underline the phrases I needed help with—cosmogenesis, noosphere, the divinization of matter—and hoped Marie Catherine could help me.

Everything he wrote made my insides quake. He'd fallen in love with matter at an early age, fascinated with rust on a piece of iron. Because he felt the Divine in every particle, he believed that we live "steeped in the burning layers" of the very God we seek, who molds and shapes us every moment of the day. He called this process "hominization," the spiritualization of nature and all living things.

Just as Father Grabys was doing in the classroom—taking all my old ideas and turning them inside out—so was Teilhard de Chardin in the chapel. Before either of these men came along, I was content with my beliefs. I had them all organized, memorized, lined up in neat little rows. Then the priests show up and turn my cart of certainties upside down.

After a semester struggling through Theology with Father Grabys, I was facing one of the greatest mystical thinkers of all time. His ideas turned on lights in new areas of my brain. I read every sentence over and over. I devoured and digested his mysterious paragraphs, struggling to make sense of his words and sentences, then attempted to translate them back to myself in a language I could understand.

After an hour of meditating, I would write down in my journal what I thought he was trying to say: Genesis did not happen once. Creation is not over. The cosmos expands continuously, and that itself is the very act of God being. God is the unfolding. The Creative Force, that God people seek, is pounding on our door day and night, penetrating us, saturating us with love. There is nothing for us to seek.

Monday I couldn't wait for recreation. I had my book and was on the lookout for Marie Catherine. What I didn't know was that I was the subject of someone else's lookout. Marie Catherine and I were being watched by our superiors on those days of joint recreation. Both Postulant and Novitiate Directors had offices with picture windows overlooking St. Ann's Circle. They could see who was with whom on those Mondays, Wednesdays and Fridays, and what they discovered was that I was always with Sr. Marie Catherine, my Teilhard talking partner.

Spending time with her was a thrill. I didn't have an intellectual relationship like ours with anyone in the Motherhouse. We talked about ideas, tried to figure out what an author was saying and apply it to our spiritual practice. Many things were new to me that fall, including the whole discipline of prayer and meditation, spiritual reading, Divine Office. There was a whirlwind of spiritual activity, much of it formulaic when it came to prayers, but for meditation and spiritual reading we were free to explore.

That I ended up ensconced in Teilhard's Divine Milieu is a mystery and a blessing.

My class with Father Grabys was challenging enough, but Teilhard's words electrified me. He brought God so close I couldn't tell where I began and God left off. My spiritual life was breaking open. I was happy to have Marie Catherine as a companion through the Unknown.

As weeks passed and we shared more time together, my affection grew. I looked forward to those days we could talk. I woke up excited about it and went to bed thinking about it. I was in love with who I was becoming in her presence, because of her, because of the ways she heard me, saw me, reflected me. I couldn't wait for my forty minutes with her on those three days a week. When I caught a whiff of her Jean Nate in the hallway, my whole body shivered. I was in love.

Then one day, only a few months into our friendship, I was summoned to the office.

"Sister, I'm afraid you are spending too much time with Sister Marie Catherine. This might be leading to a *particular friendship,* and we can't have that."

I was unclear what that phrase meant. Mary Matilda brought it up in class one day—without defining it but delivering it along with a dozen red flashing lights. I think the words "carnal" and "unnatural" were also mentioned. I wasn't paying much attention because it felt ridiculous and I'd tuned it out. But suddenly I wished I'd listened more carefully.

Marie Catherine and I hadn't done anything wrong. We only met when we were allowed to. For the most part we talked about Teilhard de Chardin—not ourselves or any desires. We didn't flirt or write love notes. But I knew I was in love.

"We're not doing anything wrong," I said. "We're just friends."

"*Just friends* don't meet at every opportunity to the exclusion of everyone else," she said snidely. "*Just friends* don't go off by themselves, huddling and whispering and letting no one else in."

"People can join us if they want."

"I watch the two of you down there, heading off on your own. I'm telling you, you're heading into dangerous territory."

"But Sister, I swear, we're just good friends," I repeated, pleading for some understanding. "She helps me understand Teilhard de Chardin!"

Nothing helped.

"You are forbidden, as of today, to go anywhere near Sister Marie Catherine. You are forbidden to speak with her anywhere at any time. And if you pass her in the hall, you must keep custody of the eyes."

I couldn't even look at her. I was officially split from my one and only best friend, from my budding beloved, from the first woman I had ever thought of as a soul mate.

This was a rule I could not abide. It felt like a crime against nature. They were taking something beautiful, so life-giving, and turning it into something perverted. Its cellular traces are still carved in my bones.

I knew what was happening in me was momentous. I knew I was falling in love. But I could not think of that as wrong. *She is my particular friend and I am lucky to have one*, is the way I saw it. People need that. So I was at odds with the whole shutdown.

I wasn't the problem. Their pettiness was the problem. Their minds in the gutter was the problem. Their refusal to help us develop sturdy relationships with healthy emotions was the problem. And I was not going to collude in the continuation of this appalling approach to human behavior.

All my life people had tried to make me feel bad about who I was and what I liked and they were doing the very same thing—trying to convince me I was wrong. Forbidding me to be me. I was smart enough to pass their battery of MMPI tests with all their homosexual-baiting questions: *Are you attracted to masculine women? Are you attracted to feminine women?*

Did they think I wouldn't see through that and know to answer NO to every one, despite what was true?

So much got triggered in that office—all those bullies from my childhood, all that blood and tears and agony, my self-hatred, my suicide notes, all my prayers for it to be different and despair that it wasn't.

My whole reason for being there was to save kids the way Sister Helen Charles saved me. On that day, in that straight-backed chair in front of that strait-laced Postulant Director, I vowed, for once, to be true to myself, and I didn't turn back.

In the chapel I entered the pew where Marie Catherine sat during prayers. I picked up her copy of Divine Milieu, took it to my room, wrote a note, placed it next to her bookmark, and returned it to her seat in chapel: *Told I can't see you anymore. Not going to do it. Will come to your room at 10 pm. We can make a plan.*

She had been given the same directions by her Novice Director, of course. No more communication with me. Custody of the eyes if she sees me. Unsettling accusations of particular friends and carnal relationships. Stuff of nightmares.

The hallway was dark and quiet, save for the soft sounds of sleeping postulants. I walked the length of the hall, opened the door to the exit stairway and climbed to the second floor, where I found and entered the room of Sister Marie Catherine. Luckily, it was the last room at the end of the hall. She sat on the edge of her bed waiting for me, shrouded in silver moonlight. We were both wearing nightclothes, black cotton robes covering our long white cotton nightgowns.

For the first time I saw her without her veil. I touched her cheeks and her short auburn hair. She wrapped her arms around my waist and pressed her face against my robe, warming my flesh with the heat of her breath. Neither of us knew what to do next. We just held on—me standing there, her sitting on the side of the bed. We held on and cried, trembling and weeping as quietly as we could.

It was our first act of resistance and the first of many nights we would betray Grand Silence. All our creative genius went toward subterfuge as we planned meeting after meeting in secret places—the trunk room in the basement, the reference stacks in the library, a tiny crawl space outside the choir loft.

In public, when I saw her coming I never looked up. Never spoke a word or took one step toward her on those days the others recreated with whomever they wanted. If anyone was watching—as they had been earlier—all they would see was evidence of obedience, a novice and a postulant happily mingling with other sisters, as if nothing ever happened, as if a revolution within was not being waged.

If we'd never been split, who's to say our relationship would have evolved to kissing and hugging? There's no way of knowing whether, without that pressure, that inhumane ruling, we would have simply remained friends, not ended up cuddling night after night in a forbidden room, on a forbidden bed, at a forbidden hour.

Our intimacy was an oasis in a barren desert. We hardly talked, hardly touched, save for the long length of our bodies, fully clothed, pressed together in solace and sweetness. Every novice and postulant was exhausted at the end of each day, and we were no different—awake long enough to find each other and give thanks for that treasure, but collapsing into sleep only moments later, to be awakened by the clanging bell.

Whatever they feared about carnal relationships never transpired between us. I left notes in her books all the time, mostly questions or statements of amazement at the mind of this mystic who wrote hymns to the earth, who affirmed between all his lines, lives that were courageous, on fire, of God—our lives, it seemed, our courage, our fire.

We survived the year without being discovered. Our conversations continued to deepen, though the decibels shrunk, as we always hid, always whispered. I wrote her poems, made her holy cards, wrote her a love song. The risks we took for that relationship never even fluttered on the Richter Scale of Risk. We never even paused to weigh the pros and cons.

We never asked, *Should we?* We only asked when and where, knowing that connections like ours were gifts from the heavens, full of grace. While I was in training for a vow of obedience, I decided day to day which rules to obey, a practice which foreshadowed trouble ahead.

What was happening to me was happening in the culture writ large, though I knew no details since we were spared the news. People my age were questioning authority, seizing their power, walking in rhythm to their own inner beats. Rules everywhere were up for grabs—in churches, on campuses, in boot camps and battlefields.

The zeitgeist favored authenticity, resistance to authority, speaking truth to power. I lived to those values as true as I could, though I learned early the consequences of speaking too much truth to the one in power.

Just as the soul cries in the presence of truth, so does the heart move in the direction of ardor. It cannot be forced to do otherwise. My emotions, for me to be whole and to grow, had to be free to explore what awakened them. They had to flow like a river through the canyons of my being. My feelings could not live in an environment of suppression. They were alive, they were of God, and they would not be silenced.

But trouble never left, for its source was in me and the conflicts only escalated as I became more and more myself.

TERRADYKETIL KITCHEN

Rainbow

Terradyketil Kitchen
drawing by Rainbow

Terradyketil Kitchen from *Common Lives/Lesbian Lives*, Issue 29, Winter 1989

BACKING FORWARD

Shari Katz

The tail-end of a hurricane caught us during our last camping adventure and forced us to sleep in our car for two nights rather than our tent. Our car, of course, was a Subaru Outback, and though we felt like authentic lesbians sleeping in it, and it was sort of fun, it wasn't so much fun having to climb out of its trunk in the middle of the night to go pee, as most women in their fifties must do every few hours. So, Noelle and I bought a small camping trailer.

Quite honestly, we hadn't meant to buy a trailer—we were just going to 'look' at the trailers. But it was exactly my birthday, and the dealer had a marginally less expensive one-year-old beauty that perfectly fit the bill. We have spent more time buying hiking boots than we did buying that trailer! We loved her on sight and couldn't imagine leaving her all by her lonesome for even one more night.

With a newly acquired hitch on our car we brought her home. On the way, the conversation went something like this:

Shari: Do you know how to back up a trailer into a campsite?

Noelle: No. Do you?

Shari: No. But let me tell you a story.

When I was 10, my family went camping on Prince Edward Island. The only way to get to the island was by ferry. There were drive-on/drive-off ferries that opened at each end and there were drive-on/back-off ferries that opened only at one end. Which kind of ferry you boarded was completely random. My father, who could single-handedly build a car from duct tape and cotton balls, could never figure out how to back up our pop-up trailer and I knew he spent the entire drive praying for a drive-on/drive-off. Sadly, the angels were not on his side. Drive-on/back-off was his destiny and not only that, we were the last vehicle to drive on, which meant that all the other passengers had to wait while we disembarked. My father spent an hour struggling to back our trailer off the ferry. The distance was only about 200 feet, and it was mostly a straight shot, and although the ferry staff could direct him, they could not actually get in the car and do it for him as it was against some insurance rule. I sat in the backseat, hot and sweaty, longing to tip over into the ocean and drown. This humiliating experience was further compounded during a visit to an ice cream parlour with a young couple my parents met. The woman insisted that the voyage to the island would have been nicer if Some Man had not kept everyone waiting for an hour while he struggled to back off the ferry! Needless to say, my parents paid for their ice creams.

Noelle looked at me and sighed.

With this on our minds, we packed up and set off on a seven-week adventure. We discussed at length the backing up rules: Noelle would be the driver and I would be the director, as I am a very bad driver (and a very good director). Our friends will not get into the car if I am driving. I also understood that while Noelle was backing up, I needed to tell her to turn the steering wheel to the right in order to direct the trailer towards the left and tell her to turn the wheel to the left because that would direct the trailer to the right. To this day, I have no idea how or why it works that way. I skipped physics in high school. Finally, Noelle would tolerate no yelling or shouting. She has a very low tolerance for public humiliation. We often imagine that, if WE were on The Amazing Race, there would be no cheering each other on, and no lambasting or shouting suggestions from the sidelines when things were not going well. Suffering in silence would be the only acceptable behaviour while we watched our loved one complete some ridiculous task like rolling a big wheel of cheese uphill.

With these rules being understood, we checked in to our first campground. "Do you have any drive-through sites?" I asked timidly. "Nope. Sorry," said the pimply teenager staffing the reception desk as he shoved a bunch of papers at us to sign—one I think explaining what would happen if we decided to park the trailer in the road and live in it there because we couldn't maneuver it into our campsite.

Viewing our spot for the first time we pretended to have a game plan. "How about passing the entrance and backing in from that angle?" I suggested. Noelle, looking like she was wishing we could sleep in our Subaru just one more time, waited for me to get out of the car to direct her.

At this point in our story, you should be told that the main amusement at campgrounds is watching people fit, or not fit, various sizes of campers into variously sized camping sites. I have actually witnessed a group of grown people get out of a campground swimming pool and hang over the fence to watch a couple back their huge trailer, a trailer with more square footage than the house we once owned, into a sliver of land. Using walkie-talkies—I kid you not—the man backed in as the woman instructed. It took them exactly 4 minutes and two tries. The bathing suited audience cheered! Surely, we could back our measly 15- foot trailer into our huge site. We didn't even care where on the site, we had a 35-foot electrical cord so we could plug in from almost anywhere. Off the gravel road and onto the site was our only wish.

Noelle timidly backed up. "Turn the wheel to the left, oops—no, to the right, no, to the left, I said." "Pull forward a bit, no back up a bit." I had no idea what I was saying, and Noelle looked like she was about to cry. Suddenly the angel my father had wished for all of those years ago knocked on the car door. "Do you want some help?" Noelle looked at her in stunned silence. "Get out of the car," she encouraged. Noelle popped out and let this complete stranger get into our recently paid-off car, a car that had 'the most expensive impulse buy ever' attached to it. I watched, hoping this woman wouldn't suddenly drive off with it all. About three minutes later, our trailer was flawlessly backed into our campsite, and as this angel started to walk away, Noelle shouted, "Wait a minute!" and dug around until she happily handed over a very good bottle of wine.

Five days later after we had eaten our fill of the best lobster Quebec had to offer, we pulled out and headed to our next destination, once again praying for an angel. "Site 80," we were told as we checked-in to a beautiful campground bordering the St. Lawrence River. I thought, let's back the trailer directly into the river. It's heavily insured and we could use the money to pay for a hotel and give up this charade of being two capable women out on the road. We weren't even a little bit butch! We looked like every middle-aged housewife from every sitcom you watched as a child.

Arriving at our site we saw that our neighbours were a fierce looking group of heavily bearded Harley Davidson motorcyclists. Noelle would never be able to conjure the courage to back up as this group looked on. I got out of the car and whispered to her, "When I say to, just back up and keep slowly backing up until I say stop. Do not stop no matter what you think." Faking confidence I strode to the back of the trailer and shouted, "Back up slowly." She started backing up and did not stop, even when the trailer began to make a U-turn and fold up against our car.

Just as it began to look like it was going to tip over, I turned to our neighbors with beseeching puppy dog eyes. The gang leader asked, "Do you want some help?" "Stop!" I yelled to Noelle and breathed a sigh of relief. My devious plan had worked. She got out and once again handed the steering wheel over to a complete stranger. After our trailer was untangled with itself, it was soon perfectly perched, and another bottle of wine was handed over. It should be noted that this 'gang' was made up of extremely gentle and solicitous people, who were wonderful neighbors for the next week, thus putting to bed our long-held and ridiculous notions about tough looking gangs of motorcyclists. Their adorable fluffy puppies should have been our first clue.

As our third week rolled around we started to get smart. We walked into the next campground office and as we were registering, I unabashedly declared, "We have no idea how to back up our camper, do you have someone around here who could do that for us?" The (thankfully) middle aged woman at the desk looked us up and down and chortled, "Drive to your site. I'll be there in a few minutes." While we waited for our next angel, I left Noelle sitting in the car and I walked behind the trailer to get a lay of the land. Before I could even start to think about what directions I would give Noelle if I were to try to help her, the car and trailer started to expertly back up. "Good" I thought, "that nice lady has arrived to back us into our spot." And yet, after the trailer was happily situated, I saw that it was Noelle at the steering wheel. "Wow! You are finally getting the hang of it," I mused, not understanding how this could have happened. Noelle laughed, "The lady stood directly in front of the car and mimed exactly what I should do. I followed her instructions like any good puppet." I sighed, "We can't keep relying on good Samaritans."

At the next campground, we again asked for help and this time two skinny, grizzled men were sent. But before they could help, these mostly toothless campground employees almost came to blows with each other while discussing how to instruct Noelle. Finally, one of them yelled, "Back up and turn your wheel the other way." "What other way, to the left or to the right?" Noelle yelled back. "Just the other way," he insisted. Noelle looked at me with a look I know only too well to mean, 'In one minute I am going to stick a fork in my eye.' I simply shrugged. These men were clearly crazy or drunk or both. I decided to pretend that I was actually on The Amazing Race and shut my mouth as we had always promised each other we would when things got stressful during a challenge. I stood back and watched Noelle keep trying to turn the steering wheel 'the other way.' There was much arguing and not much movement and just when I thought Noelle was going to jump out of the car and punch someone, I mumbled, "Turn the wheel to the left and back up a bit." She rolled her eyes at me and as she grumblingly obeyed, the trailer inched in the direction I wanted it to move. "Now, pull out again and turn the wheel even more to the left and back up." And with God as my witness, the car and trailer started to creep in sync towards the place I wanted it to go. This time, when Guy Number One shouted "Turn it the other way," Noelle knew what the 'other way' was. Forty-five minutes after Guy Number One and Guy Number Two showed up, the trailer was settled into its new coordinates. As these two men departed—without our usually proffered bottle of wine—a thought clicked into place.

When our second-to-last destination was an hour away, I whispered to myself,

"We can do it." "What?" Noelle asked. "We can do it!" Noelle laughed and kept driving. She had no reason to have faith in my declaration, but I noticed that she remained silent when I didn't brazenly ask for help upon our arrival. As she drove to our site I quietly remarked, "I think the thing is that one is not supposed to be able to back in all at once. I think it's supposed to be a series of backing up a bit more and pulling out again a bit less each time. Let's try it." After 30 minutes of maneuvering, praying and plenty of errors, we were actually in our site. Was the trailer straight? No. Were we anywhere near the electrical outlet? No. Was it almost dark out? Yes. But we were parked, and we had done it ourselves! That night we gave ourselves a very good bottle of wine.

Seven weeks after leaving Montreal, we arrived at our final campground, registered, drove to our site, and proceeded to carefully place our beloved camper exactly where we wanted her to be on our site. And then, as if we had been doing this all of our lives, we proceeded to quietly unpack and hook up, Noelle organizing the inside of the trailer and me doing everything that needed to be done on the outside. That night, as we sat in front of a rip-roaring fire I looked over at my beloved and said, "We're home."

The next afternoon, we gathered at the side of the road and watched as a young couple tried—hopelessly—to back up their trailer. They had no idea what they were doing. It was very good entertainment. Did we go over to offer to help? No way. Maybe next year....

P.S. Noelle and I have camping reservations on Prince Edward Island for this coming summer. Thankfully, there is now a bridge that connects the mainland to the island.

Home Sweet Tent *drawing by Raint*

Home Sweet Tent from *Common Lives/Lesbian Lives*, Issue 29, Winter 1989

MY WEATHER IS FEMALE

Kimberly Esslinger

I am not woke. I am dreaming.
Tossing the sheets off.
Rolling to your side of the bed.
Mzzz America, tell me how we met.
Was it under the watermelon tree?
Was it at a Krissy Keefer rant and you danced
in like a taiko brigade. Pounding. Pounding.
rain. It was August, I know that for sure.
It's always August. I would trade you
my sturgeon moon for the night stage
any day of the monsoon season
that washes us out. Drenches our tents.
Carries us away on our suitcase
because we unpacked everything.
Everything that makes us feel
safe floating down Easy Street
in the middle of the woods whistling
through a thunderstorm listing
three things we love best about ourselves.
There are these indivisible scars
we've stitched together —
a crazy Mary Shelley patchwork of us
(not this monster romantic nonsense).
We are a handmade triple goddess quilt
the grown daughters of a sexual revolution
telescopes to the cervix crunchy Birky stereotypes
stomping our way home across this very large country
where some folk's weather ain't for us.
But do you still see August in me?
Do you still smell the fire on my breath?

This is how clouds mate.

WHEN OBAMA REPEALED DON'T ASK, DON'T TELL

Jules Taylor

The day the ban on speaking about certain love
was lifted, which of you gathered
in the photo held sadness behind your photo-ready

smile, or wished, like me, your father would acknowledge
the justice of the moment instead of looking away?
Which of you knows the sting

of *you are loved*
and in the same breath, *don't tell*
anyone you love
who you love?

JAM-PACKED

Mary Vermillion

When I served on the *Common Lives/Lesbian Lives* Collective during its last two years, 1994 to 1996, we met Tuesday evenings in the back room of WRAC (the Women's Resource and Action Center), a two-story house across from the Student Union at the University of Iowa. From the outside, WRAC's back room looked like an add-on, one of its walls nearly touching the parking garage next door. Inside, the back room also seemed makeshift, serving every purpose under the feminist sun.

During Collective meetings, we huddled together on garage-sale sofas and chairs, shuffling through manuscripts and nibbling on cookies. On one side of the room, near the door, the kitchenette's dishes teetered in the drainer. On the other side of door sat a banquet table with paper cups, coffee urns, lemonade mix—refreshments for WRAC's many workshops. Propped against another wall were posters and banners, some of them loosely rolled up awaiting the annual Pride March. Hidden behind a wall of file cabinets was a cluttered desk we called our office. That back room and WRAC itself live on in my memories, jam-packed with moments when I sought to define myself.

Above the back room, up a narrow flight of stairs, was a cozy library. There, a couple years before I joined the Collective, I sprawled on thick carpets with members of a support group for bi women. I asked these women whether they thought I could savor my crush on a lesbian volleyball player and remain married to a man (a cisgender man, although no one knew that phrase then). What I wanted to ask was how I could find the courage to leave that marriage, the courage to give my newly acknowledged passion for women a chance.

A few months later in the front office of WRAC, I asked for a pro se divorce kit. Then I happily made my way to the back room, joining a coming out group for lesbians. As in the bi group, I made lifelong friends. But all support groups eventually disband, and shortly after that one did, I returned to the back room as a Collective member. Then seven years after the Collective folded (our distributor went bankrupt), that same back room was where I sought company with other SOFFAs of trans people (Significant Others, Family, Friends, and Allies). I was a significant other. A disoriented significant other, wondering who I was now that my once seemingly lesbian partner was a newly out trans guy.

So when I recently opened my email and read that *Sinister Wisdom* was publishing a tribute issue for *CL/LL*, I felt drawn to that back room—compelled to consider how my experience with the Collective shaped my identity and my thinking about identity labels. How it shaped me.

What did being a member of the Collective mean to me in 1994? Well, since it was a *lesbian* Collective and produced beautiful books—four a year filled with lesbian writing!—it meant everything. No exaggeration. I have always adored reading and writing. The most constant part of my identity is that of bookworm. Back then, I was also head-over-heels with being a lesbian, and I believed that the Collective allowed me to unite the two most important parts of my identity.

I first encountered *Common Lives* when my first girlfriend (the volleyball player) proudly showed me a back issue. She was a member of the Collective then, a fact that added to her allure. She presented me with *CL/LL* #38, Spring 1991, its cover graced by a lovely black and white photo of runes. I had never seen or heard of runes before, so this shiny new magazine confirmed one my beliefs about my shiny new identity: it was the key to all things novel and fascinating.

By the time I joined the Collective, this woman and I had parted ways, and she was no longer a member. But I had lost none of my giddy blind faith in the power of my lesbian identity. It had emboldened me to leave my short unhappy marriage with the cisgender man and was helping me shed a conservative Catholic upbringing, empowering me to triumph over all things patriarchal, and had led me to a new partner. This new partner had, in turn, urged me to follow my career bliss and take a job as an English professor at a liberal arts college (as opposed to the R1 institutions my professors thought I should seek). In short, when I joined the Collective, I felt like I had it all. Fueled by love and lesbian-feminism, I thought I had arrived. I was thirty.

Now that I'm 58, I embrace the journeying I have left to do, and I understand that identity labels can take you only so far.

Although I poke fun at my younger self and at the vast power I accorded my identity as a lesbian, it's no laughing matter. My over-investment in my lesbian identity caused me to turn my back on the love of my life just when he needed me most. It nearly caused me to lose a marriage that has brought me every joy. Fortunately, I was able to adjust my thinking about my identity before it was too late. Soon, I will celebrate my twenty-seventh wedding anniversary with Ben. It was he who was my new partner when I joined the Collective. And it was his transition that later caused me to seek out other SOFFAs in the back room of WRAC.

How was I—a woman smitten with being a lesbian—eventually able to support my partner as he embraced his identity as a man? How did I re-conceptualize my own identity? And what on earth do these transitions have to do with my long-ago time on a lesbian Collective?

My short two years with the Collective coincided with the beginning of my blessedly long relationship with Ben. Collective members came to our commitment ceremony in 1995, gifting us a silver frame that still hangs in our bedroom, encasing the wedding vows Ben and I wrote. Both the Collective and Ben gave me many gifts, gifts that Ben has spent his life helping me unwrap.

But before I can describe these gifts, I need to discuss the one thing about *Common Lives* that I did *not* like—its refusal to consider work by women who identified as bi. This policy, which was implemented before I joined, almost kept me away. But even though the policy distressed me—or maybe *because* it distressed me—it also ultimately benefitted me. It made me reflect on questions about identity and inclusion that became more urgent once Ben started transitioning.

When I opened the summer issue of 1993, I was dismayed by the Collective's response to "a bisexual woman who was upset" because they did not read her submission: *The queer community is a diverse one and we believe it has room for us all. However, we do not feel that the lesbian community has the responsibility to give up our limited access to print space to create one for bisexuals or any other group. Bisexual women and men need to create space to serve their community as we have done.*

I felt sad and angry that there was such little print space for women who love women, and I felt sad and angry that bi women were being excluded. It was obvious the policy hurt bi women, but I believed it also damaged lesbians because it downplayed the core of lesbian identity. Women loving women. The policy ignored what bi women were seeking when they submitted work to *Common Lives*: a sense of belonging, a home in the lesbian community for the part of themselves that they share only with lesbians—the fact that they are women who love other women.

Although this thinking is dated now that so many people identify as non-binary, it nudged me toward an insight that remains relevant. What I value most in an identity label is not precision, but inclusivity.

This insight became clearer to me because of the wisdom, generosity, and patience that Ben brought to his transition. He gave me time and space and encouragement to see my own identity expansively. "Just because I'm changing my identity doesn't mean you need to change yours," he'd say. "Who you are without me is who you are with me." Before and after he transitioned, he consistently acknowledged and nurtured the part of me that loves women. In fact, he helped me access many of my own passions and strengths. Over time, I realized that they can't be captured by a label and that they sure don't stem from one. Not even the mighty L in the LGBTQ+ acronym.

I'll always treasure the part of me that is lesbian. Coming out as a lesbian was a catalyst that empowered me to live boldly and authentically, but now I understand that my identity as a lesbian was not the source of my bravery. I was. Me. And my partner and our community of friends. However they identified, however I identified. (Bisexual? Lesbian? Bisexual lesbian? Pansexual, maybe?)

Right now, I identify as queer. I'm not planning to rethink this label any time soon, but obviously, you never know.

What I do know is this: the importance of discovering what matters most to you and making it your focus. In my marriage with Ben, I didn't fully understand what mattered most until I had almost lost it. I thought my partner's gender mattered to me, but it didn't. What did matter was his need to be fully himself. What did matter was our love for each other. Our relationship. Our shared history, our devotion, our ability to make each other smile and laugh every day.

And in the spirit of naming what matters, I want to say what mattered most to me about *Common Lives* and why I joined the Collective even though I disagreed with its exclusion of bi women. Although that exclusion did matter to me, what mattered more were the inclusive parts of the Collective's mission. I was and am in love with the Collective's desire "to encourage lesbians who have never thought of publishing to do so"—its commitment to "women whose lives have traditionally been denied visibility." My two years with *Common Lives* gave me sustained practice in living out this commitment. And this practice nurtures the most meaningful parts of my career as an English professor—the parts that help under-represented or timid students find and use and celebrate their own voices.

Like Ben (who would later encourage me to write mystery novels), *Common Lives* also expanded my sense of what sort of writing and professional activities matter.

It may seem like a little thing, but I loved that the magazine emphatically requested contributor bios that were personal and "*not* academic." As someone who had recently finished graduate school, I had been obsessed with my own academic bio, and it was a breath of fresh air to see a publication that insisted on recognizing people as more than their CVs, more than the peer-reviewed articles they had published.

Long before I encountered the phrase 'public scholarship,' *Common Lives* enabled me to practice it, to use my creativity and skill in the service of a community outside the academy. I felt especially proud that the Collective gave free back issues to incarcerated lesbians. It has always seemed sacred to me, the way that the printed word can touch a lonely individual, and this connection is all the more urgent when the solitary reader lives behind bars. The Collective's concern for incarcerated people reinforced a message that I received from the Sisters who were my undergraduate mentors and who taught in prisons: imprisoned people matter. So the Collective helped plant a seed that blossomed into what my students and I informally call Prison Book Club—our visits to a nearby penitentiary, where we discuss the texts we've studied in class with a small group of inmates.

My time with the Collective also fuels my belief that small groups (and small publications and presses) can make a big difference. With only six of us in that back room at WRAC we reached 2,500 subscribers. And if the magazine empowered each of those readers even half as much as it empowered me? Well, that's a lot of queer energy!

I'm grateful that the Collective gave me an early opportunity to serve part of the LGBTQ+ community, to experience the joy of lifting up queer voices. I owe a lot of my professional joy to my time with the Collective.

Maybe any time you help someone else access their voice and power, you gain at least as much as you give. Certainly, that was true of my time with *Common Lives/Lesbian Lives*—and truer still of my years with Ben.

Until I saw him gleefully savor each step of his transition, I had no idea that I could be so moved and transformed by another person's joy. No idea that I could share in such joy even as I grieved my old familiar—and simpler—way of seeing my partner and myself, seeing gender and our relationship. I had no idea I would eventually savor the complexity he helped me recognize in myself and in our world. And no idea I would take pride in an identity resembling that back room at WRAC—makeshift, multi-purpose, gloriously messy.

PAPER TRAIL

Dodici Azpadu

A man and woman claim me
        on other birth records
on the original watermarked paper
        I come alone.
A name
        foreign to me sex assigned
equally foreign.
        No tiny footprint stains
other documents or adds
        indelible burdens I am given.
Folding frays certainty. Words are fickle.
        Tell outright lies, confuse, distort
hint. I parse them every day
        and will never have the last one.

Photo Credit: Nancy Meyer

Dodici Azpadu

SLEEP MAP

Dodici Azpadu

     A dresser drawer
softened with towels.
       Toddling to makeshift
mattresses lining linoleum floors
       or to kitchen chairs
roped together. Wandering half-naked
       to warm vacancies,
you slept where you fell.

Many beds later
anxious to find a way to privacy
       you turn to avoid arms
cramping and turn again
       forearm protecting eyes
from nothing visible
       in the dark. Stopped face down
a chalk silhouette, knee bent.

     Mismatching map folds.
One-way creases. The route
       shreds At critical junctures
in deserted cities Lost

THE LAST LESBIAN BAR IN THE WORLD IS CLOSING
(LESBIAN EPHEMERA)

Kimberly Esslinger

All the old dykes are dying!
The lesbian bar is dead!
And me in my amazon flannel
so 1970s finding my way
to a dive club near a sex
toy shop in a strip mall
police patrol banging on
steamed up windows
in the backlot where
some were doing lines
or smoking pot
someone just sleeping it off
could have been me
but I was dancing inside
this was our Happy Hour,
or Hideaway, our Que Sera,
our Mona's, our Duchess,
our Tropical Paradise,
our Star Room,
our Huntress, our Never
Never Land,
doing kamikazes
sometimes lemon drops
wondering if She were the one,
the debutante or the soft
butch blonde, would she be just
a friend to run the pool table

or just run, run around in the daylight
like a pack of wolf dykes.
Turning heads once, twice,
I'm not a sir, but I'm old enough
to buy beer and smokes in
the liquor store. We can't kill ourselves
when we're this high. In the red
bar light, her kiss, her Levis,
I feel like I could live forever.

Common Lives/Lesbian Lives, Issue 31, Summer 1989
Photo Credit: Courtesy of Sudie Rakusin

MY GRATITUDE FOR *COMMON LIVES/LESBIAN LIVES*

Sue Katz

In 1970 I was part of a Boston collective of working-class lesbians. We put out one of the earliest post-Stonewall publications *Lavender Vision* (1970-1971). Although we could only afford two issues in total, that work, amazingly, continues to live on. For example, I am invited each year to lecture to Harvard students studying Activism on a piece ("Smash Phallic Imperialism") I wrote for the inaugural issue.

Some of the women in our collective had traveled to Iowa City where the feminist and fledgling lesbian movements were strong and smart. The Iowa City women had a great deal of clarity about what is today called intersectionality and we learned a lot from them about how class affects women on every level. This was evident in their newspaper *Ain't I a Woman?* (1971-1974), which came out about a year after the first *Lavender Vision*, but which survived much longer.

I had been publishing political essays in the main, but after I moved abroad in 1977, I began to dive into fiction. There were few literary outlets that would consider publishing queer tales, not the least from a writer who self-identified as a revolutionary anarcho-feminist dyke motored by class rage.

Tracy Moore, my editor at *Common Lives/Lesbian Lives* (1980 to 1996), became my first and most enduring literary cheerleader and I published a few pieces in *CL/LL* over the years. I'm not sure how many exactly, because moving continents three times has played havoc with my book collection. I do have copies of two issues with my work on my shelf—one a short story (*Big Darlene*, about a butch who killed a violent man with one blow) and one a personal essay (*The Vanilla Tourist*, about the S/M debate in Israel's closeted lesbian community). Being published in *CL/LL* was one of the especially dazzling ways in which feminism has bolstered my life.

Thank you *CL/LL* and Tracy Moore for launching my life as a fiction writer. Thank you, *Sinister Wisdom*, for marking the invaluable role of *Common Lives/Lesbian Lives*.

COMMON LIVES/LESBIAN LIVES
a lesbian quarterly

Stories, journals, graphics, essays, humor, poetry, and more . . .
The experiences and ideas of common Lesbians.

Graphic from *Common Lives/Lesbian Lives*

REMEMBERING DIRTBAG

Jesse Joad and Ann Bonham

Until the summer she went to Aspen and bussed tables, where everyone got a nickname, Dirtbag was Linda. Back in Iowa, to her friends she became known as Dirtbag, who lived in a collective on Kirkwood Avenue and was co-coordinator for the Iowa City Free Clinic.

From the Free Clinic, where Dr. Jesse Joad volunteered, Dirtbag connected patients with supportive people and organizations. One story Jesse tells is about rural women who were in the women's community because Iowa City was a magnet.

After Dirtbag died, folks came together in a giant circle to tell Dirtbag stories. One lesbian from a poor area in Iowa said, "I'd never had a watch, but when I came to Iowa City, Dirtbag got me my first one!" To many surprised looks, 15 other lesbians gasped and said something like "she gave me one too!" Those declarations were followed in short-order when another lesbian quietly said that Dirtbag had given her a pair of socks. More gasps! More lesbians revealed that Dirtbag had also given *them* socks. She was a quiet giver of gifts, material and otherwise. Linda lived with Tracy in Oxford for years, where they established a huge garden with a Rototiller—Tracy making side-money by digging gardens in people's lawns.

Linda was often found reading the paper in the many lesbian gathering places. Rumor has it that when asked what she was doing, she said "I'm attending class." Linda had many talents and favorite things to do—going to class was not one of them. At her memorial service in her hometown (which featured many of us speaking!) her dad reiterated how proud they were of her. Looking fondly at her "diploma"—which in fact came by way of the Iowa City Women's Press, rather than the University of Iowa—he said: "One of the things they can never take away from me—her diploma!" We imagine it was propped on the Knox's TV as long as they lived.

254 ♀ Sinister Wisdom 134 - Celebrating *Common Lives / Lesbian Lives*

PHOTOS OF LINDA KNOX (DIRTBAG)
Tracy Moore

CONTRIBUTOR BIOGRAPHIES

Editorial Collective
Each of the Collective members have also contributed work to this issue.

Cindy Cleary: I discovered my life-long love of organizing at five years old... After birthing two beautiful babies, I found my lesbian self in an activist, feminist community in Long Beach, CA, where I helped found and move CL/LL to Iowa City...There, I worked at the University Women's Center and was part of *Women Against Racism*...I moved to San Francisco with my partner Joan Pinkvoss, where I spent five full, amazing years with Dance Brigade...At 53 I found my way to an MFA in Studio Art and another nourishing community, where I express, through earth-based materials, moments of grace, sorrow and the generative power of the Feminine...Life is full with creative conversations, active engagement and holding each of our eleven grandchildren.

Jo Futrell: Belonging to the *Common Lives/Lesbian Lives* collective from 1992-1996 was like being embraced by lesbian culture itself, amplifying the voices of women loving women—the joy, love, anger and fierceness coming through our poems, stories and images. I have worked as a book editor, then retired from a career in EEO and civil rights compliance, investigating discrimination and harassment in the workplace. Sold my Wisconsin farm, left the hazelnut trees and prairie we planted years ago, moved back to Iowa, and found a little house near a lake. This project brought me back to my best memories of life in Iowa City. Maybe I'll start a lesbian magazine or something.

Rowan Harvey: I am a butch dyke writer who just wants to impart what little wisdom I have onto anyone who'll listen. I love gardening, sewing, lifting heavy things, and writing about gay women. I recently quit college to pursue a career in landscaping, where I'm excited for a new piece of my life to start.

Papusa Molina: I was born and raised in Yucatan, Mexico, where I now live. At 30, I moved to the US, beginning a journey into experiences that shaped who I am today: education in Chicano/a culture; work with the women of the Women's Resource and Action Center, where I found a world where being a lesbian was the norm, not the exception; friendships with Black women who introduced me to the intricacies of African American culture while helping me understand something I was beginning to name, racism in America; and my fifteen summers spent working with the Michigan Womyn's Music Festival. Now, back at home, I retired as Professor and Director of a postgraduate Institute. My writing has been mostly academic. These poems remain the only ones published.

Tracy Moore: *Ain't I a Woman?* taught me the ropes, co-founded *Common Lives/Lesbian Lives*, served on the Collective 1982-1989. Treasured coming up/coming out in Iowa City's lesbian community. At 16 an exchange student to New Zealand, got degrees, taught English, married/divorced a swell man, loved swell lesbians, didn't look back. Painted houses, raised funds for lgbtqetc organizations (loved that work). Traveled Europe, Britain, Nepal; lived in Israel with precious wife Rabbi Lisa Edwards (she attending rabbinic school while I gathered lesbian oral histories later published as *Lesbiot*.) Lisa retired after 25 years leading the oldest queer synagogue, BCC (founded 1952), in LA. Wonderful lesbian sister Wendy & wife Kim. Saved every photo. 35 years in Los Angeles. Anglo-American, Jew since '92. Eighty years old. Retired, of course.

Aaron Silander: I moved to Iowa City in the 70's to join the Women's Liberation Front. I live here still with Barbara and our aging cat Bo. We love our neighbors - artists and activists, musicians and friends in recovery. I've been sober many years, thanks to a Lesbian recovery house near downtown LA, and Twelve Step groups here at home. These are challenging times. I'm still finding my way in the world, seeking a spiritual connection and practice that works for me. Working on this project has been a gift - reconnecting with friends, meeting new writers and artists, seeing the incredible ongoing work by women who published in Common Lives many years ago. Thank you! You lift me up and give me hope.

Editorial Contributors

mj corey: I'm mj corey, a lesbian Arab American writer and psychotherapist based in Brooklyn. My work has been seen in *The New Yorker* and *Vogue*, and I am currently working on a media theory manifesto about the Kardashian family for Pantheon. My true muse, though, is my cat, Baby Blue.

Rabbi Beth Lieberman: I love to think beyond the patriarchy. A connoisseur of good stories and catalyst of cultural change, I have been involved on the editorial side of more than 500 books. I have been a fan of *Sinister Wisdom/Common Lives/Lesbian Lives* since their early days and am honored to be involved with this amazing tribute issue.

Juno Stillee: I am an artist and gardener. Queerness in all its forms excites me. I want to make a big feast for every lesbian in the world where we can all eat and celebrate. I believe in honoring those who came before me, nourishing those around me now, and working for those who will come after me. Come find me at junostilley.com.

Contributors

Dodici Azpadu, PhD, MFA: I retired from teaching poetry and fiction writing courses at UNM and now live in the Jemez Mountain with my spouse. I continue to write fiction and poetry that often falls between the cracks. My fiction has been a finalist for a Lammy, a Golden Crown Literary Award, and a New Mexico Fiction Book Award. Recent poetry has appeared in *Ad Astra* and *Bordighera, Poetas Siglo xxi–Antologia Mundial*, Fernando Sabido Sánchez, ed. I no longer keep up a website, but I can be messaged on Facebook.

Alison Bechdel: My work includes the comic strip *Dykes to Watch Out For*, which ran from 1983-2008, as well as the graphic memoirs *Fun Home, Are You My Mother?* and *The Secret to Superhuman Strength*. In some quarters I'm best-known for being the originator of "The Bechdel Test." The stage-musical adaptation of *Fun Home* premièred on Broadway in 2015 and received five Tony Awards. I live in Vermont.

Abby Lynn Bogomolny: I left my Brooklyn family of origin in 1974 after their difficult reaction to my being queer. I joined a N. Florida community of poets and musicians, became a singer songwriter and co-founded a lesbian-family printing business. Later in California, I launched Burning Bush Publications and juried its poetry prize for 11 years. I'm editor of *New to North America: Writing by US Immigrants* and author of *Nauseous in Paradise, Black of Moonlit Sea*, and *People Who Do Not Exist*. My poetry is in *Oakland Out Loud, The Freedom of New Beginnings*, various journals, and my chapbook *The Lighted Pull of Dreams*. Was English faculty at Santa Rosa Junior College for years, now I continue to write and stir the cultural soup in Northern California. www.abbypoetry.com

Ann Bonham: Starting at five years old, taking the train to visit my aunt and uncle, farmers in Muscatine, I heard their awe about the big University of Iowa. When I decided to go to graduate school, Iowa City came to mind. That decision transformed the rest of my life. I met my partner, and now wife, Jesse Joad, still treasuring our 45-years together. So many memories—some hilarious, some poignant, some surprising—all made possible by being part of the incomparable Iowa City lesbian community. Our work has taken us to Chicago, California, Washington DC and now sharing time between Seattle and Washington DC, but we are still Iowa City lesbians at heart.

Zöe Bracken: I am a New York transplant living in the East Bay Area of California. Most of my time is spent as a kindergarten teacher by day, science fiction reader by night, and a full-time dyke. My work has been previously featured in *Just Femme & Dandy, Argot Magazine, Boilerplate Magazine*, and *Process: Journal of Undergraduate Scholarship*.

Beth Brant: (Degonwadonti) was a lesbian poet, essayist, activist, and Bay of Quinte Mohawk from the Tyendinaga Mohawk Reserve in Ontario, Canada. Born in Detroit in 1941, she began writing in 1981 at the age of forty. Brant was the editor of *Sinister Wisdom* 22/23: *A Gathering of Spirit*, an anthology of Native American women's writing, and the author of *Mohawk Trail* (1985), *Food & Spirits* (1991), *Writing as Witness: Essay and Talk* (1994), and *I'll Sing 'til the Day I Die: Conversations with Tyendinaga Elders* (1995). She passed away in August 2015.

Joanna Brown: I am a writer and community-health physician living in Providence, Rhode Island, with my spouse and two sons. My poetry has appeared in such journals as *eclectica*, *Earth's Daughters*, *Gertrude*, *City & Sea* (a local anthology) and the chapbook *2Horatio*.

Marie Cartier: I have a Ph.D. in Religion with an emphasis on Women and Religion from Claremont Graduate University. I am the author of the critically acclaimed book *Baby, You Are My Religion: Women, Gay Bars, and Theology Before Stonewall* (Routledge 2013). I am a senior lecturer in Gender and Women's Studies and Queer Studies at California State University Northridge, and in Film Studies at Univ. of CA Irvine. I published the poetry book, *I Am Your Daughter, Not Your Lover* with Clothespin Fever Press (1994).

Tess Catalano: Tess was a human rights activist, singer-songwriter, massage therapist, community leader, and local legend. She lived in Iowa City, Portland, and Eugene, Oregon and passed in 1999. As friend Jill Jack memorialized her, "Tess sang from her soul, putting a voice to all of our thoughts, our loves, and our struggles. When words often failed us, or frustration overcame us, her music would heal us, join us, feed us. Tess was a large part of the waters that run through the Iowa City community, and it was her sound, her song that guided us, questioned us, and put us at ease. This is what I think she would be most proud of—she made us laugh, cry, struggle, and take pride in who we are."

Chris Cinque: As a survivor of childhood sexual abuse, indoctrinated by the-hurch to hate everything female, I came out before Stonewall in the South. I survived by becoming an artist. I wrote and performed my trilogy of one-woman plays, "Growing Up Queer in America" and co-wrote, acted and co-directed "Toklas, MN," a Lesbian soap opera, with its founder, Randa Downs. The Walker Art Center invited me to present a counterbalance to the overwhelmingly male Gay Pride Festival in Minneapolis. So, I founded and curated the first years of "Dyke Nite" there. I'm now a member of Form+Content Gallery. Randa and I live happily ever after with our black cat named Blue. See my artwork at www.chriscinque.com.

Mel Connelly: I'm an art historian, poet, and archivist whose scholarship ranges from Netherlandish still-life paintings and early modern depictions of corporal punishment to surveying feminist graffiti, researching feminist print culture in the digital age, and elevating "craft" in the Women's Arts Movement. With an art history MA from Georgia State University and a poetry MFA from Columbia University, I've taught undergraduate poetry writing. My current project is an English, lesbianized re-translation of Monique Wittig's *Le corps lesbian* while "typing up" my handwritten poems. I wrote "Do You Consider This Blue?" after coming to terms with my lesbianism, so it addresses fears of mirroring oppressive ideas in my relationships and seeing myself in lovers. Originally from West Georgia, I now live in Brooklyn with my cat, Maxine.

Lori Curry: I am an artist, writer, wife, mother, grandmother, and an out lesbian for 30 years. My paintings usually center around flowers. I love the feelings that observing their beauty evokes within me. They are not in a hurry, they grow on their time, reach maturity and die to replenish the earth. Only to re-emerge again in the spring. They are never completely gone from us. You can find me on Facebook.

Aischa Daughtery: I am a Scottish femme dyke princess, poet and miscellanist. I live and write in Glasgow, Scotland. After achieving my MA in English Literature and Sociology from the University of Glasgow, I will proceed on to an MLitt in Publishing Studies. My work has appeared in *Adjacent Pineapple*, *Bad Betty Press*, *Not Very Quiet*, *The Queer Dot*, *From Glasgow to Saturn* and more. I curate @LesbianLoveNote, a visual archive and collective on Instagram.

Randa Jo Downs: I am a former researcher/writer for a national child welfare foundation. As a theater artist I performed with At The Foot Of The ountain and co-created *Toklas, MN*, a lesbian soap opera. I wrote and performed *In My Father's Bed*, produced by Seattle's Alice B. Theatre, and published by Rain City Projects. My script was included in the Women's Studies Program at the University of Washington where I was guest lecturer. I've received grants from King County Arts Commission, Boeing Foundation, Washington's Department of Social Services, and a residency at Hedgebrook. My memoir, *Comfort, Texas*, will be published October 2024. Visit www.randajodowns.com for more information. I live in Minneapolis with my wife Chris Cinque.

Rabbi Lisa Edwards, Ph.D.: A Jewish lesbian activist—pulpit, page, online, classroom, streets. From 1994 until 2019 I served as Rabbi (now Rabbi Emerita) of Beth Chayim Chadashim (BCC), "House of New Life," the world's original queer synagogue (founded 1972), an LGBTQIS inclusive, progressive, diverse community. With five degrees (including ordination) from five institutions of higher learning, I'm no longer enrolled anywhere, but I'm still learning. My wife, lesbian activist and archivist Tracy Moore, and I have been together since 1985. Widely published on queer and Jewish topics, I am especially proud to be included in this remarkable volume, so lovingly and laboriously assembled by Tracy and the other members of the Collective.

Kimberly Esslinger: I am a Southern California hapa dyke poet and digital media artist. I write about identity, class, relationships, suburbia, and technology. My poems have appeared in *Spillways*, *Artemis Journal*, *Nerve Cowboy*, *Chiron Review*, and others. I am currently working on my first full-length collection of poems. To stay in touch, visit kimberlyesslinger.com.

Mary Aviyah Farkas: I have been a lover of God since I was eight years old. I have been a lover of women since I was twenty-five years old. I was born in 1948. In 2006 found my first wife; 18 years together, dead in bed, sans warning, no goodbye. In 2021 I published my book, *Overcoming Deepest Grief, A Woman's Journey—Grief, Acceptance, Gratitude and Joy*, a chronicle of traveling the Mourner's Path, which has won 4 book awards. I now live in Los Angeles, in love and bliss with Marsha, my wife and true *Beshert*. I am a Docent at the Holocaust Museum Los Angeles and a member of Beth Chayim Chadashim, the world's first LGBT Synagogue.

Rachel Feury: I am a crumbling Flesh Pile living in Dublin, Ireland. I worked in the animation industry for many years, before entering the wonderful world of disabling post-viral illnesses, from which I persist in my attempts at rendering the inner world external. I am heavily influenced by my political experiences—as a working-class marxist, a lesbian, a feminist—as well as the symbolic language of the spirit found in the visual art of all human cultures. You can find my work on tumblr and instagram under the username FleshPile. I am currently collaborating with writer Tara Brady, illustrating her feminist retelling of genesis 'Ishango', released in late 2023.

Ananya Garg: I am a South Asian lesbian woman, writer, visual artist, and performer. My artmaking process is a process of prayer, and a way I honor my ancestors and present community. I live in Brooklyn, NY with my girlfriend and dog.

Melinda Susan Goodman: I've been a teacher at Hunter College (mgoodm@hunter.CUNY.edu) since 1987 when Audre Lorde chose me to take over her poetry workshops. I taught 0-4th grade reading at a maximum-security juvenile detention center in the South Bronx, adult literacy in the Bronx and Brooklyn, and GED for at-risk youth in Brooklyn. I studied poetry at Hampshire College with Jamaican poet, Andrew Salkey. I hold a poetry MFA from Columbia University and an American Literature MA from New York University. I'm a proud former member of the editorial collective of *Conditions*. My poetry, fiction, and creative non-fiction have received awards from the Astraea Foundation, Key West Literary Seminar, New York Foundation on the Arts, Key West Literary Seminar, and *Los Angeles Review*. My website is Melindagoodmanpoet.com.

Morgan Gwenwald: I am one of a small group of out lesbian photographers who emerged during the early days of the gay rights movement. My work has been featured on many book covers and has filled newsletters, journals and magazines. It has been included in many exhibitions, the latest being *Art After Stonewall*. My goal has been to capture the queer world in which we live in honest and loving detail. My move to NYC in 1979 started a long-term relationship with the Lesbian Herstory Archives where I still serve as a coordinator. Early on I took up the challenge of portraying lesbian sexuality in all its diversity. I'm currently working on digitization of my negatives in preparation for a book. There are thousands!

Jan Hardy: My MFA is from the University of Pittsburgh. I've published poetry in *Sinister Wisdom*, *Common Lives/Lesbian Lives*, *Rattle*, *Calyx* and others. I edited and published *Wanting women: an anthology of erotic lesbian poetry* in

1990 and *Sister/Stranger: lesbians loving across the lines* in 1993. These days I read more than I write. I'm a White, middle-class, grandma of 6, great-grandma of 6, beyond lucky to live with my wife of 37 years and a big crazy Lab.

Rebecca Henderson: Grew up in a Norwegian-America Quaker farming community in Northwest Iowa. After obtaining a landscape architecture degree, she lived in Iowa City 1970-1985 working as an environmental consultant, and later, a self-employed bookbinder for small presses as Prairie Fox Publications, in the same building as Iowa City Women's Press. Suffering from chemical sensitivities, she moved to New Mexico where her work allowed for summer long distance walks. This piece was written toward the end of her third summer walk. There she met and married her wife, Pelican Lee. She became active in Quakerism, was a community organizer, and helped organize and lived on lesbian lands. She left earth life at age 70 in 2014. Her books, *Ingrid's Tale: A Norwegian American Farming Story* and *Long Distance Walking in New Mexico and Colorado*, are available from pelicanlee4@gmail.com.

Kate Hewett: I am a poet based in the Peak District, UK. With my wife, the musician Katie Harkin, I am the co-founder of Hand Mirror. I am sometimes on Instagram at @kateleahhewett and usually online at https://www.handmirror.online. I am currently working on my first collection. My previously published poems can be found at https://www.handmirror.online/artists

Tamara Hollins: I write poems that take a "pinch", a small thing, from fairy tales and myths as well as the narrative content of newspaper articles to portray what is uncomfortable and illimitable experienced by a body in nature with an emphasis on depth through the visual. My scholarly work, creative writing, and art have been published in journals such as *Killens Review of Arts and Letters* and *Festival Writer*, anthologies such as *Steve Kowit: This Unspeakably Marvelous Life*, and encyclopedias such as *Encyclopedia of African American Women Writers*. I earned a BA in Art, with distinction, from Hendrix College; an MA in Cultural Studies from Claremont Graduate University; an MFA in Writing and Literature from Bennington College; and a PhD in English from Claremont Graduate University.

Everlyn Hunter: I am an educator and activist who works with children and families from diverse ethnic, and socioeconomic groups. I am also an experienced collaborator with families, administrators, and governmental agencies (DCFS and probation systems). Concurrent with my professional work, I have held numerous leadership roles as a board member of non-profit human rights and LGBTQ organizations. I earned Master's and Doctoral degrees in Psychology with specializations in Clinical Child and School Psychology. I currently live in Los Angeles where I work as a psychologist and writer.

Eve Jasper: I am a full-time student and a part-time writer from the North East of England. I'm using my art to navigate myself and the world around me, with my work featured in several literary journals such as *Impostor Magazine*. While I currently write non-fiction, poetry has always been my first love.

Jesse Joad: I grew up in Iowa City and stayed through medical school, residency and fellowship, leaving in 1986 with Ann, my wife. 1970-1986 were formative years. I was part of the lesbian feminist movement, helped start a free day care center, and participated in the Quick Rising Yeast Cell and Revolutionary Art Collective and Gay Cell. My most fun event was a "lesbian rush" that Ann and I hosted, "rushing" about 50 lesbians at our house on 10 S. Governor; it was street theater, replete with lesbian songs, 'rushees' acting as sorority members, and with memorable attire. I worked for 10 years at the Free Medical Clinic, as a student and then senior physician. "Dirtbag" (Linda Knox) was a role model—still is.

Britta Kathmeyer: Born in Germany in 1963, I'm a visual artist in Sonoma County, California. With degrees in Textile Design from the College of Art and Design in Hanover, Germany, I continued my studies on a Fulbright scholarship in the US graduating with an MFA *with high distinction* from the California College of the Arts, Oakland, in 1991. Since 1988 I have exhibited work in galleries in Germany and the US. I was a senior lecturer at CCA and a member of the Independent Study Faculty at JFK University. As a visiting artist I have presented at the San Francisco Art Institute, CCA, JFK University, and the Headlands Center for the Arts. My art making art is profoundly influenced by studies of Eastern body work and Yoga.

Shari Katz: Ever since I won 2nd place in a writing competition in grade 8, I've been putting words to paper. Born in Montreal, Canada, I spent the bulk of my career in Los Angeles as a school librarian, teacher, synagogue activist, reader and travel writer. After marrying native Californian Noelle, I cajoled her back to the snowy north for a one-year temporary sojourn, where 16 years later, we still reside. At 52 I trained to become a lifeguard and have been lifeguarding at the Ritz Carlton hotel for seven years. Now heading towards retirement, I'm focused on writing true-life travel stories. On most days, I can be found with Noelle and our cat, Lily, writing, camping, planning future travels, and having a helluva good time. sharifern@hotmail.com

Sue Katz: My business card identifies me as a "Wordsmith and Rebel." I've been a martial arts master, promoted transnational volunteering, and partner-danced more than my feet could bear. A life-long activist, I was on the ground floor of the women's and lesbian liberation movements. My writing has been published on the three continents where I've lived, worked, and roused rabble, and has appeared in a plethora of publications. My fiction often focuses on the lives of LGBTQ elders, including the short story collections *A Raisin in My Cleavage and Lillian's Last Affair*, and the novel *Lillian in Love*. In honor of Stonewall 50, my first play was produced by the prestigious 'The Theater Offensive.' My first published short story was in *Common Lives/Lesbian Lives*.
https://www.facebook.com/sue.katz
https://suekatz.

Lynda Koolish: Professor Emeritus of English and Comparative Literature at San Diego State University, Koolish studied and has taught photography and other visual arts throughout the country. Her earliest photographs, primarily a celebration of lesbian and feminist culture, have been springboards to many kinds of portraits. African American literature has become increasingly the focus of her intellectual life, her photographs and her heart work. Her portraits, included in numerous publications and exhibitions, have been described as "elegant...emphatic...more than mere light and shadow, to drink in the writers' thoughts and feelings...." Koolish's portraits, both recent and going back to the 1980's, document writers essential to American letters, and in a very real sense, to a richly imagined life.

Anne Lee (1947-1981): In 1980, Anne Lee was living in Pasadena, CA with her son and her magic. I heard her read from her work in an event organized by Catherine Nicholson and Harriett Demoines, co-founders of *Sinister Wisdom*. Afterward, as lesbians gathered over tea, Anne and I exchanged amusing comments and began a deep loving connection. Encouraged by *Sinister Wisdom*, Anne, Cindy Cleary, and I left LA to join Iowa City dykes in inventing what became the founding collective of *Common Lives/Lesbian Lives*. In July 1981, a previously misdiagnosed cancer stole Anne from all of us. Anne left behind broken hearts, marvelous writings, witty sayings, and safe to say after 43 years—a lifetime of treasured memories. –Tracy Moore

Olivia Loscavio: I'm a young queer poet from the Bay Area. My goal through poetry is to transcend harmful narratives of lesbophobia and fatphobia and write new ways of recognizing what it means to be young, queer and fat. My work coalesces narratives of conflicting identities into a young woman at peace with herself. My projects explore power dynamics of interracial lesbian relationships and rejection of beauty standards imposed by white femininity in favor of a more unique, inclusive, queer beauty. I graduated from the New Literary Project writing workshops and have published poems in *Simpsonistas: Volume Two* and *Three*. None of the work I've produced would have been possible without the brave queer activists before me, and the support of my queer friends, family, and mentors.

Alison Lubar: I'm a queer, nonbinary, mixed-race femme who teaches high school English by day, and yoga by night. My work has been nominated for both the Pushcart Prize and Best of the Net, and I am the author of four chapbooks: *Philosophers Know Nothing About Love* (Thirty West Publishing House, 2022), *queer feast* (Bottlecap Press, 2022), *sweet euphemism* (CLASH!, 2023), and *It Skips a Generation* (Stanchion, 2023). You can find out more at http://www.alisonlubar.com/ or on Twitter @theoriginalison.

Sabrina McIntyre: Disabled femme lesbian, I have a casual relationship with art and a devoted marriage to lesbianism. I don't really have anything to plug so I'll leave a few reminders: All lives cannot matter until Black lives do, cops are fascists who will always protect themselves over you, and there is an active trans genocide in America. Take care of yourself, stand up for others, and fight for your beliefs.

Margarita Meklina: I am a queer writer born in Leningrad. A winner of the prestigious Andrei Bely Prize and the Russian Prize, I am unable to be published in Russia, due to the expanded anti-LGBTQ laws signed by Putin in December 2022. My earlier book, written in collaboration with Lida Yusupova, *Love Has Four Hands*, was removed from Russian bookstores. My short story collection was to be published in Moscow but is now subjected to self-censorship by the publishing house. I came to the US in 1994 with refugee status. With Anne Fisher, I curated a folio of Russian LGBTQ poetry and prose translated to English and printed by The Brooklyn Rail/In Translation. Now I am forced to abandon my native language in favor of English.

Diana K. Miller: I returned to Iowa City in retirement after working in Boston for 26 years. I've written poetry, quilted, drawn, and painted representational watercolor and abstract acrylic—my pandemic anchor. Intuitively playing with color, texture, shape, and movement brings me great joy. Art enriches our lives and sending my art into the world allows people to join in my joy. Proceeds from my work go to local charities like the Iowa City Free Lunch Program. I have Open Studios in my home and exhibit my artwork with four women from my Monday Art Group at the Iowa City Senior Center. I've been blessed to have my Monday Art Group and Louise Fletcher's international Art Tribe to inspire and support me. I can be reached at dkmilleriowa@gmail.com.

María Mínguez Arias: I am the author of *Nombrar el cuerpo* (Editorial Egales/España; El BeiSmAn PrESs/USA; 2022), chosen among the Best of Queer Lit in 2022 in Spain by Revista Qué Leer, and award-winning novel *Patricia sigue aquí* (Editorial Egales, 2018). My essays and short stories appear in anthologies and journals in the US, Spain, and Mexico. My identity as an immigrant, queer woman, and mother writing in Spanish in the US informs my texts. I work as Operations Director at the feminist press Aunt Lute Books and live in the San Francisco Bay Area with my partner and our two teens.

Cherry Muhanji: There is the rhythm of the mother, the suppressed poet and the worker. There is the rhythm of the first-time college student at forty-six, the activist, and the budding prose writer. There is the dizzying rhythm toward the Masters in African American Studies; the rapid riffs necessary for an interdisciplinary Ph.D. in English, Anthropology, African American Studies....Threaded throughout the journey was the continuing baseline of travels to China, repeated trips to Cuba, a harrowing experience in Haiti, to Tijuana where the rhythm of exploitation in the maquiladoras was palpable
....teaching...writing...the many literary awards.
But, always, always the working writer....
Strange rhythms these things.
My life has been saved many times by writing.

C. Eliot Mullins: I'm a therapist, friend of cats, lifelong Pacific Northwesterner, mother, and extreme introvert. My mid-life has been a journey of finding my people in lesbian, recovery, and writing communities. I'm a student of poetry engaging in numerous poetry classes and two year-long poetry mentorship and study programs at Simon Fraser University and Brooklyn Poets. I reside in Washington State with my wife and assorted animals, feral and tame. My poetry has been published in a variety of journals and anthologies, with links on my web site: www.celiotmullinspoet.com

Merril Mushroom: I am a 1950's bar dyke, a native Floridian, a 45-year resident of rural Tennessee, and a lifelong butch. My many stories and articles have appeared in existing and defunct publications. My play BAR DYKES was most recently performed in New York City and Los Angeles. I have been a big fan of "CL/LL" from its beginning.

Tanya Olson: I live in Silver Spring, Maryland and work as a Senior Lecturer in English at UMBC (University of Maryland Baltimore County). My first book, *Boyishly*, was published by YesYes Books in 2013 and received a 2014 American Book Award. My second book, *Stay*, was released by YesYes Books in 2019. I have received a Discovery/*Boston Review* prize and was named a 2011 Lambda Fellow by the Lambda Literary Foundation. My poem "54 Prince" was chosen for inclusion in *Best American Poems 2015* by Sherman Alexie. *Born Backwards*, my third book, is out from YesYes Books in June 2024.

Kim Painter: I am a local elected official who serves as Johnson County Recorder in Iowa City, Iowa. I am resistant to writing my own bio, which I compare to crafting a personal ad, with all the neediness and ego that implies. I have written throughout my life, finding publication in online blogs, *USA Today*, the *Des Moines Register*, and *The Daily Iowan*. In 2013 I was awarded a Harvey Milk Champion of Change award by the White House under President Barack Obama for my service as an openly gay official. I'm both proud and nettled by the fact that those awards pages were expunged from the White House web site during the administration of our 45th president, The Former Guy.

Diamond Marie Pedroza: I am a Hispanic American writer and self-proclaimed sapphic historian. In my work, I explore issues surrounding mental health, autism, and lesbian culture. I currently reside in Texas.

Jan Phillips: I am an author, speaker, artist and activist. I am the author of *Still On Fire, No Ordinary Time, Creativity Unzipped, The Art of Original Thinking, Divining the Body, Marry Your Muse, God is at Eye Level, Making Peace, Born Gay, A Waist is a Terrible Thing to Mind, Finding The On-Ramp to Your Spiritual Path.*
http://janphillips.com/ - http://www.livingkindness.org
Jan's TED-X Talk, https://www.youtube.com/watch?v=sJGGmoHVxYE

Quinn: During my years in NYC I healed from two life-threatening addictions, but for years more would suffer from depression. After leaving NYC I wandered, lived for a time in the Sugarloaf lesbian community, returned finally at age 50 to Iowa City, my hometown. Once here I grew reacquainted with my two precious daughters, did all I could to make amends for having left them when they were far too young. Eventually I helped care for three delightful grandsons. Also once back here I began remembering and healing from sexual violence I'd suffered as a tiny child. Subsequently my writing, therapy, friends and family help carry me to my current 86th year, one blessed with abundant love, joy, laughter and gratitude.

Paloma Raffle: Hi! I'm Paloma and I'm currently a Sophomore at UC Berkeley, where I enjoy discovering how I can use painting, sculpture, and other mediums to contribute to a more empathetic world focused on social justice. Outside of school, I love to row, bike, paint, sculpt, cook, read, play guitar, travel, and spend time with friends and family. You can learn more about me at palomaraffle.com.

Sudie Rakusin: The last bio I wrote was in 1992, 31 years ago; I was 42. I am still an Aries, Jewish, white, and lesbian; North Carolina is home where I do my art and live with my pitbull, Justice Grey. My feminist political and critical awareness of inequality and injustices has broadened to include the earth and her animals. We are all 'the other.' In my work, I explore ways to express this deep connection and bond, its magnificence, and all the reasons why we must fight to preserve it. My art continues to be a refuge and a place I find solace. Being grateful for this gift, I seek ways to share it and give back. My website: sudierakusin.com and EtsyStore: https://www.etsy.com/shop/SudieRakusinArt

Sandra Renew: My poetry addresses a lesbian life lived on the fringes of heterosexuality and the perils thereof. I write to reflect and highlight issues of gender, sexuality and the poetry of politics and power. My poetry collections from Recent Work Press are *Apostles of Anarchy*, *It's the sugar, Sugar,* and *Acting Like a Girl*, which won the 2020 ACT Writing and Publishing Award for Poetry and was shortlisted for the 2020 ACT Book of the Year. From Ginninderra Press are *The Ruby Red's Affair* and *The Orlando Files*. I am a founding editor, with Moya Pacey, of the *Not Very Quiet* online journal of women's poetry 2017-2021. *Not Very Quiet: The anthology*, editors Moya Pacey and Sandra Renew, Recent Work Press, was published in 2021.

Canyon Sam: I am a fourth generation San Franciscan. I won a NEA Minority Youth Arts scholarship as a teen and dropped out of university. I moved to women's land in Oregon to come out and upon return to the Bay Area in 1976 organized the nascent Asian American lesbian community. I read and published in the 70's, 80's most notably with the ensemble Unbound Feet, of Chinese American writers. In 1986-87 I spent a year in China and Tibet; my interest in Buddhism and the Tibetan cause led me to solo performance art ("A master storyteller..." Village Voice) and to write *Sky Train: Tibetan Women on the Edge of History* (University of Washington, forward by the Dalai Lama), winner of the PEN American Center open Book Award.

Stephanie Sauer: Raised in Rough and Ready, California (a real town), I learned to sew and make art in 4-H and work with language, book arts, fiber, and the space between parentheses. I wrote *Almonds Are Members of the Peach*

Family and *The Accidental Archives of the Royal Chicano Air Force,* and my work has appeared in *Lavender Review, Pleiades, Gulf Coast, Drunken Boat, So to Speak,* and *Asymptote.* I live in Brazil with Rachel Gontijo Araujo, with whom I co-founded A Bolha Editora to publish Gloria Anzaldúa, Cheryl Clarke, Audre Lorde, Adrienne Rich, Tove Jansson, Renee Gladman, Bhanu Kapil, and others in Portuguese. I teach writing in Stetson University's MFA of the Americas program and develop Lolmĕn Publications with the Shingle Springs Band of Miwok Indians.

Linda Shear: Music has been at the center of my life. As a young adult I played in bars, clubs, coffee houses, festivals and concerts – and was part of the Women's Music Revolution in the 1970's. I performed in the first "out lesbian" concert in the U.S. in 1972, formed and toured with the first Lesbian Band in the country, Family of Woman, and played on the mainstage at the Michigan Women's Music Festival two consecutive years in the late 70's. Retiring from my day job as a CPA in 2021, I have turned once again to my music. After 30 years in California, my poet wife, windflower, and I relocated back to the Northampton, Massachusetts area in April 2024. Going back home...
Google "Linda Shear Music" (soundcloud or YouTube)

Mistinguette Smith: I am a late bloomer. "Rain," my very first short story, was written in my late twenties. In the decades that followed, I went to college at 35, then graduate school; founded The Black/Land Project, a research project about Black relationships to urban land; ran a philanthropic consulting practice; remained joyfully partnered for 35 years; and settled in the lesbian haven of Northampton, MA. My poems, essays and fiction about race, land and kinship are published in many literary and academic journals and anthologies. An early decision climate refugee, I recently moved to Oberlin, OH. I identify as a Black lesbian feminist elder who refuses to quietly disappear. You can find my work at MistinguetteSmith.com.

Mi Ok Song: Mi Ok (pronounced "me-oak" two words, one name). I may be the only left-handed, Korean adoptee lesbian visual artist & published poet, living in RI. I happily live with my wife & four rescue felines, Eartha Kitty, Marvin Gray, Arlo Catrie & (non-binary) Cat Stevie Nicks. When not drawing, creating art & practicing psychotherapy, I drive my 2016 Smart Car, "HAF CAR" (because I can't afford a whole car). I am honored to be among the artists, poets & writers represented in *Common Lives/Lesbian Lives* & *Sinister Wisdom*. Please follow my art work at www.Instagram.com/averyfinecoloredline & I can be contacted at averyfinecoloredline@gmail.com.

Amy Spade: Originally from Detroit, I live and write in Oakland, California. I hold an MFA from the University of Houston. My largely formal poems have appeared in many journals, including *Nimrod, North American Review, Michigan Quarterly Review, Cottonwood* —and most recently *Lesbians Are New to Miracles.* New poetry is forthcoming in Gay & Lesbian Review and *Lavender Review.*

Jill Spisak: I have published in *Common Lives/Lesbian Lives* and am happy to have the opportunity of the thematic *Sinister Wisdom* issue that revisits that publication. I am a lesbian widow living near Atlanta, Georgia who has been writing seriously for many years and has recently begun to publish some of my work again. I love hiking, biking, paddling, sailing and generally staying active to balance the hours of sitting for reading and writing. A long-time member of WomonWrites I now find my audience at OUTrageous Voices, Quarentina, and the Atlanta poetry community centered on Java Speaks Virtual Open Mic hosted by Theresa Davis, where I have also encountered and begun to perform in national slam competitions.

Jean Taylor: Based on the land of the Wurundjeri Woiwurrung people in Bulleke-bek, Merri-bek, Naarm, Melbourne, Australia, since 1970, I have self-published my novels, short stories, plays, and poetry under Dyke Books Inc: My non-fiction books, *The Archives Trilogy*, document radical lesbian feminist activism in Victoria in the Women's Liberation Movement, 1969 - 1999: *Brazen Hussies, Stroppy Dykes* and *Lesbians Ignite!*; and, *What Are Dykes Doing?* The latest is *Just a Gran Havin' a Splendid Time: Australian Lesbian Grandmothers Anthology.* I'm a founding member of Long Breast Press, publishing books by, for and about lesbians: http://www.longbreastpress.com . I have an ongoing interest in archiving lesbian feminist material for research and posterity since joining the Victorian Women's Liberation and Lesbian Feminist Archives Inc. in 1984: http://www.vwllfa.org.au

Jules Taylor: I am a high school English teacher and poet. I have previously published work in *Closet Cases*, an anthology published by Et Alia Press, and *Lavender Review*. I live in Nashville, Tennessee, with my wife Emily and our three cats, Tedward, Mushroom and Belsnickel, and our leopard gecko, Jane.

Mary Vermillion: I am a Professor of English at Mount Mercy University in Cedar Rapids, Iowa and the author of three mystery novels. The first, *Death by Discount*, was a Lambda finalist in two categories: Lesbian Mystery and Lesbian Debut Novel. I write a blog called *Midway* that explores in-between spaces. You can find it at maryvermillion.com, and you can find me in Iowa City, where I live with my husband, Ben, and our two cats.

Sarah Walsh: I am an autistic and chronically ill lesbian who uses writing to cope with the world around me. The short story here is a comedic retelling of a true event about the first woman to win a hot wing eating contest in the state of Tennessee.

Jean Weisinger: I am a self-taught photographer based in Berkeley, California, who has traveled to England, Amsterdam, Germany, Cuba, Australia, New Zealand, Mexico, The South of the United States and South India, documenting people of color. I documented the 1990 "I Am Your Sister" conference honoring Audre Lorde. It was a privilege, and as my mother always said, it's best to give praise and recognition to one while they are alive to appreciate such an honor. In 1997, I documented a South India event where over 400,000 women from all religions, castes and classes line the streets to cook porridge for the goddess

Bhagavathi. I had an exhibit at the Alice Austen House Museum, on Staten Island, New York, in June 2023.

Sue Parker "Rainbow" Williams: Rainbow (1934-2022) was a multidisciplinary artist, musician, writer, mother, and instrument maker who devoted her entire life to art. Her drawings appear in many lesbian publications, such as *Lesbian Bedtime Stories,* the brochure for the National Lesbian Conference in Atlanta (1991), and the Orlando NOW newsletter *Changes* that she edited for eight years. Her passion for making art of all kinds was a major expression of her lesbian-feminist activism. Many of her art works are collages or constructions made from found objects, such as cigar boxes, seashells, children's blocks, or broken musical instruments. She treated her home as an art gallery and made a YouTube video tour to use as her email signature, https://youtu.be/6my5UAHiFpk

Leonore Wilson: I teach creative writing in Napa Valley. I am on the MFA Board at St. Mary's College of California, My work has been in such magazines as *Quarterly West, TRIVIA: Voices of Feminism, Dark Matter, MAGMA, Third Coast, Laurel Review, Unruly Catholic Women Writers,* etc.

windflower: I recently moved from the beautiful Mendocino coast with my wife, singer songwriter Linda Shear, and our two herding dogs. After 30 years we are back in the Northampton MA area. I co-founded the Feminist Art Program at the University of Massachusetts Women Center where I edited/published Chomo Uri and produced the first National Women's Poetry Festival in 1976. My poems appear in various literary journals and anthologies, including international publications. In March, my poetry book, AGE BRINGS THEM HOME TO ME, was published by Finishing Line Press. I have a deep and abiding commitment to maintaining a relationship between artistic integrity and political expression and am constantly working to find this balance. I am also a photographer celebrating the poetry of nature.

Jacqueline Woodson: ...award winning writer of books for adults, children and adolescents...
...Young People's Poet Laureate and MacArthur Fellow...
I write, catch, and eat with my right hand. Everything else—batting, shooting a basket, holding a golf club, etc. is done with my left.
I have a lot of my writing memorized so I don't have to carry my books everywhere.
I once wrote a book in two weeks and it only needed a little revision.
The next book I wrote took four years.
I have only lost at checkers once. I have only won at chess once.
Even though I can walk to a Brooklyn Nets game from my house, I'm still a die-hard Knicks fan.
I love it when it's quiet and sunny.
Fall is my favorite season.

Sinister Wisdom 2025 Calendar
Advance Order Today!

Sinister Wisdom is proud to release our calendar. As part of our year-end fundraiser, the 2024 *Sinister Wisdom* calendar celebrates the best of lesbian-feminist herstory and features features new Sapphic, sinister art.

The *Sinister Wisdom* 2024 calendar is a limited edition, get your copy toay!

$20 for one

$80 for five (including shipping and handling)

Order online at **www.SinisterWisdom.org/calendar**

Or mail a check to
***Sinister Wisdom*, 2333 McIntosh Rd., Dover, FL 33527-5980**

Sinister Wisdom
A Multicultural Lesbian Literary & Art Journal

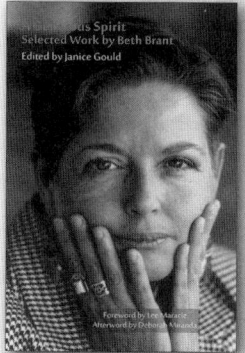

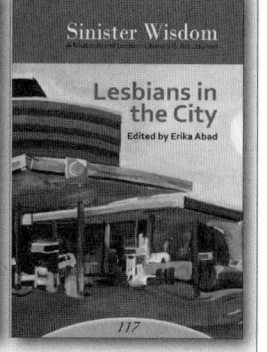

SUBSCRIBE TODAY!

Subscribe using the enclosed subscription card or online at www.SinisterWisdom.org/subscribe using PayPal

Or send check or money order to
Sinister Wisdom - 2333 McIntosh Road, Dover, FL 33527-5980

Sinister Wisdom accepts gifts of all sizes to support the journal.

Sinister Wisdom is free on request to women in prisons and psychiatric institutions.

Back issues available!

Order Sinister Wisdom's Sapphic Classics

Crime Against Nature — Minnie Bruce Pratt

Living as a Lesbian — Cheryl Clarke

What Can I Ask: New and Selected Poems 1975–2004 — Elana Dykewomon

The Complete Works of Pat Parker

Sister Love: The Letters of Audre Lorde and Pat Parker 1974–1989 — Introduction by Mecca Jamilah Sullivan, Edited by Julie R. Enszer

For the Hard Ones: A Lesbian Phenomenology / Para las duras: Una fenomenología lesbiana — tatiana de la tierra

A Sturdy Yes of a People: Selected Writings — Joan Nestle

Sapphic Spirit: Selected Work by Beth Brant — Edited by Janice Gould

selected poems by lynn lonidier — Edited by Julie R. Enszer

Notes for a Revolution
A great gift!
A spiral-bound blank book
for journalist, list-making,
and record-keeping.
$14 plus shipping and handling
Order your cipy today!

Eruptions of Inanna: Justice, Gender and Erotic Power — Judy Grahn

Order online at
www.sinisterwisdom.org
Or mail check or money order to:
Sinister Wisdom
2333 McIntosh Road
Dover, FL 33527-5980

Sinister Wisdom 134
Fall 2024

Publisher: Sinister Wisdom, Inc.
Editor & Publisher: Julie R. Enszer
Guest Editors: Cindy Cleary, Jo Futrell, Rowan Harvey, Papusa Molina, Tracy Moore, Aaron Silander
Graphic Designer: Nieves Guerra
Board of Directors: Roberta Arnold, Cheryl Clarke, Julie R. Enszer, Sara Youngblood Gregory, Yeva Johnson, Briona Jones, Judith Katz, Shromona Mandal, Joan Nestle, Rose Norman, Mecca Jamilah Sullivan and Yasmin Tambiah.

Cover Title: *Iowa City*
Artist: Lisa Schoenfielder
Medium: Mixed media drawing
Year: 2023

Lisa Schoenfielder: I am an artist living in La Crosse, Wisconsin. I recently retired after 34 years of University teaching in Iowa and Wisconsin. While living in Iowa City I was active in the lesbian feminist community contributing my artworks to various events and publications including Common Lives/Lesbian Lives. Like many artists, I like to collect images from books and magazines. Unknowingly, this developed into a research method of sorts when I started to place the images in plastic sleeves and store them in 3-ring binders. My notebooks grew into a collection of visual diaries that continue to be a resource for my work.